it's in his
heart

A RED RIVER
VALLEY NOVEL

it's in his heart

A RED RIVER VALLEY NOVEL

SHELLY ALEXANDER

Montlake
Romance

Text copyright © 2015 Shelly Alexander

Published by Montlake Romance, Seattle

www.apub.com

Amazon, the Amazon logo, and Montlake Romance are trademarks of Amazon.com, Inc., or its affiliates.

ISBN-13: 9781477829905
ISBN-10: 1477829903

Cover design by Laura Klynstra

Library of Congress Control Number: 2014922409

Printed in the United States of America

To my husband, the sweetest man and best chiropractor on the planet. Thank you for insisting I buy my first laptop so I could start writing down my stories, and for living out an incredible romance and happily-ever-after with me for the last twenty-five years and beyond. I love you.

To Lola, our English bulldog, who has brought truckloads of love and laughter to our household.

And to the town of Red River, New Mexico: You are my muse and my refuge. While the characters and establishments in my novels are formed solely from my imagination, the real people and places of Red River are no less wonderful. I've taken a few creative liberties with the geography to make the setting work to the advantage of the story, but in real life, Red River is one of the most magical places on earth.

Chapter One

Ella Dennings had a *bone* to pick with the *Albuquerque Enquirer*'s Most Eligible Chiropractor two years running. She snorted. Jeez, she *cracked* herself up.

Okay, get a grip. Humoring herself seemed like a good idea while stuck in a muddy ditch in the middle of the night. She could really use Cooper Wells's help right now, even though he wouldn't be at the cabin when she arrived. And it was for the best. Ella had made sure she'd have the cabin to herself. Her late husband's best friend owned half the vacation retreat, but spending the summer in Red River under the same roof with him was the *last* thing she wanted.

Now, if she could just get her car out of the damn ditch and actually make it to the cabin herself. Unfortunately, her BMW wasn't built to four-wheel itself out of the mud.

"I should've traded this thing for a four-wheel drive," she grumbled, even though it wasn't true. When she drove the Beamer, Bradley's presence washed over her like he was in the seat next to her. Maybe she imagined it, but his scent still filled the plush interior and eased the dull ache in her heart every time she got behind the wheel.

"I think it's time to brave the storm on foot, Winston. We may not get out of this ditch any other way tonight."

The overweight English bulldog occupying the passenger seat panted toward her, his oversized tongue hanging a good six inches out one side of his flattened snout. It resembled a wagging slab of roast beef, and a glob of slobber rolled off, making a splat on the console. Ella didn't know whether to laugh or cry.

She snapped Winston's black leather leash onto his matching spiked collar.

I will not cry, I will not cry, I will not cry. Both hands gripped the leash, and she counted to ten, a little trick she'd learned while teaching history at Bella Vista High. One of the roughest schools in Albuquerque, she'd had to outmaneuver the less motivated students with a few tools in emotional restraint. Either that or she would've quit on the first day of classes when a saggy-pants sophomore offered to get her high between classes.

"I. Will. Not. Cry," she whispered into the darkness. A giant tear the size of the raindrops pounding the windshield slid down her cheek. She swiped at it. How could she possibly have any tears left? She'd cried an ocean the last two years since Bradley had been gone. Dabbing her eyes with a sleeve, she glanced at Winston. "I'm pretty pathetic, huh?"

Winston cocked his head to one side, whining as if he understood.

Bradley's car, Bradley's dog. He'd been a true dog lover and never minded one bit the smeared windows or sticky seats the way she did. Now she was going to Bradley's cabin in Red River to spend one last summer and finally—hopefully—say good-bye.

The familiar sting of sadness settled in her chest.

Ruffling the wiry fur on top of Winston's expansive head, Ella sucked up her resolve. "Yeah, I know you miss him as much as I do." She chucked the canine under the chin and winked in his direction.

"But, we've still got each other." He burped and resumed his tongue-wagging pant. "God, I *am* pathetic." She wiped a gob of slobber off her hand and leaned against the window to study Winston. He rested his oversized head on the console and stared up at her with giant, adoring eyes.

Her attention returned to the deserted road, and she flicked on the wipers again. The cabin wasn't more than a half mile farther. But in this rain, at night, and on foot, it might as well be on the other side of the universe.

She blew out a heavy breath, making her overgrown bangs flutter, and stared into the black sheets of rain.

Cooper Wells. Bradley's buddy since their pimply faced youths. They went through high school and college together, then on to chiropractic school. Afterward, they'd both returned to Albuquerque to set up their own practices, and they stayed best friends until Bradley's diagnosis.

A vein throbbed at her temple.

Just the thought of Coop inspired a desire for margaritas. A whole pitcher would be great just about now. Except that after two drinks, she usually ended up dancing on the nearest table with a lampshade on her head. Cooper Wells just wasn't worth the embarrassment or the hangover.

"Ancient history," she mumbled. It didn't matter anymore. Bradley was gone, and her association with Cooper Wells ended with Bradley's passing. Except for the cabin, which was her reason for being here in the first place. It was time to let the cabin go, too. Bradley would've wanted Coop to have it. They *did* buy it fifty-fifty long before she and Bradley married.

Ella stared at the windshield, now completely obscured by the heavy rain, and sighed. Of course she arrived on one of only ten days out of the year when it rained in northern New Mexico. Traveling to a cabin located two miles down a dirt road would've been too easy in nice weather.

Shoulders sagging, she thumped her forehead against the steering wheel. *Final score: Muddy Ditch – 1, Stupid Redhead That Didn't Check The Weather – 0.*

A bolt of lightning cracked open the sky and revealed the jagged silhouette of the Sangre de Cristo Mountains. She and Winston both jumped.

Her heart thumped against her ribs. "Ready or not, it's time."

Winston's head popped up.

Ella pulled up the hood of her flimsy windbreaker, zipped it up to her nose, and looked at Winston. Opening the door, she stepped into the watery ditch and sank half up to her knees in mud. Still in the car, Winston pulled on the leash.

"Oh, no you don't." She tugged harder against his sixty-five-pound girth. "If I've got to do this, then so do you."

His tongue disappeared into his flattened face, and he dug all four paws into the expensive leather seat.

"Seriously? You're seriously going to make me carry you?" She cursed, not really under her breath. "I should've gotten Bradley a Chihuahua. At least they can swim, and they don't weigh as much as a small elephant."

She tried to pull one foot free from the mud. A loud, sucking *squish* sounded, and one shoeless foot appeared.

"Are you freakin' kidding me?" She glared at Winston. "I just bought these!" He sneezed and resumed his wild-horses-couldn't-drag-me-outta-here stance.

"That's it, buddy boy. You're coming whether you want to or not. And once we're out of this ditch, you're walking your prima donna butt the rest of the way to the cabin."

With a "humph," she hoisted the stubborn bulldog from the car and stumbled back under his weight. Thick mud clung to her feet like cement weights, and she lost her balance. A loud splash sounded as she fell backward, Winston clawing to stay on top of her like she was his lifeline. With both arms wrapped around him, her car keys began to slip from one hand. When she eased her hold on Winston to tighten her grasp on them, he clawed his way higher and pushed her down into the water.

Ella sputtered and gasped for air. One arm flailed to regain control, and the keys jarred loose. With a plop, they disappeared into the same watery grave as her shoe.

Where was a crane when you needed one? Or Animal Control?

Mumbling something about a Chihuahua, Ella picked her way up and out of the ditch, each step squishing and slurping. She walked the hydrophobic dog, now stiffened in protest, to higher ground and sat him down on the rain-soaked road. Then she waded back, dropped to her knees in the murky water, and searched for her keys.

Her hand brushed against metal, and she grabbed for it. Falling back onto her butt, she squeezed her eyes shut and rested her forehead against the keys fisted into one hand. Several calming breaths later, she forced herself up and sloshed to the car. She retrieved her purse from the front seat and kicked the door closed with a shoeless, muddy foot.

"And another thing," she said, marching back to Winston to grab his leash. With a gentle tug, she and the obstinate dog set out toward the cabin. "You're going on a diet as of right now."

Coop stirred from his peaceful slumber but refused to open his eyes. He turned on his side, willing his interrupted dream of the curvy Megan Fox to restart right where it had stopped.

A low growl sounded at the foot of the bed, and his eyes popped open. He lay still, listening. The eleven-month-old boxer's shaky growl quieted, and Coop heard nothing except heavy rain pelting the rustic cabin.

He rolled up to rest on one elbow as the dog moved closer, trembling. "What's the matter, Atlas? Probably a raccoon. Go back to sleep, boy." He scratched the dog behind the ears and lay back down.

Atlas whined like a baby.

"Are you really that big a chicken? Come on, grow a pair." Coop rubbed his sleepy eyes. He should have gotten a German shepherd or a rottweiler. A poodle would've been a better guard dog than Atlas. A boxer had seemed so manly, so alpha. He had imagined doing a five-mile morning run with Atlas lumbering along with him.

He sighed, his head rolling to one side so he could look at his fifty-pound marshmallow. A chick magnet that all the ladies deemed as "sweet." Great. Just what he needed—a cutesy dog who quaked at his own shadow and drew the attention of "aww"-ing females.

Females. He groaned. Better they stay in his dreams from now on. The real ones caused far too much trouble. Turning onto his side, he punched his goose-down pillow, anxious to get back to said nocturnal fantasies.

A loud thump had Atlas growling again, and Coop sat up. "Shh," he murmured and listened into the darkness. Atlas scooted under the covers, cowering. Slipping out of bed, Coop inched to the window. With one finger, he pulled on the blind. The darkness gave away nothing, making him more aware of the chilled dampness that infused the air around him. Coop tensed, the back of his neck prickling.

He should have left the porch light on.

A crack of lightning illuminated the rural landscape, revealing a hooded shadow just as it moved onto the redwood porch to the left of his window. He pulled back, letting the blinds close. *Think. Think!* His eyes scanned the dark bedroom, searching for something, anything he could use as a weapon. Shifting to the door, he pulled his prized baseball bat, Old Faithful, from behind it.

His bare feet moved silently across the hardwood floor, and he headed down the hall. With Old Faithful raised high and ready to swing, he eased into the entryway. The front door knob jiggled, and the lock clicked. Adrenaline coursed through him. As the door swung open, he surged toward the intruder. Half into the swing, the overhead light switched on, flooding the room with one thousand volts of eye-stabbing electricity. His recoil shifted his momentum upward, and Old Faithful crashed into the wall just above the intruder's head.

Coop pulled Old Faithful back, ready to swing again. Now face-to-face with the prowler, familiar green eyes, rounded with fear, greeted him. Long, soaking tendrils of auburn hair escaped the confines of the hoodie, each lock finding a home against milky white skin.

Unfortunately, those deep feminine pools of green didn't register any recognition of him, and she screamed. Loud.

Hell. Before he could explain, apologize, even berate his best friend's widow for not calling to let him know she was coming, Ella raised her keychain, and a sparkly pink bottle streamed pepper spray right into his eyes.

Chapter Two

The baseball bat that nearly took off her head clattered to the floor. Ella's attacker—all five feet eleven inches of him, dressed only in a tight-fitting pair of midnight-blue boxer briefs—stumbled backward, clawing at both of his eyes. Disjointed strings of cuss words and something about her being a she-devil streamed toward her. Heart lodged in her throat and pounding like a bass drum, she swung her drenched purse off one shoulder, whipped down the side zipper, and reached for her Taser.

Wait a minute. She heard her name, and her head popped up. Her adversary with the extremely well-defined abs staggered a few more steps back and fell into the recliner.

Oh, God. Not thinking of the bling-covered pepper spray still in one hand, she tried to cover her gaping mouth and almost coated her tonsils with the fiery liquid. She forced her hand away. Another onslaught of colorful vocabulary cinched it. She knew that voice.

"Coop? Is that you?"

"Of course it's me," he growled back. "Who else would it be?" He pulled one hand away from his face, and the familiar chiseled jawline and the trademark mole next to his left eye made her cringe.

His hair had grown longer, but the sandy-blond color still reminded her of caramel.

"Oh, my gosh, Coop. I didn't know you would be here."

He tried to open one exposed and very swollen eye, but flinched with a groan and covered it again.

She bolted toward him. "Let me help you."

This time he managed to pull both reddened eyelids into small slits. "No!" He drew back against the leather chair, and it tilted off balance. Catching himself, he pointed in the general location of her hands. Which one, she wasn't sure, since they were both outstretched toward him. "Stay away from me with those things."

She stopped her advance. *Jeez, some people. You try to throw them a lifeline, and they still let themselves drown.*

Coop stared at the weapons in her hands, and she glanced down at them, too. "Oh." Ella let her hands fall to her sides. "Now that I know it's you, I'm not going to use them on you." Her weight shifted, eyes flitting to one of Bradley's amateur wildlife photos that still hung on the wall. "Well, not again, anyway." She cleared her throat and forced herself to meet his glare.

"Out of the two of us, I'm the only one that's been pepper sprayed tonight, so I'm not taking any chances."

She hadn't seen Coop since Bradley's funeral, and he was already ticking her off. Typical. She discarded her purse, Taser, and keys—decorative pepper spray and all—onto the coffee table, her feelings of remorse quickly dissipating. "And out of the two of us, I'm the only one that's been attacked with a baseball bat tonight, so consider yourself lucky." In no particular hurry, she disappeared into the kitchen and reemerged with a wet cloth. "Here," she said, kneeling beside him. "Let me put this on your eyes."

She raised the rag toward his face, and he recoiled. Well aware that Cooper Wells had never liked her and never wanted Bradley to marry her, Ella hesitated. His unspoken disapproval seared her like a hot poker. Always had. Even though she stopped trying to be his friend a long time ago and avoided him like a bad case of the shingles, his distrust still stung.

Who was he to disapprove of *her?* He should've been happy for Bradley, glad his best friend was happily married. But no. Coop resented her for taking away his running buddy, even though Bradley hadn't enjoyed the single life half as much as Coop.

"Do you want the wet rag, or not?" she asked, all compassion now neatly tucked away for another time when it might actually be deserved.

Slowly, he moved his hands away, giving her access. She placed the cloth over his eyes and molded it to his nose and forehead.

"I've never been pepper sprayed before." Sarcasm threaded through his voice. "Any idea how long the burning will last?"

"About thirty minutes or so. Just don't rub your eyes. It'll make it worse."

Silence descended again, and Ella watched the rise and fall of his muscled chest. What the heck, his eyes were covered. Why not sneak a peek? She absorbed his athletic build with an appreciative scan from head to bare feet. He really was a gorgeous man. As much as it pained her to admit it, she could see how he so easily seduced women of all ages, shapes, and cup sizes within seconds. Too bad he felt it necessary to be such a prick to *her.*

Speaking of . . .

Her eyes went to the package just below his waist. He really did fill out those boxer briefs nicely. In fact, he could easily be a model for men's underwear. Move over, David Beckham. Long, powerful legs stretched out beside her, his upper arms bulging while he held the wet rag to his eyes, that caramel mane was tousled just enough to look sexy as—

"See something you like?"

She jumped, and her eyes flew to his. With the rag lifted a fraction he stared back at her. *Oh crap, oh crap, oh crap.* "Uh, no!" C, R, A, P in capital letters. "I just wanted to see if you were hurt, uh, anywhere else." She bit her lip.

Oh, God. What would Bradley think? Yes, his dying wish had been for her to move on. Find someone else and marry again. He knew how much she wanted kids. But, ogling Cooper Wells? Her gaze fell to the ground in shame.

He dropped the cloth back onto his eyes. "What are you doing here, Ella? Don't you have history students to teach or whatever?"

"It's summer, and I quit my teaching job three years ago." Her words clipped out at a sharp pace. "To take care of Bradley, remember?"

He swallowed, his mouth thinning into a hard line just below the rag.

Really? He didn't remember *that?* Unbelievable, even for a self-absorbed . . .

Coop lifted the cloth again. His puffy red lids caused her conscience to rear its foul head. Guilt threaded through her.

"Didn't you get my message?" she asked, trying to sound contrite.

Chicken that she was, she had called his home phone before leaving Albuquerque when she knew he'd be at work. After the long and detailed message she'd left—which had been cut off, forcing her to call back twice to finish it—she felt certain he would stay away and give her the peace and quiet she so desperately needed to close this chapter of her life. So, why was he asking *her* for an explanation? As far as she was concerned, he had some explaining to do.

"What message?" His voice dripped with suspicion, and his posture tensed.

Well. Obviously, he *hadn't* gotten her message that could easily qualify as a dissertation for a doctorate degree. A knot started to form just below her breastbone.

A hefty bark sounded from the porch.

"Oh, God. I forgot Winston." Ella ran for the front door, which still stood ajar.

Leading her muddy canine inside, she gave the knotty pine door a shove, and it thudded shut. She frowned at the dirty paw tracks left in Winston's wake, but couldn't deal with that mess right now. Not when she had a much bigger problem staring right at her, by the name of Cooper Wells.

"You remember Winston, right?" Ella asked. Coop's brow furrowed. "No? Oh, I keep forgetting you were too busy to visit Bradley much." A muscle in his jaw flexed. *So there, Mr. Hotshot. Your power shift failed.* "I got Winston for Bradley when he was sick. He always wanted an English bulldog. I tied Winston up outside to wash the mud off, but I guess it doesn't matter."

Ella looked around the messy cabin. Okay, cleanliness obviously wasn't one of Coop's virtues, not that she thought he had any virtues to begin with. "Looks like the floor hasn't been cleaned in . . . well, ever."

Winston growled and yanked out of her grasp. "Hey!" Ella yelled, but Winston bounded toward a trembling mound of fur in the corner of the room.

A muffled groan sounded from Coop's direction. "That would be my dog, Atlas."

"Atlas." Ella smiled, remembering the first time she'd met Bradley. After hiking the La Luz trail her first year in Albuquerque, she'd limped into his office as a new patient. Pointing to her X-rays, he'd explained the misalignment of her spine, starting with the top vertebra—the atlas. "Only a chiropractor would come up with a name like that." She shrugged thoughtfully. "Or an English Lit major."

Several creases appeared over Coop's brows.

"Haven't you read Ayn Rand?" His blank stare answered her question. "Oh, forget it." Reading apparently ranked right up there with cleanliness on Coop's list of priorities. Figured.

The cowering pooch rolled onto its back, whimpering. Winston pounced and licked the other dog's snout while humping away.

Coop groaned again. "I didn't think this night could get any worse."

"Winston's neutered," Ella reassured him.

"Wouldn't matter if he wasn't," Coop muttered. "Atlas is a *he*."

She couldn't help it. A rumble of laughter started somewhere deep in her gut and echoed through the cabin.

Coop glared at her. His head fell back on the headrest, and he covered his eyes again. "What happened to you, anyway? You look like hell."

"Thanks. You really know how to flatter a girl." She looked down at her mud-streaked legs and shoeless foot. When she wiggled her toes, mud squished out. Yeah, she looked god-awful. "The road coming in was so muddy the Beamer slid into a ditch and got stuck. I had to walk the rest of the way here."

"You drove Bradley's BMW up here in this weather?" An accusation hung in the air.

She bristled. "I didn't know it was going to rain." She crossed both arms across her chest. "Besides, I got rid of our truck. I can't relocate to a different state driving both."

"So if you're moving to another state, what are you doing in Red River? And couldn't you have called to tell me you were coming?"

"And you could check your messages once every decade or so."

There went that muscle in his jaw again.

A wheezing snore emerged from the corner. Winston and Atlas cuddled. Winston was fast asleep and both looked content. Well, they'd just seen more action in two minutes than she'd seen in the past two years. Too bad she didn't smoke. If she did, she'd offer them a cigarette.

"I'll pull your car out of the ditch tomorrow, so you can be on your way."

Tomorrow? Three and a half years had passed since Bradley's terminal cancer diagnosis. She'd come here to make peace with losing him before starting over somewhere else. She planned to give Coop her share of the cabin when she left, but she sure wasn't going to let him push her out before she was ready.

She wouldn't be asking for much, just a little time in this secluded mountain retreat that had meant so much to Bradley. Before she turned the property deed over to Coop, she had to give her heart a chance to mend. It was her only hope of finding love again, of building a new life—a life that she hoped would include children and a man just like Bradley.

Coop's presumptuous statement needled her like a burr under a horse's saddle. She narrowed her eyes. If he couldn't give her a little space, then maybe she'd keep her share of the cabin. After all, he hadn't offered to buy her out yet. Even if he did, she didn't have to sell.

One foot tapped against the wood floor. "What makes you think I'll be leaving tomorrow?"

"I'm here, for starters," he sputtered.

She shrugged. "You'll have to go back to Albuquerque in a few days, right? You've got patients to see."

He glowered at her. "How long are you planning to stay, then? A week, two maybe?"

Time to dig in and stand her ground. Ella planted a hand firmly on one hip and leveled a solid stare at him. "Try the whole summer."

She looked good. Too good. Even with her hair plastered around that heart-shaped face and black sludge oozing from the perfectly painted toes of one foot, *Cinder-Ella*, as he had secretly dubbed her when she and Bradley first started dating, looked incredible.

In the beginning, Coop understood Bradley's physical attraction to Ella. Her anal-retentive routine soon wore thin, though. She couldn't handle a spontaneous act of fun if her life depended on it. When Bradley told him she didn't much care for Red River because it reminded her too much of all the country bumpkins back in her hometown, well, that was just nauseating.

He stared at the bedroom ceiling and listened to the shower. With the bathroom next to his room, he could hear her moving around, even knew when she picked up the bottle of liquid soap and set it back down. She was in there, all steamy and wet, rubbing handfuls of Old Spice body wash all over herself. He had forgotten what a great body she possessed. A little short for his taste, not scary thin, just filled out and rounded in all the right places. The rain-soaked Nike running shorts she wore had molded to her thighs and hips, reminding him of how fit she was. Not so muscular that she lost her feminine allure, but just enough to look healthy and lush.

After the hot water washed her clean and warmed her up, she would put on the T-shirt he'd offered her. What else could he have done, since her luggage would have to stay in the car until morning? That ill-timed act of chivalry now had him in a state of misery. The minute he'd handed the white undershirt to her, his overactive imagination produced images of what would be underneath. Or, more precisely, what wouldn't be underneath.

He swallowed hard.

"Jesus, she's my best friend's widow." *And she just attacked me with pepper spray, so get over it.* Besides, Ella seemed like the type to prepare for any eventuality. If she carried pepper spray and a Taser in her purse, she probably had a veritable department store of extra clothing tucked in there, too.

Lifting his head, he looked down at the tented sheet.

Nope, not getting over it anytime soon. His head fell back on the pillow.

His latest experience with a member of the opposite sex should've rendered him incapable of such an intense reaction. That nightmare had led to this self-imposed exile to Red River.

She thinks she's staying all summer. Coop snorted. As if he'd let that happen. It was too late to argue about it tonight. Plus, he needed time to come up with a good reason *why* she had to leave. Immediately. He couldn't tell her the truth. Not unless she'd already heard about his situation. God, he hoped not. Since he hadn't been arrested yet, his attorney had managed to keep it out of the news. No, he doubted she knew, or else she'd have been her usual smug, condescending self. When it came to him and his confirmed bachelor lifestyle, she let her disapproval glow like radioactive waste.

She never made an appearance at the cabin when Bradley was still alive. She probably thought the "hicks" here were beneath her. She usually made Bradley take her on some ridiculous historical vacation. Okay, she *was* a history teacher. He'd give her that much. But she'd made it clear that Red River wasn't up to her lofty standards, which had always been fine by him. He'd preferred that Bradley come alone, so they could do guy stuff like fishing and rafting. So they could drink beer at night with their feet up on the coffee table, and burp or scratch themselves without Cinder-Ella staring down her nose at them.

So, why now?

The shower shut off. After a few minutes of Ella doing whatever women do in bathrooms, the door opened, and footsteps retreated down the hall. The wood planks creaked under her feet. She called for Winston to follow, and her door clicked shut.

He ran two fingers across his bloated eyelids. Tomorrow, the first order of business would be to drag her car out of the ditch, then get her on the road and out of his life.

Chapter Three

Ella yawned and wandered into the empty den, Cooper Wells far from her thoughts. She grabbed a crocheted afghan off the sofa and tugged it around her shoulders. Pulling the front door open, she whistled to Winston. "Come on, boy, go outside." Winston hustled outside for his morning constitutional, and Ella snuggled deep inside the handmade-by-Granny blanket, stepping out onto the wooden porch. The crisp mountain air filled her lungs and bit at her bare feet.

For several years she'd stayed away from the cabin after her fateful run-in with Cooper Wells. But after watching Bradley wither into nothingness, his rural hideaway, where he'd come to relax and recharge, was the only place she wanted to be right now. Red River—where the Ute and Jicarilla Apaches once roamed, and prospectors had carved countless mines looking for precious metals—sat nestled into a lush, green valley and held a serenity that brought peace to her wounded soul.

Winston shuffled up onto the porch and let out a low growl, cutting his eyes up at her.

Chuckling, she bent to scratch him. "You ready to eat?"

He barked.

"Stupid question," she said, and walked back into the kitchen, her bare feet slapping against the linoleum. Rummaging around in the pantry, she found a bag of dog food. *Thank you, Atlas.* She pulled a large bowl from the cupboard and filled it. While Winston devoured the kibble like a vulture having his first meal in a week, Ella searched through the disorganized cabinets.

The French press coffeepot she bought for herself and Bradley when they were dating lay hidden behind a haphazard mound of mismatched pots and pans. She pulled it free and circled her finger around the lip of the carafe. It definitely failed the white-glove test. The gray dust coating her fingertip confirmed it hadn't been used since the first, and last, time she visited. She gave it a good washing, and then foraged around the messy kitchen, locating the necessary ingredients to make coffee—the only thing she could successfully create in the kitchen.

When she finally held a steaming cup in hand, she ambled through the lower level, reacquainting herself with the place. Definitely a guys' weekend retreat. An eclectic collection of country and rustic furnishings filled the den and dinette. A wrought-iron staircase spiraled upward to a loft that offered several sets of bunk beds and a bathroom that hadn't worked since before she met Bradley. As photography was one of Bradley's hobbies, several of his nature photographs still garnished the walls.

Bradley had loved this place. The solitude of Red River had been his refuge since he started coming here with the Wells family in his adolescence. He would've loved nothing more than for her to share it with him, but she'd disappointed him. She and Coop, the two people Bradley cared about most, had let him down in the worst possible way.

She stopped at the bar separating the kitchen from the dinette, and cleared off a barstool that was stacked practically to the ceiling with Coop's miscellaneous junk. She'd really have to give this place a good cleaning, and soon, just to make it livable. After she gave Coop full ownership and left for destinations still to be determined, Coop could dirty it up to his heart's content. While she lived here, though, the clutter had to go.

Ella perched herself on a barstool and sipped her coffee. The afghan slipped off one shoulder, and she pulled it back on, angling her stool toward the large picture window, which offered a grand view of the babbling stream that ran through the back side of their property. The log she had sat on to watch Bradley fish for trout still lay there, clumps of blue fescue grass growing up around it.

A loud snore reverberated from the corner. Ella laughed. Finished with his breakfast, Winston had found a cozy spot on top of the floor vent and curled into a ball for a nap. His back legs moved in rhythm, and Ella shook her head. Probably dreaming of Atlas.

Even though she only intended to stay the summer, the cabin felt nice, comfortable. Like home. It needed a little tidying up, granted. Glancing around the lower level, which had everything from clothes to sports equipment strewn around, she lifted a dirty sock from the other barstool with two fingers. Well, maybe it needed to be disinfected and some of the contents torched, but still, it would be cozy once she cleaned and organized it. She tossed the sock aside and wiped her hand on the afghan with a grimace. Still, the cabin was comfy and intimate, and Red River had always reminded her of the coziness and tranquility of her home in East Texas, without all the family drama and obnoxious demands for her to stay and help work the ranch.

She shuddered at the thought.

She stared down at the dark brown liquid and rolled it around in her cup. Steam curled up and teased her nostrils. Warmed her soul. A great way to start the day, especially in the mountains where a chill always hung in the morning air, even now in early June. Unfortunately, her favorite drink couldn't dispel the guilt she still carried.

The truth was she loved it up here. During that one and only visit to Red River, she'd fallen in love with the town, its charm, the quaintness, and the familiarity of everyone knowing each other. It was kind of cute, actually. Safe. Secure.

Coop's Toyota Tundra, with its oversized off-road tires, churned into the driveway, her BMW in tow. His beefy truck circled the cabin and pulled to a stop in front of the window, blocking her scenic view of the stream and ending her nostalgic walk down memory lane. Bradley's image faded like mist, leaving her with a view of mud-encrusted steel-belted radials. Filth covered both vehicles, but hers didn't even resemble the same car she left in the ditch last night. Instead of midnight blue, it had transformed into a sludge gray. Not a fleck of blue paint could be seen through the thick grime.

Coop jumped out of his truck and headed for the house, Atlas bounding after him. Coop's caramel hair feathered against the breeze, and his faded jeans went taut over muscled thighs with each long stride. Behind him, his younger brother, Calvin, got out of the truck, and Ella smiled. A younger version of Coop, Cal had darker hair and a boyish face just as handsome as his older brother's.

Cal walked to the Beamer where their dad, Butch, sat behind the wheel. Cal pulled suitcases from the backseat, and Butch popped the trunk and got out to retrieve its hidden treasures.

Butch's resemblance to his two sons was uncanny. With graying hair and a small spare tire around his middle brought on by age and retirement, Butch wore a jovial smile.

When Coop's boots landed on the wooden porch and he stomped the mud off, Ella twitched. She bristled, waiting for the inevitable confrontation.

"Hi," he mumbled when he charged through the door, a muddy clump dangling from one hand. Then he just stood there. He blinked once. Then twice, his eyes traveling down her bare legs. Swallowing, the muscles in his contoured neck flexed, sending a strange tingle through Ella's chest.

She tugged the afghan tighter. "I, uh, didn't have any of my own clean clothes to put on, so I borrowed more of yours. I hope you don't mind."

When she uncrossed her legs, Coop blew out a heavy breath, and his eyes grew darker. With his dislike of her emanating from his very pores, Ella's nerves got the better of her. She babbled out a lame explanation. "Uh, I don't usually rummage through other people's things, but I found these hanging in the bathroom and they smelled relatively clean." She opened the afghan like a flasher to reveal his running shorts and the T-shirt he'd loaned her to sleep in. And yes, she had smelled them before putting them on and found no offensive odor. After searching the medicine cabinet, she doused them with body spray anyway. "I'll wash them before I give them back."

"Yeah. Fine." His hazel eyes clouded over, and several wrinkles appeared between his brows. "The Beamer runs, but the roads are so rutted and muddy we had to pull it here. It'll be a few days before you can get on the road again."

She tensed. "I told you last night. I'm staying the summer."

"No." Coop scrubbed a hand over the faint shadow of stubble on his jaw. "You're not."

She placed her cup on the bar and stood to do battle, but Calvin burst through the door with Butch on his heels. Each carried suitcases in both hands and under their arms.

"Great to see you, Ella!" Butch roared. He dropped his load, then converged on her, swinging her around in a bear hug.

"Butch! It's been too long. Haven't seen you since you moved up here permanently." When Butch put her down, she turned to Calvin and ruffled his hair. "You're so tall, kiddo. I blinked, and you grew up." She nudged Butch. "Handsome, too. You got your stick out, Dad, to scare off all the pretty girls?"

Calvin kicked the floor, shoving his hands in his pockets. His ears burned bright red, like any seventeen-year-old boy's would when talking about girls. "Good to see you, too, Ella."

Butch tossed his chin toward the mound of purple paisley luggage. "Looks like you're stayin' a while."

***

Ella glanced Coop's way, a smile on her plump, rosy lips. They danced when she spoke, and he wondered for the millionth time how they would taste. Again. "Oh, yes," she said. "I'm here for the summer."

Okay, been there, tasted that. Focus, idiot, she has to go.

"Hey, hey! That's great, Ella," Butch bellowed.

Coop wanted to roll his eyes. Why did his father make such a fool of himself around women? Especially those with a superiority complex. Luckily, none of his five short-lived marriages had stuck. The minute one of them said a cross word to Coop, they were history. He was a good dad, but when it came to women, he could be obtuse. Okay, dumb as a stump would be a better description, but hey, Butch deserved *some* credit for being a five-star father. Why it took his dad five failed marriages to figure out that he should probably stay single still perplexed Coop, because Coop decided he'd never marry by the time stepmom number two left.

As the familial traitors gushed over the unwanted intruder, Coop couldn't keep his mouth shut. As usual.

"Why?" he asked.

Three sets of cheerful eyes turned on him. Merriment faded from the emerald-green pair.

"Excuse me?" Ella asked, crossing her arms over her chest.

"Why are you here for the summer?" Coop tried to sound civil, but his dad's glare told him he failed.

She shot Coop a look that could wither a full-grown oak tree. "I do own half this place."

"That still doesn't answer my question," Coop ground out.

"I wasn't aware that I answered to you," Ella shot back.

Butch cleared his throat. "Uh, why don't we sit down and figure this out. Is that coffee I smell?"

Ella turned a charming smile on Butch. "It is, Butch, and there's just enough left for you." When her eyes returned to Coop, those upturned lips melted downward into a frown.

Coop held up the muddy object in his hand. "This yours?"

Ella's brow wrinkled. "It vaguely resembles the shoe I lost last night in the ditch."

He tossed it to one side, and it rolled toward the door.

"Uh, thanks, but you could've left it on the porch," she mumbled.

"The handsome prince brought Cinderella her shoe," Cal teased.

Coop tried to incinerate his little brother with a glare. Neither Bradley nor Ella ever knew he had pinned her with that nickname, mostly because he never meant it as a compliment. He'd already been a crummy friend to Bradley, in so many ways. If Cal gave him away now, Coop would siphon off the gasoline from his truck every night for the entire summer. Keeping his cocky little teenaged butt home might teach him a thing or two about family loyalty.

Butch rattled around in the kitchen, making a cup of coffee. Cal plopped into the recliner, kicking his feet up while he dug out his phone. He held it high. "Reception here still sucks. Too bad you don't have Wi-Fi."

"Oh, I brought a router." Ella folded herself onto the sofa and meticulously propped her bare feet up on the coffee table. "Best one on the market. It can catch a signal from Colorado. The cable company will be here day after tomorrow to hook it up."

Coop's gaze raked the length of those long, graceful legs that stretched from here to heaven and . . . "Wait. Cable? Oh, no." He shook his head. "If you want all the conveniences of city life, then go back to Albuquerque."

"I can't."

Butch joined them in the den, and sat next to Ella. He sipped his coffee. "Mmm, Ella, you always did make a killer cup of coffee." Then he gave Ella's knee an affectionate pat like she was his long-lost daughter.

"Dad," Coop fumed. "Do you mind?"

"Mind what?" Butch's blank expression made Coop almost sympathetic toward his mother and four ex-stepmothers. Well, not his mother. She was so much like Ella. Always looking down on Red River and the people here. Always wanting to go on an adventure, live the lifestyles of the rich and famous. Please.

Coop pinched the bridge of his nose. "Why can't you go back to Albuquerque?"

She fidgeted with a ring on her left hand, turning it in a complete circle. Her wedding ring. Guilt pinged his chest.

"I've sold the house and put most of my belongings in storage. I'm leaving New Mexico." She gave Coop a determined stare. "But first, I'm spending the summer in Red River. It's the last thing I need to do to say good-bye to Bradley."

And there it was again. The guilt card.

Yes, Bradley had been his best friend. Yes, Coop owed him. Big. But he absolutely, unequivocally, could not live under the same roof with Ella for the next three months. Not no, but hel—

Wetness shimmered in her eyes and dampened the silky lashes that brushed her cheeks every time she blinked.

No, no. Not tears. Anything but tears.

She sniffed.

Coop closed his eyes. Yep, he just went down in flames.

"Aw, Ella. You're too pretty to cry," cooed Cal, looking bashful. His teenage crush announced itself in his lovesick puppy stare.

Butch grabbed a napkin off the coffee table and handed it to Ella. She looked at it like it might be diseased, then used a tiny corner to dab her eyes.

"Now, now, sugar," Butch soothed her. "This is your place as much as Coop's, and you should stay as long as you need. I'll even fix up that old bathroom in the loft for you. That way you'll have some privacy."

"And some cleanliness," she said in between sniffles. "Thank you, Butch, but I don't want to put you to all that trouble."

"Nonsense, young lady. I'm retired, and Cal and I live up here year-round now." Butch thumped his chest and chuckled. "It'll give this old man something constructive to do."

Coop made a mental note to remind his dad that blood was supposed to be thicker than water. After he sold his condo in Albuquerque to help pay for his legal fees, Coop had moved here to be near family. Thought it would ease the blow of his tarnished reputation back in Albuquerque, where most of his "friends" had stopped returning his calls. Apparently, neither his father nor his little brother understood the meaning of family allegiance.

Butch draped his arm around Ella's shoulders. "Bradley was like a son to me. I darn near raised him."

Ella sniffed, and dabbed, and nodded and sniffed some more. "He loved you like a father. He always said you were the reason he became a chiropractor—because you were a chiropractor." She gave

Coop a dismissive glance. "And, of course, because Coop wanted to be one, too."

Butch laughed. "Yessiree, always partners in crime. They looked out for each other since they were kids." He hesitated and lowered his voice almost to a whisper. "And . . . you know . . . Bradley's parents got into that cult stuff. Always leaving him alone 'til all hours of the night, forgetting to pick him up from school because they were at a 'meeting.'" He did air quotes with his fingers. "Even gave away all their money to the cult leader, then wanted Bradley to support them when he went into practice. That kid worked like a dog putting himself through school."

"I'm glad he had you, Butch. Thanks for looking out for him and for helping him with tuition. He never forgot it."

"We'll be here for you, too, Ella, as long as you need us." Butch gave Coop one of those looks. The look that said, *Do what I say or I'll make sure you regret it for the rest of your natural-born life.* "Right, Coop?"

Coop tried to unclench his locked jaw. "Sure. We'll manage. I guess."

A whimper drew his attention to the floor vent in front of the window. Atlas lay on his back, Winston doing his best to have his merry way with him. Atlas licked Winston's wrinkled face. Well, if Coop and Atlas were both going to get screwed, at least one of them should enjoy it.

Chapter Four

Ella and the three Wells men drove into Red River, the gargantuan tires on Coop's truck rattling her brain. Was he *trying* to hit every pothole in the county? Hells bells, she needed her own four-wheel drive.

Still, she enjoyed the scenery as they tooled into the city limits. She'd arrived after dark, with only the moon to cast a glow over the sleepy little town where the sidewalks rolled up at a certain hour. This morning the white crest of Wheeler Peak towered overhead, dwarfing the rest of the mountain chain. Tourists ambled along the sidewalks, and the strips of businesses that lined the streets boasted red-barn or wood-siding facades, giving the town a historic feel. Nothing had changed since her only visit to Red River all those years ago. Not one thing. And that was part of the nostalgic charm of a small community woven so tight that it became a sanctuary of sorts.

When they pulled up in front of the Red River Market, the town's only grocery store, Ella bailed out of the backseat and considered walking back to the cabin. She clutched the truck bed with one hand, letting the fresh air settle her motion sickness.

Butch climbed out of the front passenger seat. "You okay, Ella? You look a little green."

"I'm fine." No way was she going to admit to getting carsick. She wasn't about to give Coop the satisfaction of thinking she was that much of a wimp.

"Coop, give your keys to Cal," Butch said, easily commanding his boys.

She envied their closeness. Even though Butch had been unlucky in love, he did a great job with his two sons. An amazing feat, considering he had pretty much raised them on his own. As a high school teacher, it wasn't hard for Ella to spot the difference between the kids who had involved parents and those who didn't.

"Cal," he directed, "you help Ella with her grocery bags. Load them in the truck when she's done shopping. It's cool enough for them to keep awhile in the truck." He turned to Ella, and his tone melted to one of affection. "You take your time, Ella. When you're done, you and Cal meet us across the street at the Gold Miner's Café. Breakfast is on me, you hear?"

"Yes, sir." She smiled at him. Butch had a warmheartedness that her father never possessed. An affectionate side that always touched her. Just like Bradley. She glanced at Coop, who stewed with his hands in his pockets. Amazing how different Butch's oldest son turned out. Cal got more of his father's "happy" gene than his older brother.

Her phone beeped.

"Finally," Cal sighed. "We've got reception again." He pulled his phone from his pocket and fired off a text.

"Thanks, Butch. We shouldn't be long," Ella said. She watched Butch and his brooding firstborn head across the street to the café. A Jeep puttered down the street, waving at the Wells men as it passed. Butch waved back, but Coop kept both hands hidden in his pockets.

Faded Levi's hung low on his narrow hips, and Ella pulled in her bottom lip, her eyes grazing over his nice bottom. A blue plaid flannel shirt covered a plain white T-shirt that stretched taut across his broad shoulders, the shirttails flapping in the breeze. She gave her head an infinitesimal shake. What a waste; that perfect male body paired with such a sour personality.

Turning away, she scrolled through her missed call log. Her parents and her sister, Charlene. Ouch. Probably wanting to know if she arrived in Red River safely. They were also more than likely plotting some sort of family conspiracy to get her to move back to East Texas. She'd call them later, after she had a few dozen more cups of coffee.

A couple of missed calls from close friends back in Albuquerque, also probably wanting to check up on her. She sent them a quick group text. *Got here fine.* Well, mostly, but the details were too long to type in a text. *No cell reception at cabin. Call on landline.*

She checked her voice mail. Cynthia Caldwell's name popped onto the screen. Ella glanced up at Cal. "Uh, Cal. Why don't you go on in, and get a cart for me. I'll be right there."

"Sure." Cal ambled into the small market with a teenaged swagger.

She hit the Listen button, and Cyn's voice crowed through the line. "Violet! How's my favorite *New York Times* Bestselling Erotic Romance Author? Girlfriend, I'm still on cloud nine about it," her editor gushed. "Just making sure you got to . . . where is it you're staying for the summer? Anyway, your deadline for book three has been moved up. Wanton Publishing has decided to fast-track the next release because sales for the first two books have shot through the roof! Send me what you've got so far. And don't forget, we need an excerpt for book four, like yesterday. That should have the preorders flooding in." Cyn cackled. "Did you see this morning's top news story?"

Ella turned and looked both ways down the street, her chest tight.

"A chick fight broke out at a Book-Mart in Cleveland. Apparently, two of your fans tried to grab the last copy of *New Mexico Naughty.*" The excitement in her voice made Ella's embarrassment grow, and heat eased up her neck into her cheeks. Even the tips of her ears grew hot. "Really, haven't these women heard of e-readers? I'll just bet book three debuts even higher on the bestseller list than the first two. Well, tootles, and call me soon." The message ended, and Ella looked around to see if anyone had guessed her dirty little secret. Even though she wasn't on speakerphone, she felt exposed. Like after having a dream where she was naked in a public place.

Jeez, Dennings, grow up, she scolded herself, because really, she was a *grown* woman for crying out loud. Why should she care if her real identity got out? Except that she'd been a role model for her high school students and had grown up in the Bible Belt sitting in the front pew every Sunday because her dad was a deacon. Her family would probably disown her, and if she ever wanted to return to the teaching profession, she might be hard-pressed to find a school district that would hire an erotic romance novelist to teach impressionable teens.

But if she was careful, no one would ever find out.

"I can't tell Ella, Dad," Coop insisted, for about the hundredth time since they walked into the Gold Miner's Café.

Caricatures of famous visitors hung on the wood-paneled walls. Most of the glossy wood tables were occupied with patrons wanting the best home-cooked breakfast in town. Chatter was high, but heads were down, eating and talking at the same time because the food was just too good to let it get cold.

"Tell me what?" Ella stepped from behind a group of customers who loitered in the aisle to exchange pleasantries with another table.

She sat down next to Butch, and Cal plopped into the chair opposite her. "That you're hiding out in Red River until your legal problems back in Albuquerque are resolved? Something to do with a woman scorned, I think Cal said."

Coop blinked; he tried to speak but nothing audible came out. Then he leveled a deadly look at his little brother. Definitely siphoning off the little rat's gasoline tonight.

Cal shrugged. "Sorry, dude. She asked when you were going back to Albuquerque. I had to tell her."

"Really? Did you tell her my shoe size, too? Since you two are so chummy, why don't you tell her what brand of underwear I use?" Coop wanted to smirk, because she'd probably already figured that out. The way she checked him out last night when he was wearing nothing *but* underwear, she probably knew the brand, size, and thread count.

"Sorry, bro. Ella's prettier than you. Besides, news travels faster in this town than a class-five forest fire. It's just a matter of time before someone else tells her." Cal waved at a cute little waitress that looked about his age.

"He has a point," Butch offered, and Coop wanted to throttle the both of them.

He raked a hand over his face. "I'm not *hiding out.*" He hesitated. He didn't want to have to explain this to Ella of all people. "My license to practice has been temporarily suspended, so I had to close my office. Until the investigation is over, I moved up here for some peace and quiet." He shot her a scowl. "Which has now been interrupted."

"Hi, Cal." The server came over, notepad in hand, and tossed her black ponytail over one shoulder. Retrieving a pen from the back pocket of her tight-fitting jeans, she gave Cal a dimpled smile.

"Hey, Kaylee," Cal said. His cheeks flushed, and his mouth turned up in a bashful grin.

"What can I get you guys?"

While Ella looked over the menu, Cal and Butch ordered their usual fare. Coop asked for a protein-only plate, a large glass of milk, and a coffee. He turned to Ella, who studied the menu like a textbook. Her elegant nose turned up just a bit at the tip. Light auburn hair the color of autumn leaves was neatly tucked behind one ear. Those intelligent green eyes skimmed across the page.

"I'll have a large stack of buttermilk pancakes, two dollops of butter instead of one, extra syrup, and whipped cream on top." Ella closed her menu and handed it to the server. "Oh, and a large glass of orange juice."

Coop stared at her, aghast. Some things never changed. Ella still ate like a man. "That's what you're eating? How can you consume all that sugar so early in the morning?" My God, that meal contained enough sugar and carbs to send a diabetic to the hospital.

She turned a furrowed brow on him. "Instead of worrying about my eating habits, why don't you concern yourself with your own problems?" One corner of her mouth turned up in a cocky smile, and Coop's eyes locked on to her lush mouth. "Because from what I hear, you have so many."

"I'm innocent," Coop said, still staring at her pink, plumped lips. The very ones that always emitted smart-ass remarks when speaking to him.

One of her perfectly arched brows raised high.

"No, really. I didn't do it," he barked, finally breaking the spell that her mouth cast on him every time it formed an O. Amazing what one little letter could do to a man.

Kaylee returned with their drinks. Placing each one in front of its recipient, she spoke to Cal. "So, are you going to summer school?"

"Uh, yeah." His grin faded. "I have to retake English and History."

"I guess I'll see you there, then." Kaylee finished delivering the drinks and fidgeted with the extra straws on the tray.

Cal's eyes rounded. "You're going to summer school? You're a straight-A student."

She flashed a shy smile at him. "I'm taking extra classes in the summer so I can graduate early. I want to go to nursing school."

"That's an admirable profession, Kaylee," Butch praised her.

"Thanks, Dr. Wells. I'll be right back with your order." Kaylee bebopped over to another table.

"Cal, do you mind if I ask why you have to retake classes?" Ella said.

Embarrassed, Cal traced the pattern on the tablecloth with a finger. "I didn't pass. I have a hard time keeping up with the amount of reading we have to do in those subjects." He glanced up at Ella, and Coop guessed his little brother was trying to gauge her reaction. Relief washed over Cal's face when he saw understanding in Ella's schoolteacher eyes. "I'm dyslexic."

Ella nodded, compassion etched into her expression. Coop had to give brownie points to Ms. Overachiever for that. It had been painful watching his little brother struggle with the same learning disability he had grown up with. If it hadn't been for Bradley, Coop wouldn't have graduated high school, much less gone on to college and chiropractic school. He would've never made it without constant help from his best friend. Unfortunately, Coop and Butch both suffered with the same affliction, making them useless to tutor Cal. Embarrassed by his slow and choppy reading, Cal wouldn't accept help from any of the reading specialists Butch tried to hire, so he never got the same help that Bradley had given Coop.

"I happen to be an okay teacher," she said modestly. "At least that's what I've been told by most of my students. How about I tutor you?"

"Really?" Cal asked.

A ping of gratitude blossomed in Coop's chest.

"It would be my pleasure. I haven't taught since Bradley got sick, and I miss it."

Their food arrived and Ella dived into her pancakes like one of the guys.

Butch stirred sugar and cream into his coffee. "Thanks, Ella. That would be great."

"Sure thing. It's the least I can do for you fixing up that bathroom for me in the loft." She shot a cloudy look in Coop's direction. "Since I'm going to be here for three months, I really need my own space."

Coop's ping of appreciation evaporated.

"Oh, and Kaylee's cute," Ella said to Cal, a smile in her voice, "and she likes you."

That was it. Ella went too far. Coop couldn't tutor his brother in academics, but he could certainly offer him some friendly advice when it came to women. "Trust me, they're nothing but trouble." He waved a fork toward Kaylee delivering food to another table. "Learn it now, and save yourself a lot of heartache and even more money." Nope, Cooper Wells would never again fall prey to a conniving female. No more. *Nada.* He was officially off the market and planned to become well acquainted with his hand. The real thing just wasn't worth it. Ever.

"Coop, did it ever occur to you that not all women are evil beings sent from the bowels of hell to ensnare you in their wicked plans to take over the world?" Ella asked.

"Nope. Never." He cut into his food.

She rolled her eyes, then shoved another chunk of sugar-on-a-plate into her mouth. She chewed, swallowed, and wiped her mouth with a swipe. "Maybe, just maybe, it's the kind of women you hook up with."

"What's that supposed to mean?" He feigned insult, but he knew exactly the kind to which she referred. The kind who looked good but would never inspire a long-term commitment from him. No, marriage wasn't for him, and neither was cohabitation.

His mom leaving him and Butch behind had been hard enough. Oh, she'd begged Coop to move with her to California, but ten-year-old boys weren't usually real anxious to leave their friends. Or their fathers. Then came the revolving door of wives filtering through Butch's life, the last one giving birth to Cal just before cleaning out Butch's bank account and disappearing.

No, Coop would be content staying single. And after what happened with his last presumed girlfriend, Kim, he didn't even care to date anymore. Kim Arrington had come to him begging for help, and that's what he'd tried to do. She set the trap, and he walked right into it like a dolt.

"It means stop dating bimbos," she said flatly. Picking up her glass, her lips formed a perfect little O around the straw, and she drew on her OJ.

Coop sputtered.

"She's got a point." Butch shrugged.

"Enough with the points, Dad."

"Why are you holed up here?" Ella doused her pancakes with a little more butter and syrup. "With all this time off, I'm surprised you're not backpacking around Europe or surfing on the Mexican Riviera. There's a whole big world out there, you know."

"Not my style. I can do all the adventure-seeking I want right here in Red River."

Ella cut off another chunk of pancake and swirled it around in the inch-deep syrup. "Cal didn't tell me exactly why you're being investigated. He left that honor for you." When she molded her mouth around the fork and her eyes closed in savory appreciation, he tried to ignore the tug below his belt and the heat gathering in the same spot. Damn this place for making such good pancakes. "Care to share?" she said around a mouthful of carbs.

Coop speared a piece of green chili turkey sausage with his fork, shoving an entire link in his mouth. Staring at his plate, he chewed in silence.

"She's gonna find out, bro. You might as well be the one to tell her."

Butch sucked in a deep breath, gathering steam to speak, but Coop cut him down with a glare.

"Don't say it," he growled at his dad.

Butch showed Coop both palms. "I'm not going to say that Cal has a point." When Coop speared another organic sausage, his dad added, "But he does."

"You're a lot angrier than I remember, Coop. You really should get some help with that," Ella said.

Coop surrendered and dropped his loaded fork onto the plate. "I was trying to help her out. Besides, we only dated a few months," he said.

"And?" Ella tapped an index finger on the table.

"Kim needed help," Coop explained.

"Oh, you actually ask their names now?" Ella said, and both Butch and Cal snorted.

"As. I. Was. Saying." Coop drew in a deep breath and fought to keep his temper in check. "Kim came to me with a sob story about how she needed to save money to go back to school. She needed a job, needed a place to stay. Her roommate was doing drugs. Obviously, she couldn't go back to her apartment because of the druggie types that were going in and out at all hours of the night. It wasn't safe. So I gave her a job."

"You gave her a job? In your office?" Ella's regal brows snapped together.

"There were tears. Real ones. What was I supposed to do?" Coop defended his honor, since his family obviously wasn't going to jump in on his behalf.

A hearty laugh bubbled through those ample lips. "You fell for that?" The mirth that danced in Ella's eyes irritated him to the bone.

"It was supposed to be temporary. Only for a few weeks until she found another job. Then she would move out, and we could go our separate ways."

Ella blinked at him several times. "You let her move in with you, too?"

"It was temporary!"

"Uh-huh. I suppose you bought some oceanfront property from her, too."

"Do you want to hear this, or not?"

"Alright, alright, go on." Ella downed another gulp of sugar-in-a-glass.

Coop rubbed his eyes. "After six weeks, she still wasn't gone."

"Big surprise," Ella mumbled as she polished off another thousand carbs or so.

"By that time, I really didn't want to date her anymore."

"Another shocker," she added a little above a whisper.

"But she wouldn't move out. Finally, I told her she couldn't work for me anymore, I boxed up all her things and changed the locks at the office and at home."

"Uh-oh, you fired her." Ella said. "I bet that set off World War Three."

"Try a mushroom cloud," Butch piped up, making a bomb-dropping whistle and finishing off with a perfect imitation of an explosion, with hand gestures and everything.

"Instead of picking up her things at the office the way I asked her to do, the police showed up. She accused me of sexual . . . misconduct."

Something flickered in Ella's emerald greens. "Coop, are you saying you could go to prison?"

He dragged a hand through his hair. "I haven't actually been arrested yet. The police are investigating, but my attorney assures me they don't have enough evidence to make any charges stick. It's really my word against hers."

Another glint of dark emotion raced across Ella's flawless features. Concern, maybe? Nah. Disapproval, more than likely.

And damn it, this time the irritating woman had a point.

Whatever. He wasn't about to admit it to her. And there was no way he was going to prison for something he didn't do.

Chapter Five

A late-morning breeze whispered through the giant cottonwoods, gently stirring their leaves. Snow still capped Wheeler Peak, as it did most of the year, but fresh pine-scented air and moderate temperatures declared summer had arrived in the Red River Valley.

Coop baited the hook and threw it into the stream. As the water took it, he pulled out more line and let it snake downstream. Tossing a look over his shoulder toward the cabin, he stewed, an ocean of conflicting emotions raging inside him.

When he recited the whole embarrassing mess to Ella, disapproval emanated from her and encircled him like a nasty wool blanket that had been left out in the rain, all itchy and irritating. But he didn't see a shred of doubt about his innocence in her gaze. She didn't recoil and excuse herself like most of his "friends" in Albuquerque. When the story first broke, his phone stopped ringing, and he became a social pariah. But Ella just shrugged and said it was bound to happen sooner or later, him being a man-whore and all.

Come to think of it, he should've taken that as an insult, but his heart had thawed toward her a little. She believed him, which was quite unbelievable, actually. And then she came back to the cabin and moved her ass right in with him, instead of hauling that nice little back end straight out of town.

Ella was inside, unloading two shopping bags of junk food, unpacking an alarming amount of feminine paraphernalia, and settling into the cabin for the entire summer. Not the typical reaction from a woman if she thought her housemate might be guilty of a crime.

Coop's stomach soured. Any idiot that had to force himself on a woman was a monster. God, he hadn't forced a woman to do anything against her will, ever. Unless you counted the time in high school when he made Caitlyn Thompson, a very popular cheerleader, go out with a geeky member of the chess team because she'd lost a bet to Coop.

Ella opened the back door to let the dogs out. Atlas ran to him, sniffing around the can of worms. Winston made it down the steps, then hesitated, looking across the backyard at them. Probably deciding the stream was too far out of his range, he flopped on the grass by the steps.

Coop chuckled, shook his head, and returned his attention to the stream.

Granted, most of his romantic liaisons had been shallow and superficial, but that didn't make him a pervert. Admittedly, it probably made him an asshole, but he could live with that. But sexual misconduct? No way. That kind of behavior was so far beyond disgusting that it made his stomach turn.

Ella hadn't batted an eye, though.

Not true. Actually, she'd batted two very beautiful green eyes, but the point was, not even a hint of doubt had flickered through those deep pools of shimmering emerald.

It was so much easier being angry with her. Why'd she have to go and be so nice . . . sort of?

It was a conspiracy. He was convinced of it. Regardless of what Ella said, women possessed closely guarded answers to the secrets of the universe, and men would forever be kept in the dark. No wonder his dad had struck out all five times he got up to the plate.

Coop reeled in his line and recast it. Dragging a hand over his whiskered jaw, he tried to tamp down the sorrow he felt over Bradley's absence. Coping with his legal problems would be so much easier if Bradley were here to listen. "I miss you, buddy," he mumbled to the stream. It was times like these that made Bradley's death so painful.

Coop's line jiggled, and he tugged on it. The line went taut, and Coop reeled in a nice-looking brown trout. Putting it on the stringer, he reloaded his hook and walked a little farther upstream. When he found a nice rock with a deep pool around it, he tossed the bait into the water again.

Normally, a little fishing helped clear his mind, but today . . . today the thing that chewed at his conscience couldn't be escaped. Ella's very presence was a constant reminder of what a lousy friend he'd been to the best guy he ever knew.

When Bradley got sick, Coop couldn't accept it and refused to talk about it. With the patience of a saint, Bradley kept calling, even when Coop withdrew, seeing him less and less. A year after the diagnosis, Coop's cell phone rang, and he let it go to voice mail when he saw Bradley's number on the screen. The New Message signal beeped and he played it back.

Ella's voice sounded in his ear. "Coop, uh, hi." She hesitated, just as uncomfortable with him as he had always been around her. "Bradley can't get out of bed. The doctors don't know how much time he has left. He's lucid most of the time, but the oncologist said that will deteriorate as the cancer spreads through his brain." More hesitation, then she drew in a heavy breath. "Listen, he really wants to see you. It might be a good idea if you come by soon, you know, while he still knows who you are." Her voice cracked, and it took a second to regain her composure. "Your dad's been visiting once a week. Cal's been with him a few times. Butch said he's planning to retire soon and move to Red River permanently, so he wants to spend as much time with Bradley as possible before moving away." She sniffled. "Bradley knows he doesn't have much time left, Coop, and he wants to see you." A few seconds passed in silence. "I'm asking you to come see him before it's too late. Please."

The emotions woven through that last word tore at Coop's heart, forcing him to face the truth. The loss of the best friend he had ever had, the sadness of a young woman mourning for her husband and for herself, a brilliant young man cut down in the prime of his life— all of those things and many more knifed through him, and he felt his very soul tear from his chest.

For the first time since his mother walked out the front door, suitcase rolling behind her, Coop had sat down and cried like a baby. Then he got dressed and went to see Bradley.

Ella finished organizing the pantry and started on the kitchen. With both hands planted on her hips, her eyes raked the cluttered countertops. She breathed deeply. This was going to take a while. As she plotted her plan of attack, the landline rang.

"Hello?"

"Hi, sweetie," her mom's voice sang through the receiver.

"Hi, Mom."

"Obviously, you got to Red River in one piece." Her mother's usual sweet Southern drawl turned to a scold.

"I'm sorry I didn't call." Ella paused. "I've kinda had my hands full since I got here."

"Is everything alright, hon? Do you need money?"

"No! Mom, I'm fine. I already told you and Dad that Bradley had plenty of life insurance, and I got a fortune for the house." Not to mention the royalties from her book, which had already made her as rich as Midas.

Deafening silence made her shift from one hot-pink running shoe to the other. Like a six-year-old wanting to get out of time out, she offered a halfhearted explanation. "It's just, you know . . . I'm trying to get settled in. How's Dad?" Ella changed the subject.

"Oh, he's as ornery as ever, honey. When're you movin' home?"

She cringed. "I told you I'll come for a visit in the fall, but I'm not moving back to Texas, Mom."

"Why not? There's plenty of teachin' jobs around here. You need to be back with your family now that you're alone. We can't take care of you when you're way out there."

"I don't need anyone to take care of me, Mom," Ella ground out. "I'm a big girl."

"Well, now you've got your sister, Charlene, madder than a hornet," her mother harumphed.

"What did I do wrong this time?" Ella asked with resignation, because she'd *always* done something wrong.

Her mother snorted her disapproval. "You've got your niece, Kendra, wantin' to follow in your footsteps. Says she's movin' away. Applying to colleges out of state."

Ella stilled. If her churchgoing family found out about her new profession, they'd likely not want her around her nieces and nephews at all. Moving home would be a disaster if the truth came out, because she'd be banned from the entire dry county by chapter three of book one. Once they got to chapter ten . . .

Oh, thank the angels in heaven for pen names.

"Your father and Henry, Jr., just walked in from checking the cattle," her mom said, and Ella was never so happy to change a subject. Except for maybe when her mom tried to give her "the talk" on her eighteenth birthday, as if Ella hadn't already figured out where babies come from.

The cattle. Oh, joy. "Tell them I said hi," said Ella, guilt threading through her. Those cattle had supported their family and put her through a bachelor's degree, but then her dad had insisted she become a veterinarian and help work the ranch.

Ella shuddered.

Working in cow dung in hot, humid temperatures just hadn't been her dream career. Seemed more like a nightmare to her.

Her mom repeated Ella's message to her dad and brother and then got back on the phone. "They want to know when you're movin' home."

Ella rolled her eyes.

"Listen, I've got to run. I'll call soon." Ella had to get off the phone before she said something she'd regret. She loved her family, but every phone call was charged with disappointment and her failure to become what they expected her to be. And the incessant demands for her to move back to East Texas drove her insane.

"Isabella, your dad said we'll drive out there and help you move back. Just let us know when."

Wow. Some of her family came to Albuquerque when she graduated from UNM. That was the only time in seven years they'd visited her in New Mexico until Bradley's funeral.

Ella glanced out the picture window over the sink. Coop shuffled toward the cabin in muddy rubber boots, a string of trout in one hand, a fishing pole in the other, and a scowl on his face.

"Gotta go. A storm is headed my way, and I need to prepare for it. Love y'all!" Throwing in a "y'all" always earned a few brownie points and eased her mom's disapproving tone.

Her mom sighed, issued a discontent farewell, and Ella pressed the End button.

Ella stared out the window at the storm in question. Right. A wicked-hot storm by the name of Cooper Wells. How in heaven's name was she supposed to prepare for that?

———

The next morning Coop took Atlas for a long run to work off some tension. Tension also known as Ella Dennings. During the few days she'd been in Red River, the cabin had started to transform into a feminine nightmare. He couldn't find half his stuff because the entire downstairs had been rearranged.

Taking the steps onto the porch, he adjusted the waistband of his nylon running shorts and reached behind his neck to grab a handful of T-shirt. He pulled it off to wipe the sweat from his face. His breaths still heavy, he stood in front of the back door and sniffed the air. What was that smell? His forehead creased, and he opened the door.

The sterile odor of cleaning products nearly singed his nose hairs.

Atlas bounded in and joined Winston in the den. Coop looked around the room. A vase filled with fresh-cut wildflowers sat in the middle of the table. He rolled his eyes, surprised the flowers hadn't wilted from the ammonia fumes that filled the air.

Bright yellow placemats adorned the table with matching cloth napkins that were gathered into fans and tied with artificial pieces of straw. Each mat and napkin was perfectly aligned. No way would he use something that . . . dainty to wipe his mouth. Paper towels worked just fine.

He swiped at the perspiration on his face again and tossed the damp shirt onto the table. The shirt tumbled across two of the placemats and sent the mats and napkins sliding askew. He smiled. *Better.*

An awful bellowing sound that was an apparent attempt at singing came from the kitchen. He recognized the lyrics, but the tune was so far off-key it didn't resemble a real song. Coop peeked over the bar.

Oh, this was just too good to pass up. He walked around the bar into the kitchen and leaned against the cabinet. Arms folded over his bare chest, he crossed his legs at the ankles and watched Cinder-Ella cleaning under the kitchen sink. On all fours. Wearing cutoff denim shorts. With an iPod and earbuds blocking out the real world, she howled a Blake Shelton tune.

Now that wasn't something Coop saw every day. Or heard. Thank God.

Coop wasn't sure if he would ever be able to listen to his favorite country singer again. The sound of Ella's unpleasant voice could have scarred a man for life and caused PTSD by the end of the song.

She bawled out the chorus, and Coop's head jerked back. Atlas whimpered.

Her butt wiggled in rhythm to the music only she could hear, and a tiny swatch of her blue silk panties made an appearance from under her shorts. Coop's mouth went dry. His head involuntarily angled toward his shoulder, and he took in the view.

Yep. Too good to pass up.

With the toe of his running shoe, he nudged her foot and recrossed his ankles. Ella glanced over her shoulder, and her eyes turned to saucers. She jerked up, her head connecting with the plumbing.

"Hells freaking bells!" she yelled. Really loud. Grabbing her head, she scooted backward out of the cabinet and collapsed onto the floor. A tank top that rode up just above her belly button revealed a flat stomach, heaving in pain. Legs pulled up, an elbow rested on each knee, yellow rubber-gloved hands clutched at the top of her head.

She looked up and glared at him, a sexy shade of pink seeping into her cheeks.

"Sorry," he said. Except for the knot she was going to have on her head, he really wasn't all that sorry, but it seemed like the appropriate thing to say.

"What?!" she yelled with earbuds still in.

One corner of Coop's mouth slipped up, and he pointed to his ear.

"Oh!" she yelled and pulled the earbuds out. Her voice returned to its normal volume, her eyes darted away from him. "Um, you scared me."

"Yeah, sorry about that." *Not really.* "What, no pepper spray this time?"

The pink in her face deepened, a stark contrast to the black smudges of grime streaking her cheeks. And Coop had a sudden urge to take his thumb and wipe her creamy skin clean. Softly and gently with the pads of his fingers.

He coughed.

"I'm considering a holster for my Taser." She tried to get up, but her bare foot slipped on the damp floor that she'd apparently just mopped, and she slid back onto her bottom. "So don't sneak up on me like that again."

Coop pushed himself off the counter and held out a hand. "Let me help. And I didn't sneak up on you."

She studied his hand for a second, then took it with a reluctant expression. He pulled her to her feet, grasping her rubber-gloved hand.

"Do I want to know what's on that glove?" he asked and released her hand.

Ella looked at both palms. "I don't think *I* want to know. Have you ever had this place cleaned? I mean really deep cleaned?" She looked up at him; a few messy strands of hair escaped her ponytail and hung across her eyes. She swiped at them with her forearm, but missed because of the cumbersome gloves. Then she blew at them, but they settled back into the same spot.

Coop shrugged. "A few times. Maybe."

Ella's silky brow arched.

"Okay, once."

Her brow went higher.

"I think."

Coop's gaze anchored to the stray locks that dangled over her face. He reached out and grasped one before he could stop himself and tucked it behind her ear. Her eyes went soft. And dropped to his lips. Then those green emeralds slid lower and took a nice long tour over his bare chest. He found himself holding his breath.

"You're . . ." She swallowed. "You're all . . . sweaty." Something flared in her eyes. Something akin to . . . physical attraction? Yeah. He'd been with enough women to recognize that look. But seeing it in Ella's eyes shocked him. And seemed to shock her even more, because she took a step back. Her eyes still roamed his chest, though.

"I'm busy, did you need something?" Her tone gone hard, she turned away from him and snapped off the gloves.

"Nope." He went to the pantry. Every item was lined up in perfect order. "What'd you do to my stuff?"

"Organized it." She sprayed the already-spotless counter and wiped it down.

"I can't even make toast because I can't find the bread," he huffed.

"It's in the section labeled *B*."

He turned a frown on her.

"Just kidding." She marched over to the pantry and gave him a miniscule push to move him out of the way. "And you say I need to loosen up." She lifted some sort of wood contraption with a small roller door and shoved the bread at his chest.

"What is *that*, and where did it come from?"

"It's a bread box that keeps our bread fresher. I got it at the market when Cal and I shopped for groceries. I picked up a few other things to brighten the cabin up, too. This place could use it."

"This place is fine." Coop popped some bread into the toaster and got out eggs and bacon. "Want some breakfast?" He'd never had a problem with the cabin, why should she?

Ella bent and started replacing cleaning supplies under the kitchen sink in precision rows. "No thanks. I already ate cereal." She stood just as Coop turned to put something in the sink and they bumped into each other.

"You're in my way," she ground out.

"I was here first. Remember?"

"That's real grown-up, Coop. Are you going to stick your tongue out at me, too?"

Maybe. He inhaled. "Look, I just need to fix something to eat before I go to Cal's summer school parent-teacher conference." Maybe he should ask her to make a schedule for taking turns in the kitchen. Although why she'd need to spend much time in the kitchen was beyond him, because coffee and a bowl of cereal seemed to be the extent of her culinary skills.

Her expression went blank. "You go to Cal's conferences?"

Coop stepped around her and got out two frying pans for the bacon and eggs. "Of course. I helped Dad raise him since Cal's mom didn't stick around." Coop tossed two slices of bacon in the pan and cracked some eggs into a small bowl. Since he was so much older than Cal, he'd stood in the gap where a mother was glaringly absent.

He looked up to find Ella staring at him.

"That's . . . really nice."

Coop shrugged. "Don't most parents do the same thing?"

She snorted. "No. Actually, they don't. I'm a teacher, Coop. Trust me, I know."

He scrambled the eggs with a fork. "It's not the same as having a mom to orchestrate a birthday party, or participate in the PTA, or show up at his Little League games with homemade cookies decorated to look like baseballs." He poured the eggs into the pan and turned on the burner. "But I try."

"Sounds like the voice of experience." Ella tucked the mop and bucket inside the pantry all nice and neat.

Coop's jaw hardened because it was none of Ella's business that his mother hadn't been around.

"I could get cleaned up and come with you. Since I'm a teacher, I might be able to offer some insight into Cal's learning disability. It might be a good idea for his summer school teacher and I to collaborate since I'm tutoring him." She snatched her phone off the counter and thumbed at the screen. "I'll have to rearrange a few things on my schedule, but it's no problem to do that for Cal."

Oh, no. There wasn't much he could do to stop her from invading his space in the cabin. She owned half the place, after all. But he wasn't going to let her take over his responsibilities with Cal, even if she was trying to help. She could stick to tutoring his little brother. Coop and his father could handle the rest.

"You have to rearrange your schedule?"

She glanced at her phone. "Well, yes. Today is cleaning. Tomorrow is laundry. The next day is—"

"You've got to be kidding me?" *A schedule*? In Red River?

She crossed her arms over her bare midsection, and the tank top pulled taut over her bustline. Coop's tongue darted out to lick his lip and he bit down on it. *Ow.* That kinda hurt. But he had to stay focused.

"You know what? It's probably not a good idea for me to go with you. The point is to focus on Cal."

Fine by Coop. Mission accomplished. He didn't want her at the conference.

"I'll just let Butch and Cal know that I can meet with his teacher on my own, if it would help."

Wait. But before he could inform her that there was no need for her to meet with Cal's teacher, she stomped down the hall, into the bathroom, and slammed the door. The shower turned on.

The toast popped up, and the smell of burnt eggs chaffed his nose. He snatched the pan off the burner. He stared at the empty hallway, then back at his browned eggs. With a deep exhale, he tossed the pan in the sink. Now she was even hogging the bathroom. Maybe one of her silly schedules *would* come in handy so he could actually have some time in the shower when he needed it.

Chapter Six

Finally, the road dried out enough for Ella to drive her car into town. She tooled down Highway 578 through Carson National Forest with the sunroof open, enjoying the clear blue sky and crisp mountain air.

She'd made good use of the five days she was homebound by cleaning and organizing the cabin. Butch called a few times to check on her and ask if she needed anything.

So far, sharing a cabin with Coop hadn't been the hurricane-force disaster she'd expected. Since he gave her a wide berth like he would a skunk on a country road, she'd had the place pretty much to herself, but it was time to get out and explore a little.

She slowed her speed. With summer vacation season in full swing, the souvenir shops lining Main Street brimmed with tourists. Vacationers in comfortable tennis shoes, sun hats, and T-shirts from every university in Texas and Oklahoma ambled along the worn sidewalks and crossed at every intersection.

Texans and Okies loved Red River. It served as a year-round playground where they could escape the harsh summer climates of their home states and enjoy the winter wonderland of the southern Rockies from November to March. There were probably more Texans in Red River than there were in Texas, and it kind of reminded her of home.

Flipping the blinker, she sat at the four-way stop that ran down the side of Joe's, where Butch offered to meet her for lunch. A two-story building with a red barn facade, it sported a neon sign that flashed its name and several brands of beer. A family wearing University of Texas paraphernalia moseyed through the crosswalk, giving her a friendly wave. She waved back, and they stepped onto the sidewalk, then she eased into the gravel parking lot behind the building.

She got out of the car, and the fresh air filled her lungs, the atmosphere so crisp it almost crackled. She walked around to the front of the building and ascended the wooden staircase that bent to the right. Reaching the top, she stomped a little mud off her hiking boots against the planked, covered porch that lined the front of the restaurant

Ella walked into the darkened entryway. A waitress scurried by. "You can sit anywhere," she said.

Ella blinked, trying to bring the interior into focus. The cavernous room tripled as a restaurant, bar, and dance hall. A few hours past lunch, only a dozen or so diners filled the red-checkered tables and booths. She picked out an empty booth in the back corner and headed for it. Peanut shells crunched against the old wood flooring with every step.

As she walked toward the back, she passed two ladies sharing a booth, their heads together, bodies leaning in to whisper. Each held a book. One of the books was closed, and the title *Southwest Sizzle* glared up at her, the author's name, Violet Vixen, emblazoned across the bottom in scarlet letters.

The late-twenties woman sported perfectly coiffed black hair cut into a chic angled bob. She caressed the cover with French-manicured nails.

Her midforties companion swished a shoulder-length perm around in agitation. Her copy open, she pointed to a section of text.

"See. I tried this with Hank last night, and he got angry. I mean, really. We've been married twenty-five years, and we need to spice things up. I'm not dead yet, ya know."

Ella altered her course and slid into the booth just behind them. If curiosity killed the cat, then Ella was about to die a horrible death, because she just *had* to hear what local readers were saying about the books.

"He got angry? What did he say?" asked the younger woman in a loud whisper.

"He said our sex life has been fine for a quarter century, and he wasn't about to lock me to the bed with a pair of fuzzy red handcuffs. Then he went and slept on the couch." The older woman harrumphed loudly.

Ella's cheeks burned hot. Grabbing a menu, she pretended to browse the selections.

Honestly, she couldn't blame this Hank guy. Ella and Bradley had never done any such thing. Their sex life had been loving and affectionate; it had seemed spicy enough without handcuffs or blindfolds. So when she sat down next to Bradley's bed and started writing a romance story to fill the empty spaces of time during his long stretches of medicated sleep, she had shocked herself with what flowed onto the page.

A very hot, sexy story, using the pen name Violet Vixen, burgeoned into a full-length novel about a librarian and her fantasies. Fantasies that Ella imagined living out with Bradley. *Living* being the operative word. That's why she kept writing, outlining a second and third book. Her imagination ran wild with what she wished she would have done, still could have done, with Bradley if not for his rapidly declining mind and body.

"Andy loved the handcuffs." The younger woman's voice dropped low, and Ella leaned back to hear. "And he wants to try more."

Turning her head slightly for a better angle, Ella snatched peripheral glimpses of her unknowing subjects while analyzing the menu.

The familiar crunching of peanut shells sounded, and the server approached.

"Hi, I'm Miranda. What can I get you?"

"Oh, I'm waiting for someone," Ella whispered.

The waitress smiled, a dimple appearing at each corner of her mouth. "Okay. Can I bring you something to drink while you wait?"

"Um, how about a Coke."

"Will do." Putting the order pad and pen back in her apron, she stepped to the next table.

"You two ladies need anything else? A male blow-up doll? A whip?"

"Oh, bite us," the older erotica reader admonished. "You've read it, too, Miranda."

The server gave them a slinky laugh. "Yep, and I can't wait for the third book to come out next month." Her voice turned a little frustrated. "I can't believe the first book left us hanging with their breakup. After all the great sex, what woman in her right mind would walk away from that?"

The younger woman's hands flew to her ears. "Don't tell me! I haven't gotten to that part yet." She began to hum, her hands still clamped over both ears.

Miranda huffed and scurried away.

"I can't believe she just gave away the ending," one of them complained. "They better get back together for more hot sex in the next book, or the readers might riot."

Ella giggled. Her hand shot to her mouth, but it was too late. The two ladies in the next booth went quiet. Crap.

Ella turned to see two pairs of eyes peering at her over the booth.

"Hi," she said, unsuccessful at squelching the guilt in her voice. "Sorry. I couldn't help but overhear."

"Have you read them?" The fortyish woman held up the book.

"Um, yes. I'm familiar with it." Ella tried evasive tactics so she wouldn't have to lie.

"I'm Donna." She pointed a finger at her companion. "This is Brianna." Brianna waved. "You new in town?"

"My name's Ella Dennings. Nice to meet you both."

Ella didn't miss the quick look that passed between the two women.

"I'm here for the summer, actually," Ella said.

"We're driving into Santa Fe when the next book is released. It'll take a while for any of the stores up here to carry it," Brianna said. "You could come with us, if you want."

Ella shook her head. "I switched to an e-reader when my husband got sick. I didn't have much time to browse the bookstores."

The front door opened, and Butch's voice rang out a greeting. "Hello, ladies."

He trudged through the peanut debris, followed by two other men. Ella stood, and Butch gave her a fatherly hug. "I see you've met Donna, Red River's postmaster, and Brianna, the owner of Shear Elegance two doors down from here." He greeted both of them.

Butch hooked a thumb at the two men behind him. "I picked these two stragglers up. Anybody know them?" he said playfully.

Donna pointed to one of the men. He was about her age, lean and tanned from working outdoors, and he wore a straw cowboy hat, well-starched Wrangler jeans, and brown Roper boots. "That one there is mine. Hank's his name. I'm the better half."

He took off his hat and nodded at Ella. "Ma'am." Hank and Donna's accents gave away the fact that they were transplants from the Lone Star State.

"I'm Ross." A tall, burly guy stepped from behind Butch and offered his hand. "I don't have a better half yet," he drawled.

"Nice to meet you, Ross. I know how you feel."

"Why don't we get a bigger table, and y'all can join us," Donna offered.

Ella's hand fluttered to her hair, which she smoothed back with a palm. Starting over, meeting new people—people that probably knew Bradley because of the time he'd spent in Red River with the Wells family—pulled her way out of her comfort zone. Catapulted, actually.

Ella let out a deep sigh. Would she ever be able to let go of Bradley and function on her own again?

She doubted it, but she was here in Red River to at least try.

Coop entered Joe's using the side door. He pushed through the swinging door and joined Dylan McCoy behind the bar.

"Hey, man." Coop hitched up his chin.

"Hey," Dylan said. His dark brown hair hung in waves to his shoulders, and a small diamond earring glinted from his left earlobe. "You're here early." Dylan dried another glass and placed it on a shelf with a hundred other identical glasses.

Bartending at the busiest establishment in Red River had been a great distraction for Coop. With his legal bills gradually draining his savings and whittling away the sizeable profits from the sale of his condo, the extra cash to cover his spending money didn't hurt, either.

"You're dad's here." Dylan waved his dish towel toward the table across the room. "Who's the redhead with him?"

Wariness deep in his gut, Coop's eyes trekked across the room. Butch waved him over, then leaned over and said something to Ella, whose back was to Coop. She glanced over her shoulder and frowned.

Without looking away from Ella's flowing locks of fire, Coop said, "She's my cabinmate from hell."

"Dude, must be tough. She's hot."

Coop stabbed him with a glare.

"Just sayin'." Dylan shrugged and dried another glass.

Coop turned his attention back to the chattering table of familiar customers. Now would be as good a time as any for Ella to find out he worked here. Unless, of course, his dad or Cal had already informed her, being so chummy with her and all. He walked toward them, a sense of dread lodging somewhere inside his rib cage in the form of a lump. Or heartburn.

"Hey, good-lookin'," Donna teased as he approached.

"Hey." Coop looked around the table, nodding a generic greeting.

He stood at the end of the table where Donna and Brianna sat, each with a book. He glanced at the opposite end, where Ella devoured a large plate of chili cheese fries.

"Pull up a chair," Hank offered.

"Thanks, but my shift is about to start, and I'm working a double tonight."

Ella's head shot up. So, she hadn't heard that he worked here.

"That's right. Tonight's a big night at Joe's, with the dance and all," said Ross. "Ella, you coming?"

"Um," she looked uncertain, dabbing her mouth with a napkin. Amazing how she could eat like a man and make it look dainty.

"Come on, now," encouraged Donna. "Everybody will be here. It's the annual firefighters' dance to raise money for the fire department."

Butch agreed, cutting into his chicken-fried steak. "It'll be another good chance to meet more of the locals."

"Sure, alright." She agreed with a reluctant nod. "It's been a long time since I went dancing."

"Honey, if you can two-step, then this is where you should be tonight. A pretty girl like you won't sit down the whole night," Donna said.

Coop's jaw twitched.

Ella downed another fry and wiped her fingers clean. "You don't grow up in East Texas without learning to two-step."

He'd watched her and Bradley dance once. Growing up in a strict religious home, Bradley had been uncomfortable, his movements stiff and unsure. But Ella, she moved across the dance floor with graceful, fluid motion. He had been envious that night because Bradley had such a great dance partner and Coop . . . didn't.

"Good. It's settled, then," Brianna said. "Wear cowboys boots, if you have some."

"What are you ladies reading?" Coop asked.

Hank groaned and pushed back his chair. "You had to ask, didn't you?" He shot Coop an accusing scowl.

Brianna turned a light shade of pink and looked down. Donna perked up, leaning forward like she had a juicy secret.

"It's a worldwide sensation," Donna said. "This young, pretty, extremely anal-retentive librarian in Albuquerque meets a hunky chiropractor, and she completely transforms into this wild sex machine."

Huh. A strange sensation prickled Coop's gut.

"That's it," Hank said. "I'm leaving if y'all are gonna talk about those trashy sex books."

"Sex books?" Coop couldn't hide the shock in his voice. "You ladies read that stuff?"

Ella hadn't spoken to him since he walked up, but now her green eyes bored into him like two bullets. "Why is it that men have read girlie magazines for decades and it's deemed manly, perfectly acceptable in most societal circles until recent years, but if a woman reads a romance novel, it's criticized?" Her emerald eyes held his.

Was that a question? He wasn't sure, and before he could figure it out, his eyes sank to her pursed lips. They looked ripe, full . . .

They started moving again, but Coop couldn't quite make out the words spilling from them.

"Coop?" Donna said, snapping him out of the spell.

He looked around the table. "Huh?"

No one spoke but Ella. "I said how is reading those books so different from . . ." She glanced at Butch, then pushed her plate back. "You know what? Never mind."

"See what you started, Hank?" Donna accused her husband.

"Me? I just said I wasn't gonna sit here if y'all start up with those books again. It's not proper dinner conversation. Coop's the one that brought it up in the first place."

"Well, get used to it, mister, because the ladies and I are meeting here twice a week for lunch to discuss them. Sort of like a book club. And these books," she picked up her copy and waved it in the air, "are just the first two in a long series."

"Then I guess I won't be joining you for lunch anymore," Hank said, slamming his hat down on his head. He stood up.

"I guess you won't." Donna pushed her chair back. She stood, fists planted on her hips. "And I guess you can sleep on the sofa again since you like it so much." Donna stormed out with Hank on her heels.

Ella threw her napkin over her chili-smeared plate. "I'm leaving, too." She stood, grabbing her purse. "Thanks for lunch, Butch. Next time it's on me." She turned to the others still seated and said her good-byes. She ignored Coop.

"We'll see you tonight, Ella," said Brianna, trying to sound cheerful, but the elephant in the room was hard to ignore.

As Ella strode to the door, her posture rigid, Ross stood up and gave Coop a slap on the back. "Good goin', buddy. You really have a way with women," Ross said. "Remind me not ask you for advice on how to make a good impression on a gal."

Joe's front door swung closed after Ella stepped through it. Coop shook his head. "Why would you want to do that? Women are nothing but trouble."

Ross put his hat on and flipped the brim. "Maybe, but a woman as pretty as Ella is the best kind of trouble a man could ask for." He threw a tip down on the table. "I'm kinda glad you can't see it. Gives a guy like me a better chance."

Ross walked to the door and tossed a nod at everyone. "See y'all tonight."

Not if I see you first. Coop wouldn't allow himself to say it out loud. Even he could see how childish his favorite high school barb was. He should be glad someone was interested in Ella. If she started dating, it might get her out of his hair. She dominated the cabin, as it stood now. Constantly cleaning, making the place smell good. Walking into the bathroom was like entering the Twilight Zone. Even her toothbrush was pink and her soap smelled all fruity. And what was she doing on that laptop half the night? When he lay in bed, he could hear her banging away on the keyboard until all hours.

He stayed out of the cabin as much as possible to avoid Ella. Dating would get her out of his way and at least give him some privacy. He should cheer Ross on. The big guy would be doing him a favor.

So, why did he want to smack Ross for even suggesting it?

Chapter Seven

Just before Bradley proposed, he and Ella drove up to Red River for a four-day weekend. The first day they spent a few hours on the slopes, then returned to the cabin and built a fire. Bradley uncorked a bottle of white wine and made pasta with clam sauce while fresh snow fell, blanketing the mountainous landscape.

It was a winter wonderland, and by far the most romantic day of Ella's life. She wanted him, needed him. Badly. The glass of wine having gone to her head, she patted the empty seat next to her, and Bradley joined her on the sofa.

Her schoolteacher inhibitions tossed to the wind, she kissed him deeply and passionately and pulled at his sweater.

"Come on." He tried to rise, tugging her with him, but she tugged back.

"Make love to me here. In front of the fire."

He laughed. "The shades are open."

"So?" She pulled him back down. "Your cabin's surrounded by trees."

He settled on top of her. Wrapping her long legs around his waist, she ran her palms under his sweater and caressed his back.

He nuzzled her neck. "I need to get you tipsy more often."

She giggled. "It doesn't take much to get me tipsy. Then you can have your way with me."

"I noticed." He nipped at her earlobe, and a shiver lanced down her spine.

When it was over, Ella lay on the sofa wrapped in an afghan. Content. Life was perfect.

Bradley's phone went off, and he stepped out of the bathroom in search of it. "Hello." He listened. "This is Dr. Dennings. What can I do for you?"

Ella sat up and reached for her wine as Bradley listened to the caller. He was so good at it. Always listening, always caring about others. It wasn't any wonder that his patients loved him.

"Alright. Since Derek referred you and it's an emergency, I'll see you in a few hours. Until then, put ice on it."

Ella's heart sank. Their romantic weekend was over before it really got started. She got up to pack, wrapping the blanket under her arms to cover her breasts.

Bradley snapped the phone shut. "Hey," he whispered. "Where you going?"

"We're going back to Albuquerque, aren't we?"

He enfolded her in his arms, pulling her flush against him. "I am. You're not." He pecked her nose with a kiss. "I'll be back early in the morning, and we can pick up where we left off."

"You're sure?" Ella asked, because she wasn't in the least bit certain.

"You won't even know I've been gone. Promise." He covered her mouth with a deep kiss.

An hour later, Ella still lay on the sofa, enjoying the fire. She didn't often relax so completely, but here in this place, how could she not? Especially after such tender lovemaking.

She stared into the fire, the flames holding her captive, and dozed. When she woke a few hours later, the fire had died out and a wicked chill hung in the air. She bundled the blanket tighter around her nakedness and went to the basement to check the furnace.

Well, frick. After finding the pilot lit and fully functioning, Ella stood staring at it with one hand on her hip and the other clutching the blanket to her chest. What now? Bradley wouldn't be back until the morning, and she didn't have a car to go find a warm motel. She'd just have to pull on some thermal underwear and tough it out.

She took the first two steps, but the basement door opened above her and a figure in winter gear stood at the top of the stairs. He took one step down, saw her at the bottom, and lost his footing. A string of cursing echoed off the dank walls as Cooper Wells tumbled downward and landed at Ella's feet.

"Ah!" He grabbed at the back of his head.

"Coop?" Ella bent to help him. "What happened? What are you doing here? Bradley said you weren't coming this weekend. Have you been drinking?"

"For God's sake, *Cind—*" He hesitated. "One question at a time. And, no, my neck's not broken. Thanks for your concern."

"I came down here to check the furnace," Ella explained. "The heat isn't working."

"Probably because the thermostat wasn't turned on. I checked it as soon as I walked in."

"Oh." Ella bit her lip, her cheeks burning even in the cold basement. Checking the thermostat hadn't even occurred to her.

Still grabbing at the back of his head, his eyes closed. "Jesus, that hurt."

"What happened?"

He looked at her through one half-opened eye. It dipped to her chest. "Uh, you took me by surprise, that's all."

It's In His Heart

She pulled the afghan up as much as possible. "Bradley said you wouldn't be here this weekend."

"When I saw how much snow Red River was getting, I came to go snowboarding."

"You could've called." She tried to adjust the afghan again.

"I did. Bradley was on his way back to Albuquerque and thought it was a good idea I come up tonight so you wouldn't be alone."

His furious stare raked over her, and a glint of something new dawned there. Something different, softer. Coop's glower faded, his sensual hazel eyes anchored to her mouth, and the sexy De Niroesque mole under his eye twitched. Instead of recoiling, her tongue traced her bottom lip as she took in his tousled caramel hair that always looked as though a woman had run passionate fingers through it. His breath hitched, and lust flared in his eyes, turning them a dark shade of green.

Then, Ella did the unthinkable.

She lowered her head and kissed her boyfriend's best friend.

His reaction was instantaneous. Lips warm and ready, he took control of the kiss and pulled her against him. His padded snow jacket cushioned her breasts, and she melted into him as he encircled her in his arms. One of his hands drifted down her back, flexing and caressing until it cupped her bottom. The other threaded through her hair. Pressing her into him, he deepened the kiss.

He tasted earthy and intoxicatingly male. He explored her mouth with his tongue, and she followed his every stroke. In spite of the freezing basement, the air around them sizzled with need. She settled against him with a soft moan, and he pulled her hips into his, his rock-hard groin confirming his desire. His fingers pulled at the blanket, tugging it upward. A shiver raced up her legs as, inch by inch, he bared her to the cool night air and to his warm, searching hand. When his palm settled over her bare bottom and caressed,

65

a low growl came from somewhere deep inside him, and his kiss became primal and urgent. His grip on her was firm, like he didn't want to let her go. And for an instant, she didn't want him to, either. Her brain clouded, a sensuous moan escaped from the back of her throat, and it startled her.

That was her, right? The room spun around her, and she fought to regain lucidity.

Frick. It *was* her.

She pushed herself off him.

"No! I can't." Her shaky hands fumbled with the blanket that had slipped dangerously low.

Coop's scowl returned, and he pulled himself off the basement floor.

"I'm sorry." Ella looked at the cinder block walls, the wood beams that ran across the ceiling in perfect increments, anything to avoid Coop's stare. She eyed the stairs, wanting to make a run for it, but Coop stood in between her and the only escape route.

"Can we . . . pretend this never happened? Please."

He analyzed her for a moment, conflicting emotions playing across his face. None of them looked positive.

"I wouldn't want to hurt Bradley. Especially over something foolish that didn't mean anything," Ella plowed on.

Coop gave a slow nod. "Right. It was just one of many kisses I've had this week. It wasn't even that good."

His tone had turned retaliatory, and Ella couldn't blame him. She had initiated the kiss, not him.

He certainly hadn't tried to stop her, though. How far would it have gone if she hadn't pulled away? And could she trust him to keep it quiet? Maybe she should tell Bradley herself. But that would cut him deeply—his best friend and his girlfriend fooling around when he wasn't looking. And he actually had thought it was a good idea for Coop to be looking out for her while he was gone.

She was an idiot. A two-timing, traitorous idiot.

"I need to go upstairs." She gave him a pointed look.

He stayed rooted in place for several long, torturous moments. The furnace kicked on, drowning out the deafening silence. Finally, he stepped to the side, waving her through with a bow. Mocking her.

She darted up the stairs and into Bradley's room, slamming the door in her wake.

Tucked safely into her room, she put on one of Bradley's T-shirts and dug a pair of lace panties out of her suitcase. The black pair that drove Bradley crazy with desire. Pulling a handful of the shirt to her nose, she inhaled his scent and rubbed the soft cotton across one cheek. She loved sleeping in his shirts. It was so intimate, like a security blanket or a shield of protection.

Then she paced the floor. How could she have done such a thing? She had just humiliated herself and betrayed Bradley. And with his chauvinistic, philandering best friend, no less.

The lavender hue of twilight filled the window by the time Ella finally dried her eyes and climbed under the covers. She drifted into that fitful limbo between wakefulness and sleep with Bradley's scent comforting her and Coop's taste tormenting her. A few hours later, Bradley slid into bed, wrapping her in his warmth. She snuggled into him and buried her face in his chest.

"I missed you," she whispered. "I don't like it when we're apart."

"Good, because I kept wondering something during the drive back up here." He kissed her, tender and sweet. "Maybe we shouldn't be apart." He caressed the tip of her nose with his. "Will you marry me?"

"I love you, Bradley." Her voice quivered. The memory of how her body had responded to Coop's scorching touch and steamy kiss just a few hours ago haunted her. Her eyelids slid shut, and she pulled her lower lip between her teeth. "Yes, I'll marry you."

Bradley let out a shaky laugh. "Whew. There for a second I thought you were going to say no."

Ella shook her head. "I want us to spend the rest of our lives together. I love you." A tear slipped down the side of her cheek.

"I love you, too, babe." He trailed kisses from her ear to her mouth. "Now, where were we?" When his hand found the small swatch of lace around her hips, he moaned. "Oh, yeah. That's where we were."

Ella swallowed. "Coop might hear us."

Bradley tucked one hand between the lace and her skin. "Coop left early this morning. There was a note on the counter. Something came up in Albuquerque."

"Oh," she squeezed her eyes shut and buried her face against Bradley's neck.

He rolled her onto her back and covered her. "At least he stayed the night. It made me feel better about leaving you."

They spent the rest of the weekend at the cabin alone. Bradley fished in the stream out back while Ella looked on, bundled in several layers of down. They had a snowball fight, trekked to a meadow to take pictures of a herd of elk, and made sweet love every night. But Ella never visited the cabin again after that. Even after they got married, she encouraged Bradley to go without her. Claiming she didn't like the small-town culture, Ella stayed behind when Bradley wanted to go to Red River. It was a good chance for him to spend time with Coop and do guy stuff, she'd say.

Bradley accepted her excuses, but she knew he always wondered why. He guessed she was holding something back. He just never knew that *something* was the betrayal of his future wife with his best friend.

Chapter Eight

Ella shuffled through the well-worn clothes hanging in her closet. She really needed to go shopping. An updated wardrobe hadn't been a top priority the past several years, and she certainly hadn't been dancing since before Bradley was diagnosed.

According to Brianna, cowboy boots were in order for tonight's dance, so she pulled her black buffalo calfskin Luccheses from the back of her closet. They weren't for traipsing through cow dung on the ranch; these babies were for scooting across a dance floor in style. She ran her fingers across the hand stitching. It had been a long time. Her dance steps were probably more than a little rusty, but hey, wasn't it like riding a bike?

She dabbed on a little makeup, hoping the ancient tubes of goop weren't expired and breeding some sort of skin-eating bacteria. New makeup was probably in order, too. She picked up a tube of mascara. At least she thought it was mascara. Hard to tell, since it was so old the label had rubbed off. Twisting off the cap, she withdrew the wand, and a dry black clump of tar came out.

Ick. No way was she putting that on her face.

Ella tossed it in the trash and then put on a white gauzy sundress.

The night air was cold year-round in Red River, so she added a jean jacket. The last touch was a pair of gold hoop earrings, a small dainty necklace, and her wedding ring. After sliding it onto her finger, she held up her hand to look at it.

It was a beautiful piece of bling. Bradley had insisted on buying her a nice-size engagement ring and a band of diamonds to match. Soon she'd have to take it off permanently. Definitely before she left Red River. She sighed. But not tonight. Not yet.

Actually, she didn't plan to stay at the dance that long. A little time out of the cabin would be nice. Then she'd head home to work on her third book, *Rio Grande Romp*. She only had a few chapters left to write, and since Wanton Publishing had it on a crash schedule for earlier release, she needed to finish it in the next few days. Cyn Caldwell would probably be calling soon, also insisting on the excerpt for book four.

A wave of panic swept through her. She'd outlined book four but hadn't even started writing it yet. How on earth was she going to come up with an excerpt? She blew out a heavy breath. She'd have to think of something. Soon.

Her new career and its demands were all so daring, so breaking-the-rules.

So totally not like her.

That's what made it so exciting. She'd never lived life on the edge. The biggest risk she'd ever taken had been applying to grad school at UNM without her parents' knowledge and moving to Albuquerque with student housing and an on-campus job already lined up. And that had scared the hell out of her. She hadn't been sure she made the right decision until she met Bradley.

Now, it seemed her life consisted *only* of unexpected twists and turns and surprises around every corner. She had no plan, beyond spending the summer in Red River. Just the here and now, and the future would work itself out somehow.

Ella snatched a comb and a hair band from the dresser and tried to pull her overgrown hair into a fashionable knot.

Financially, she could afford to take risks. Emotionally? Completely different story. How could she move forward without Bradley? He'd been her security blanket. Without him, every step was like walking a tightrope with nothing below to catch her if she fell. And loving another man besides him? That terrified her.

With a frustrated sigh, she gave up on her hair and let it tumble loosely around her shoulders.

Maybe instead of running out of the dance tonight, she'd stay and try to have a good time. Meet new people. Have a drink and enjoy dancing. Fun hadn't been on her agenda in a long while.

Fidgeting with her ring, she slid it off her finger and studied it.

The past two years, her friends in Albuquerque coaxed her out to dinner or a movie once in a while just to get her out of the house. But she'd refused to go dancing. The idea of facing the singles scene shook her already battered sense of security.

Maybe it was time. She'd come here in the first place to let go of Bradley and move on as a single woman. A confident single woman, right? A few friendly dances in this little town wouldn't be the same meat-market atmosphere as the bars in a big city. It might be a good start.

She drew in a breath, and slid the ring back on her finger.

One step at a time. Dancing and fun tonight. Taking Bradley's ring off forever . . . she still wasn't sure when, but not yet.

Ella stared at her reflection in the mirror. She certainly wouldn't be the belle of the ball. A trip to the salon wouldn't hurt. She'd make an appointment with Brianna soon. For tonight, though, there wasn't much she could do to improve her appearance.

"What do you think, guys?" She struck a pose for the two dogs that snuggled in the corner on top of a fuzzy blanket. Winston broke wind and rolled onto his side, a loud wheeze sounding through his flattened snout. Atlas snuggled closer to him.

"That good, huh?" Ella's shoulders sagged.

Grabbing a tube of pink lip gloss, she swiped the wand over her lips, then twirled in front of the mirror. This was as good as it got for tonight, anyway. And really, whom did she need to impress? Nobody.

"See ya, boys. Don't do anything I wouldn't do." She stared at the snoring dogs.

Ella slung her purse over one shoulder and walked into the kitchen. The T-shirt Coop had loaned her the first night she arrived still sat on the counter, laundered and folded into a perfect square. He hadn't bothered to put it away. Ella ran her hand over the soft cotton.

If she didn't care to impress anyone tonight, then why was she wondering about Coop?

Blowing out a frustrated breath, Ella slammed the door behind her and peeled out of the drive, headed to town.

Coop shoved the tap handles back and tried to pretend Ella wasn't in the room. Kind of hard, since she'd fixed herself up so nicely and scooted past him every dance with a smile on her face so broad it lit the room. Light makeup emphasized her sculpted cheekbones, deep green eyes, and full lips. Tiny little strings that knotted into a bow over each shoulder had him guessing she wasn't wearing a bra.

When Ross dropped her into a dip and she came up laughing, the nice bounce of her chest confirmed Coop's guess, and his teeth ground together. He tried to shake it off and concentrate on the streams of beer that trickled to a stop.

She looked good. That feminine dress was way different than her usual faded jeans and running shorts. The transformation drew his attention every time she moved.

Coop ran a hand through his hair and focused on the two old buzzards in front of him. Butch and his buddy Orland sat at the bar, each drinking a beer. Friends since his dad came to Red River on vacation twenty years ago and hired Orland as a fly-fishing guide, they were inseparable. Coop plunked full mugs down in front of them. They clinked them together, making another obnoxious toast. Coop shook his head and wiped his hands on a towel. He'd be driving the both of them home tonight.

The annual Firefighters' Charity Dance had drawn a big crowd. Anything sponsored by the fire department usually did, since northern New Mexico was so heavily forested, and the local economy could die out completely from one stray spark from a campfire or a careless flick of a cigarette butt. Every table full, and C and W dancers working up a sweat, Coop and Dylan kept the drink orders flowing, but Coop's irritation grew every time he heard Ella's throaty laughter drift in his direction. His jaw clenched a little tighter every time Ross turned her on the dance floor and her white dress drifted upward to reveal slender legs.

"Hi, Coop." Sandra Edwards appeared in front of him. She propped her elbows on the bar and leaned over, offering him a nice view of her considerable cleavage. Her voice purred like a seductive kitten. "Buy a gal a beer?"

Coop averted his eyes. "No can do. It's for charity, so everybody's responsible for their own tab." *And I'm supposed to stay away from women like you. Women in general, actually.* Coop frowned and glanced in Ella's direction.

Sandra's bottom lip puckered, and she dipped her shoulders lower so that her buxom chest poured out of a skimpy top.

Coop didn't take the bait. He had to get rid of her. He'd heard stories. Of course, he couldn't believe everything he heard; he'd learned that very painful lesson because of Kim Arrington. Being the victim of malicious gossip made a person think twice before listening to rumors. But the way Sandra constantly cornered him like a cat pawing at a mouse, he had to believe there was some truth to her sexual notoriety. And that meant trouble for him, with a capital T.

"Sandra, Doc Holloway hasn't danced all night." Coop waved his hand towel toward Red River's young and eligible medical doctor sitting on the far side of the room. "If anyone can coax him onto the dance floor, it's you."

She looked over at Dr. Blake Holloway, and her smile turned predatory.

Guilt washed through Coop for throwing the good doctor under the bus to save himself.

Sandra stood up straight and pushed out her chest. "See ya later, then." She winked at Coop and set off for her new target.

Poor man. Doc was a nice guy. Coop would have to make it up to him somehow.

Another fast two-step started, and the dance floor filled. Ross led Ella into a turn like a master. She could dance, that was for sure, and irritatingly enough, it turned him on as much as the teasing glimpses of her firm thighs.

They maneuvered past him, and her laugh evoked a pull in his chest. She was having a little too much fun, in Coop's opinion. After just two drinks—because yes, he'd been counting—she'd gotten loud and flirty. Ross was a nice guy, but he was a *guy*. His attraction to Ella was obvious, and with her inhibitions dropping like a rock, Ross might get the wrong impression. And the thought of Ella doing anything with Ross beyond dancing rubbed Coop the wrong way. The fact that it bothered him so much chafed him even more. Ella Dennings wasn't his problem.

Except that she was. On so many levels.

The hem of her white dress fluttered like tissue paper as Ross spun her under his arm. When she tossed her head back and laughed like a little girl on a merry-go-round, Coop's fists clenched. The song ended and Ross pulled her close, dipping his head to whisper into Ella's ear. Coop pulled the hand towel from his shoulder and tossed it on the bar. He threw up the hinged counter and started for the dance floor.

"Whoa there, partner." Orland blocked Coop's exit with one outstretched leg. "I wouldn't do that if I were you."

Coop glowered at his dad's buddy. "You're not me, and how do you know what I'm about to do?"

Orland chuckled and looked at Butch.

"It's written all over your face, Cooper," his dad said, before sucking down a quarter of the mug. Butch wiped a trickle of Budweiser off his chin. "You've been watching Ella ever since she walked in, and your face turns a deeper shade of red every time she dances with Ross."

Coop grew indignant. "It does not."

"Does too," Orland slurred.

"You're drunk," Coop accused.

"And you're an ass," Orland countered.

"I'm taking your keys away if you order another drink."

"You do that. Won't change you being an ass." Butch downed another quarter of the mug and burped.

"I was just going over to see if she's okay. She's not much of a drinker. How does that make me an ass?"

"Bull. You were going over to make a fool of yourself by butting into her business," Butch said. "You've made it clear that you don't want her around, so who she dances with, dates, or sleeps with isn't any of your business."

A vision of Ella naked with Ross made him bristle, and he cursed under his breath.

"You don't get it both ways, son," Butch said. "Trust me, I know."

Coop blinked at his dad. Everyone tiptoed around Butch's failed marriages, most of all, Butch himself. One could argue that Butch often lived with his head in the sand. Coop's mom and all four step-moms had certainly said so, often telling Butch that denial wasn't just a river in Egypt. So his levelheadedness threw Coop for a second.

Before Coop could respond, an arsenal of cell phones went off around the dance hall. Several of the men retrieved theirs from their pockets. Fire Chief McCoy signaled to the DJ to shut down the music.

"There's a fire out at Powder Puff. All fire department employees and volunteers who haven't been drinking alcohol need to report to the fire station ASAP."

The dance floor cleared, and half the men at the dance streamed toward the door. The tension in Coop's jaw eased when Ross left with the other volunteers.

"I think I've had too much to drink, Orland," Butch said with a belch. "How about you?"

Orland shook his head. "They'll have to fight this one without me."

"I'd call the sheriff and have you both arrested if you tried," Coop promised.

Coop's gaze followed Ella as she joined her group of friends at the table. Miranda, Joe's best server, approached their table with her pad and pen and wrote down orders, then headed back to the bar.

"Another round of drinks for the Red River Reviewers." She turned in their orders. "They're discussing those erotic novels again." She raised a silky black brow. "In detail. Brianna's husband doesn't mind, but Hank's threatening to leave, and his face is as red as a tomato." Coop handed her the drinks, and she stacked them onto the tray with steady precision. "Someone go rescue the poor guy before he strokes out."

Miranda tossed her wavy black hair over one shoulder and returned to their table to deliver the drinks.

Coop put both fists on the bar and stared at the back of Ella's tawny red hair, the light giving it the same color as a new copper penny. He leveled a glare at his dad and Orland. "I'm going over there, and if either of you old coots try to stop me, I'm cutting you off for the rest of the night."

"Are you going to behave?" Butch asked.

"I'm not five, Dad." Coop dried his hands and put the towel down.

"Then I'll expect you to act like it, and be nice to Ella."

Coop rolled his eyes and signaled to Dylan at the other end of the bar.

Dylan nodded back. "I've got this."

Coop walked up behind Ella, and her words bit at him. "Sure I want to get married again. I want kids. I miss sex." She giggled.

Donna saw Coop's approach, and with a wicked smile, said, "Coop's available, and you two share a house. Sounds convenient to me. Maybe you could have sex with him while you're here for the summer."

Ella let out a mocking laugh. "Please, he's the last man on earth I'd sleep with. Not even if he begged." The table fell silent. Donna paled a little at her joke that had gone seriously wrong. Ella babbled on, "I don't understand what the ladies see in him. He's overrated."

Brianna made the "cut it" sign across her neck, but Ella kept on talking, completely oblivious.

Coop stepped up beside Ella's chair, stance wide, arms folded over his chest. She didn't notice and took another sip of her drink. Everyone at the table stared blankly at him except Ella. She was still immersed in her own alternate plane that revolved solely around herself.

"I guess it's a good thing I've never had to beg for it."

Ella choked, spewing Coke across the table. A little even came out of her nose, and Coop smirked. He gave the rest of the table a gratified smile. When Ella tucked her hair behind one ear with a quivering hand, Coop almost laughed. Her profile glowed bright red, almost matching the color of her hair, and she stared down into her drink, stirring it with the little red swizzle stick.

"Hey, cutie," Donna said, changing the subject.

"Hey, yourself." Coop winked. "Any of you ladies care to dance? I hear your husbands might need a break from the conversation."

"They'll just start up again when the dance is over," groused Hank. "Ella here just lost her dance partner, though."

Ella's head shot up. "I'm done for the night."

Oh, no, you're not.

"You're not ready to call it a night, are you, honey?" Donna nudged Ella. "Go on and make Coop's night."

Ella's face turned a deeper crimson. "I, uh—"

Coop eased her out of the chair with a hand on her upper arm. "Great idea. We'll see you later." Coop pulled her onto the dance floor as Lady Antebellum's "Just a Kiss" came on. He tugged her into his embrace and initiated a slow, sensual two-step. She followed his lead and melted into the song like she was born to dance with him.

"You don't strike me as the two-stepping type," Ella finally said.

"Why's that?" Coop changed his angle to see if she'd follow. And she did. To perfection.

"You're not exactly a cowboy."

"Don't have to be a cowboy in western boots to like country music." Her green eyes darted around the room, never meeting his. "Besides, girls love a guy that can dance. It was incentive to learn."

She let out a condescending snort.

He eased her a little closer and lowered his head to whisper against her ear. "Since you don't find me in the least bit attractive, it's safe to dance this close." A miniscule shiver coursed over her, causing her to shimmy against him ever so slightly. She drew in a sharp breath. He suppressed the urge to do the same, the friction of her full breasts against his chest sending his mind reeling. With a steady smile, he pulled her even closer. "You won't be tempted by my overrated charm."

"I . . . I'm sorry. I didn't know you were standing there." She swallowed against his ear. "I don't drink much, and I've had a couple. Did Bradley ever tell you I don't hold my alcohol very well?"

"He may have mentioned it." Coop tried to sound bored. Bradley had mentioned it plenty, not that he needed to. Coop had witnessed firsthand the effect alcohol had on her when she and Bradley were dating. When she laid the sexiest kiss Coop had ever had on him while she was wrapped only in a blanket in the cabin's basement. "I don't really remember."

"Well, I'm sorry."

"So you said."

"Can we just dance, please?" Her tone changed from remorse to annoyed in a nanosecond.

"Whatever you say, Ella."

In a smooth, fluid movement, he molded her body to his and dropped one hand way south of her waistline. She let out a small gasp. His head dipped, and he rested his cheek against hers, angling his mouth so his breaths whispered across her ear. She shivered in his arms, making him tingle everywhere his body met hers. The feel of her pliant in his arms like putty, quivering under his touch, made him want . . .

He swallowed, choking back the gravel in his throat. Because God Almighty, he wanted to take her creamy earlobe between his teeth and nibble.

His eyes squeezed shut for a moment, and he regrouped.

For one, he was taking a very long sabbatical from women. Part of his plan to stay out of trouble and, hopefully, out of jail. Second, this was Ella. Not only could he not sleep with his best friend's widow, but he absolutely would not complicate their already absurdly complicated situation.

They shifted directions and her thigh slid between his for a second, brushing against the inside of his legs.

Wait. What was that last thing? Coop tried to refocus.

He let the music and the mood take them, and they traversed the dance floor like they had danced together forever. She melted perfectly into his embrace, matching him step for step. Ella's skin pebbled under his touch when he ran his hand down the length of her upper arm. But she wasn't cold. Her body grew hotter and more flushed against him with every intricate combination of steps, every turn and twirl. They expertly maneuvered around the few other couples still on the floor.

As the song lilted to its end, Coop took a step back from her, his hands still holding her hips. She looked up at him, her green eyes round as saucers. Deep pools that he could get lost in. Her lips parted, but she didn't speak. When his gaze dropped to her mouth, she swayed into him. Just like when he found her in the basement all those years ago, wearing nothing but a blanket.

He stepped away from her. "Thanks for the dance, Ella." Turning, he nodded to the table of open-mouthed friends who had watched him dance Ella around the floor like they were making love to the music. He walked back to the bar, well aware that Ella's hot gaze stayed anchored on his back.

Chapter Nine

"Thanks for being the designated driver. It's really nice that you look out for your customers like that," Ella said. When the truck hugged a wide curve, she grabbed for the dash.

"Are you going to be sick?" Coop asked.

"No, it's just your truck rides a lot rougher than my Beamer. Why do you have such big tires, anyway? Is it a guy thing? I've heard the macho types compare the size of their trucks to the size of their . . . anatomy." She'd seen the size of his *package* her first night at the cabin when he greeted her at the door sporting nothing but a baseball bat and a pair of fitted boxer briefs. Yeah, his package was way more impressive than the size of his truck.

Coop laughed. "I got these off-road tires put on because they come in handy up here when it rains or snows. You won't find me stuck in a ditch during a storm."

Smart aleck. She glanced at him, the illuminated dash casting a glow on his chiseled features. But he was an incredibly good-looking smart aleck, to be sure. She shook the thought from her mind.

"Speak of the devil." He flicked on the wipers. "It's starting to sprinkle."

The rain pelted the truck harder, and the wipers squeaked back and forth across the windshield.

Ella groaned. She didn't want to be stuck at the cabin for three days every time it rained. She had things to do, like tutoring Cal. "I hope this doesn't keep up. It'll mess up my schedule, and I'll have to rearrange my calendar."

Coop glanced at her a second too long and had to swerve back into his own lane. "Why are you so obsessed with schedules? What exactly is *on* your calendar? You're not even working."

"Just because I don't have a nine-to-five job, doesn't mean I'm not busy. And staying on a schedule is what any responsible person does," Ella said.

"Jesus, Dennings, you're such a Girl Scout."

"And that's a bad thing?"

"Oh, not bad," said Coop. "Just boring and predictable." He pulled up in front of the cabin just as the sky opened up completely. The heavy rain pounded the truck.

"Says the man who may likely end up with a criminal record. You should try a little anal-retentive caution, Coop. It might keep you out of trouble."

His breathing flared, but before he could come back with another retort, she changed the subject.

"A covered garage would be nice," Ella groused. "I can pay for one, you know."

"We don't need a garage." Coop's annoyance was obvious. "You won't melt, and the cold rain might finish sobering you up."

"I'm plenty sober. I only had two drinks."

"That's probably one and a half too many for you." He jumped out of the truck.

Ella still sat there, staring straight ahead into the darkness. Coop ran for the porch and took the first two steps. He stopped and looked back at the truck. Sloshing through the rain, he ran back to her door and opened it.

"Are you going to sleep in here?"

"Maybe. What's it to you?"

"It's my truck, that's what. Come on, it's just a little rain."

Ella could care less about the rain. She was still ticked about that dance with Coop and the effect it had on her. His put-down just added insult to injury.

Predictable? Boring? Okay, maybe a little predictable, but still. She folded her arms over her chest.

"You really do suck at drinking. Do you want me to carry you? Because I will if you don't get out of my truck right now."

"No," she said, fighting off a grin, a plan forming in her head. She shouldn't. She really, really shouldn't.

But oh, heck yeah, why not?

"That won't be necessary." She slid out of the seat and planted both boots on the soggy ground, leveling a stare at him. The rain soaked through her thin white sundress within seconds, and the gauzy material stuck to her thighs. "Satisfied?"

Coop's gaze dropped to her chest, and a flicker of lust ignited in his eyes. Her nipples hardened under his stare.

You asked for it. "I forgot my jacket at Joe's." She slammed the truck door closed and brushed against him as she walked past. She sloshed across the wet yard with a sway in her hips. When she got to the front door, she turned to him. Coop still stood by the truck, staring after her. She knew exactly what she looked like. The flimsy white material clung to every inch of her body, revealing her braless bust and the white lace panties underneath. "Are you going to just stand there, or are you going to unlock the door? My keys were in my jacket, and I'm freezing."

"Oh, uh, yeah." He snapped out of the trance and hurried to the door.

Coop turned the door handle, but it didn't open. He jiggled the handle violently, then stared at it, confounded, when it stayed firmly shut.

A smile slid across Ella's mouth, and she sucked in her bottom lip to hide it. "Um, Coop," she purred, shifting her weight so her thigh brushed against his. She leaned toward him just enough to invade his personal body space.

He turned a stormy expression on her.

"I think you have to unlock it first." She gave him her very best coy smile.

"Huh?" His eyes dropped to her breasts, then darted back up to meet her gaze.

She nodded to the keys in his hand. "With the key."

Coop followed Ella's line of sight to his hand. "Oh. Yeah." He fumbled through the keys and found the right one. He tried to shake the celestial vision of Ella's flimsy white dress soaked and molded to her like a fitted glove, but since she slid out of his front seat and the rain did its dance all over her, he could think of nothing else except how perfect she was.

When Ella scooted one boot right up next to his foot and shifted her weight so that her thigh grazed his, he dropped the keys.

"Damn," he cursed.

"What's the matter, Coop. Can't you hurry? I'm freezing." Her voice purred, and she moved a little closer.

Freezing? How could she be cold when heat rose off her shivering body and wrapped around him like a vise? Or a noose that might strangle the life out of him if he wasn't careful.

He bent to reach for the keys, and so did Ella. Her hand landed on top of his as he grasped the chunk of jangling metal in his palm.

He turned to look at her with a flame-throwing stare. "What're you doing?"

"Me?" She sounded suspiciously flirtatious. "Just trying to help." She stooped lower, giving him a grand view of her magnificent cleavage.

His vision blurred.

As she stood up, she ran her hand up the length of his arm and stopped at his bicep. "You know I never really noticed how much you work out." Her fingers lingered on his upper arm, her thumb playing with the raindrops that moistened his skin.

He jerked away and unlocked the door. Atlas and Winston barreled outside to find a tree. Not feeling very gentlemanly, Coop strode inside first. He couldn't let her see the effect she had on him. He wouldn't give her the satisfaction. "I'll start a fire," he said over his shoulder.

"No," Ella said, and Coop stopped in his tracks. He turned to face her, mesmerized by her tone, her mood, her body language. Not to mention her full breasts that strained against wet, sheer fabric. "I'm not boring." She trekked toward him.

"What?" he asked and swallowed. Hard.

"And I'm not predictable." Her hand rose to the bow on one shoulder, and she pulled it loose.

"What the hell are you doing, Ella?" Coop demanded, panic rising in his chest, eyes glued to the round pink nipples that jutted toward him.

Her fingers went to the other shoulder and untied the strings on that side, too.

"You said I was boring and predictable." She eased up to him and placed a hand on his chest. "A Girl Scout, isn't that what you called me?"

"It was a joke, Ella."

"Really? Because I don't think it was." Her index and middle fingers slowly walked a trail down his chest. "I think you've never liked me because I represent everything you're afraid of."

"I . . . I'm not afraid of you." He managed to form the words, but he didn't really believe them. He was terrified of Ella Dennings and every single thing she represented.

"Sure you are," she whispered. "Responsibility, stability, long-term commitment." His stare anchored to her plump lips, and he watched them move. "But most of all, you're afraid that you might be wrong about me."

"You're one thing I'm very right about." Good God, his throat was starting to close.

"Are you sure about that?" she taunted him. "Because I don't think a Girl Scout would do this." She took one of his hands and guided it to her breast.

Instinct took over, and Coop's hand closed over her lush flesh. She instantly warmed to his touch, the peak hardening into his palm. Her breath caught. So did his, and he raised another hand to capture the other breast. Her nipples grew harder with each stroke, and his mouth went dry.

No, no, no!

He willed his hands away, but they didn't move. His fingers just kept caressing the flesh that molded beneath his palms like it was made for him. Firm but soft at the same time. The rise and fall of her chest quickened. God, how he wanted to pull down her dress and explore them with his mouth. Wanted to see her in all of her rain-soaked naked glory, arching into him as he pulled on a rosy, peaked nipple with his teeth.

He meant to back away. He did. Instead, both hands found a steady rhythm as they coaxed and caressed her. She looked up at him, uncertainty flaring in her gaze. For a fleeting moment, Cinder-Ella was gone, and the Ella that Bradley must've known looked back at Coop. The vulnerable, sensitive, loyal Ella that made him want to take her to bed and spend the entire night kissing every inch of her soft, beautiful body.

Her left hand caressed down his arm to where his hand still molded around her breast. The light caught Ella's wedding ring, and the big diamond Bradley had given her glinted at Coop. His brain shifted into overdrive, and he took a step back.

"Ella, this can't happen."

Her expression turned to a smile. "Now who's the Boy Scout?"

Coop's jaw clenched. She'd played him just like he played her during the dance. "You knew I wouldn't do it."

"So that makes you the predictable one, doesn't it?"

"I just didn't want to get pepper sprayed again."

Ella walked to the hallway and turned back to him. "Before you go calling me names again, Coop, you need to remember something. You might think I'm boring and predictable, but that's what kept me at Bradley's side when he needed me. I didn't let him lay there alone when he was dying. I wasn't out partying or planning how to spend the life insurance money while he wasted away in our bed. Day after day, month after miserable month, I was there for him. Where were you?"

All he could do was stare back, because she was right.

Ella spun on her booted heels and disappeared down the hall.

Chapter Ten

Something metallic thumped against Ella's head. She could've sworn the throb came from some sort of blunt instrument. She patted her hair with one hand. No, no bludgeoning on the outside. It was last night's two drinks that caused the dull ache that pulsed against the inside of her head.

She cracked one eye, and the morning sunshine streaming through the slats of her window blinds stabbed at her brain. Flinging an arm over her face, she groaned.

Oh, God. No. Memories of her putting Coop's hand to her breast caused another dull pain to ebb and flow through her head. *Way to go, Dennings.* What had she been thinking? Well, that was just it. She *hadn't* been thinking at all.

Coffee. That's what she needed. She pulled herself up to a sitting position and ran her tongue over fuzzy teeth. *Yuck.* The dresser mirror was directly across the room, and she tried to bring her reflection into focus. A messy auburn mop and eyelids slightly stained from last night's makeup made her cringe.

She couldn't let Coop see her like this. Not after last night. But the bathroom was just too damn far away right now. She needed java.

Then she could shower and get dressed. Too bad a shower couldn't wash away the memory of her behavior, too.

The clanging of pots and pans had her dropping her hurting head into both hands. *Great.* Coop was in the kitchen. Why couldn't he find something to do outside the cabin, like most every other day since she arrived in Red River? Throwing back the covers, she got out of bed. She pulled on a pair of yoga pants and an old T-shirt, then went to the mirror to smooth her hair.

She looked at the logo on her T-shirt. *Chiropractors Do It Properly Aligned.* It was Bradley's favorite. After he passed, Ella often slept in his T-shirts. At first, they smelled of his cologne, wrapping her in his presence. One by one, all those shirts had been laundered, until two years later they no longer held the familiar scent of security and contentment.

Shame washed over her. Last night, when Coop's hands were on her, Bradley hadn't even entered her mind until Coop had the sense to step away. She fanned her hand and fiddled with her wedding ring.

She rubbed her eyes. Her headache wasn't going away on its own. She needed pain relievers and caffeine. She'd just have to suck it up and face the music that waited for her in the kitchen.

Breathing deep, Ella took another look in the mirror.

Oh, my.

What sounded like the pantry door slammed in the kitchen, and she jumped. *Crap.* She couldn't stay holed up in her room forever. Squaring her shoulders, she made for the door and tried to rub the last remnants of makeup from her eyes.

The first thing Coop noticed was Bradley's old T-shirt that hung loosely around Ella's small frame. Bradley bought it when they went to a chiropractic convention together just before he was diagnosed. Coop looked away and poured her a cup of coffee. From the look of her, she needed it. She sure didn't look like Cinderella out of a fairy tale this morning. She looked like hell.

"Here." He handed her the piping hot mug.

"Thanks," Ella mumbled, taking the mug like a reluctant, mistrusting child. She sipped at it and made a face.

"I thought you liked coffee."

"This isn't coffee. It's dark brown water."

"You can always do without."

She eased onto a barstool. "This will do for now. Thanks."

He nodded and turned back to the stove. "I'm making you an omelet."

Her grimace deepened. "I usually eat Cap'n Crunch."

"Yeah, I noticed the ten boxes of cereal in the pantry." He cut his eyes at her.

"You don't like Cap'n Crunch? That's un-American." She tried to *tsk* but flinched, one palm covering her forehead.

"I love Cap'n Crunch, I just don't eat it."

"And you call me boring."

He sucked in an exasperated breath. "It's pure sugar. It'll make you feel better if you eat a lot of protein today." He flipped the frothy mixture. "And you need to drink lots of water. That'll help more than coffee."

"Aspirin." Ella rubbed her temple. "Aspirin will help, too."

Coop retrieved a bottle from the pantry, popped the lid, and shook two tablets onto the counter in front of her. A light blush tinged her cheeks.

"You know you really shouldn't drink. It doesn't seem to agree with you." He couldn't help but rub it in. After spending a sleepless night thinking of her softness, of how her breaths quickened under his touch, how could he not be a little sarcastic?

"Good tip." She downed the aspirin with a swallow of coffee.

He turned back to the pan and dished up a perfect gourmet omelet. He set the plate down in front of her and started on his own.

"Thanks," she managed.

"For what?"

"For the aspirin. And for this." Ella waved the fork at her plate and looked at him as though she were seeing him for the first time. "You're good at taking care of people." A little makeup still smudged on her eyelids, they fluttered and her reddened eyes wandered over his face, then down his chest, which caused it to tighten. She cleared her throat and looked down at the omelet. "It really does smell good. I can make good coffee, but I've never been much of a cook."

Really? Coop would've never guessed by the all the cereal boxes and frozen dinners.

"I like to clean."

No kidding.

She forked a chunk of egg into her mouth and chewed. Swallowing, she said, "How about I clean the cabin and you cook."

"There's nothing wrong with this place. It's clean enough." Coop flipped the cheesy egg mixture to the other side and steam sizzled from the pan.

She blinked at him. "It's a pigsty. Every time I straighten it up, you mess it up again."

He glanced over his shoulder into the den. It did kind of look like a hurricane had gone through the place, but he was a bachelor. Men weren't supposed to be all clean and prissy.

"Bradley said he ate dinner with you and Butch almost every night because his parents were gone to prayer meetings."

A smile spread across Coop's face. He dished up his omelet. "I learned to cook after my mom left. Dad worked all day, so I made dinner for us just about every night."

"Bradley said he would've gone hungry if not for you cooking for him."

Coop shrugged and sat down next to Ella. "He was a resourceful guy. He would've figured out how to survive even if I hadn't been around." As soon as the words left his mouth, he wished he could reach out and take them back. Ella sucked in an audible breath. Staring at his plate, he said, "I'm sorry. That came out wrong."

Half an omelet still on her plate, Ella snatched it up and walked to the sink. Setting it in the sink, she said, "Thanks for breakfast. I'll clean this up later." Then she went back to her room and closed the door.

Hell. Would he ever find a way to coexist with her? They'd been doing an awful war dance around each other for years now, like two opponents in a fencing match. Parry and thrust, parry and thrust. He'd be glad when the summer was over and she went on her way to . . . *anywhere else.*

Chapter Eleven

After sleeping off the headache, Ella showered and grabbed her laptop. The cabin was empty, and Coop was nowhere in sight. Winston whined to go out, so Ella cracked the door, giving him free rein to go in and out as he pleased.

She positioned herself at the table so she could look out the window, and fired up her Mac. With Coop's truck gone, she had a peaceful and expansive view of the stream. Her fingers went to work.

The way Coop had held her in his arms on the dance floor, molding her body against his, his breaths against her ear sending shivers down her spine, had ignited her body into flames she had no way of putting out. Then when she'd challenged him, put his hand on her breast, and he'd tugged and massaged both into aching peaks . . .

Hells bells, she was getting worked up thinking about it. The entire night had caused a whole new set of fantasies to play through her mind. Fantasies that would go unsatisfied. Again.

Frustrated, she banged away at the keyboard, letting those fantasies drench the pages on her laptop, the same way she'd done when Bradley was ill.

Hours later, Ella finally typed "the end" to book three and sent the manuscript zinging through cyberspace to her editor, Cyn. After clicking on the magical Send button, Ella looked up from the keyboard and stretched. The sun had started its afternoon descent, casting a dusky haze across the backyard and leaving the cabin in shadows. She got up and cleaned the dishes from the morning's breakfast. Just as she stacked the last plate in the dish rack, the landline rang.

"Hello, stranger!" a familiar voice hollered into her ear.

"Marilyn!" Ella yelled back.

An English teacher at Bella Vista High, Marilyn had sauntered into Ella's history classroom on the first day of school to say hi. Two days later when Marilyn, all five feet one inch and a hundred and ten pounds of her, broke up a fight between two teenaged linebackers without so much as smudging her hot-pink lip gloss, she'd won Ella's respect forever.

"How the heck are you?" Marilyn asked.

"I'm good," Ella said, and almost broke into tears. She missed Marilyn and the other ladies in the Circle of Trust.

"Well, I was out with the girls for our monthly lunch and couldn't wait another day to hear how things are going up there. So, how's mountain life? Are you lonely yet out in the sticks?"

Tears stung Ella's already-puffy red eyes. "I miss you guys." Her voice shook a little. "How's Bella Vista?"

"Still brimming with studious students eager to learn," Marilyn said, her voice dripping with sweet sarcasm. "I'm taking over the yearbook next year. Mrs. Riggs retired." Her voice dropped to a whisper as though someone might overhear. "Thank the Almighty. Now if I can just get the teenage boys on staff to take pictures of something other than girls in short shorts, I'll be in business."

Ella laughed. "How are *your* kids?"

"Rowdy as ever. When they get too far out of hand, I call Becca and Carissa. They come over and untie me before the boys burn the house down."

They laughed. Becca and Carissa were in the Circle of Trust, and were definitely capable of lassoing Marilyn's rambunctious adolescent boys. They could also be counted on to be there for a young grieving widow.

"So how's life in Red River?" Marilyn asked.

"I'm settled in." That's all Ella could think to say, with visions of Cooper Wells licking his lips while she all but undressed for him.

She'd fully expected him to push her away. His warm hands had closed over her aching flesh instead, his smoky gaze locking with hers, and she'd wanted to follow through for a moment. Then she'd panicked, and thank the angels in heaven, Coop had come to his senses for the both of them.

At least her stupidity had given her the inspiration to finish *Rio Grande Romp*. She'd fired off the last few chapters while the creative juices were still flowing after last night's near-romp.

There was a brief silence before Marilyn finally spoke up. "Okay, what's eating at you?"

"Huh?" Ella stammered. "I . . . I . . . nothing!"

"Yeah, sure. You're talking to *me*, so spit it out."

"No, really, it's just that, uh, uh—"

"Don't make me drive up there," Marilyn threatened, and Ella knew her closest friend in the world would do just that if Ella didn't give her something more substantial. Anything.

Ella sighed. "I'm not exactly alone, that's all."

"Who's there with you? Please tell me it's not your co-owner, Cooper Wells." Marilyn sounded suspicious. "Because you said you took care of reserving the cabin for yourself for the entire summer."

"I thought I did. Apparently, Coop's not big on checking messages."

"El, there's something I need to tell you."

Ella closed her eyes, braced for what was coming.

"I just heard some interesting gossip about Cooper and why he left Albuquerque and moved to Red River."

Ella tried to sound calm. "Okay, I know what you're going to say."

"Oh, phew," Marilyn said. "So, when's he leaving?"

Ella bit her lip.

"Ella?" Marilyn prodded. "He *is* leaving, isn't he? Because you can't stay with someone who's been accused of a crime."

"Oh, come on!" Ella grew defensive. Coop's irresponsible life-style had gotten him into this mess, and it certainly wasn't her place to jump to his defense. But much to her chagrin, she couldn't stand hearing anyone give merit to the accusations that'd been leveled against him. They just weren't true. This morning, she'd seen his caring, compassionate side when he took care of her like he'd always done his patients. Bradley told her Coop's playboy lifestyle was just an act. A self-defense mechanism against getting hurt again after his mother walked out on him and his dad. Ella never believed it until this morning. "You know as well as I do that Coop isn't guilty."

"Maybe not, but it's still not a good idea to live under the same roof with him. You could buy out his share of the cabin. Rumor has it he sold his swanky Nob Hill condo to help pay his legal fees. It'll give him some extra money and you'll be alone."

"You have no idea what Red River and this cabin mean to Coop. Selling this place is the last thing he'd ever do." She blew out a sigh. "Coop is harmless. I'm sure of it, and frankly, I'm a little offended that you don't trust my judgment."

The other end of the line went silent, and Ella got a little scared. Marilyn was probably already concocting a plan to recruit the other Circle of Trust members and drive up to Red River to toss Coop out on his ear that very night.

"Besides, he's never here," Ella added, to pacify the well-dressed lynch mob leader on the other end of the line. Marilyn, Carissa, and Becca made a pretty intimidating mob, now that she thought about it. Their strategy and plan of attack every Black Friday was downright terrifying.

"Doesn't his dad live up there?" Marilyn asked. "Can't Coop stay with him while you're there?"

"Butch's cabin only has two bedrooms, and Coop's a grown man. He's not going to sleep on the couch or share a room with his teenaged brother for months."

"Maybe I should drive up there," Marilyn said, more to herself than to Ella.

"You're acting like I'm living with him in the carnal sense, for goodness' sakes. I don't need a mother hen to rescue me. It's sweet of you, it really is, but I'm fine. Coop is fine. We hardly see each other, and he has as much right to be here as I do. He's half owner of this place, and he was technically here first."

Marilyn hesitated.

"Come on, it's fine. I promise the minute it stops being fine I'll pack up and put Red River in my rearview mirror. Fair enough?"

A reluctant sigh came through the phone. "All right," said Marilyn. "But I swear, if I hear any more gossip about him or if I hear any tension in your voice when I call you—eeeevery siiiingle daaaay—" she drew those three words out for melodramatic effect, "I'm coming up there. And I just might be packin' heat."

Right. Marilyn hated guns, but she wouldn't hesitate to bring the US Marines, the ACLU, and a few radical feminist groups if she thought it would help get her way. Ella smiled at the phone. "Deal." She laughed. "I really do miss you."

Ella hung up the phone and whistled for Winston since Atlas must have been with Coop. "Let's go for a walk, boy." The beautiful day had turned into an even more beautiful evening. A little fresh air and sunshine might loosen the aching muscles in her back that had tightened after sitting in front of the computer all afternoon.

By the time Winston waddled down the steps and over to the stream, Coop's truck crunched down the gravel-and-dirt drive and pulled to a stop next to her car. Atlas barked and pawed at the glass. As soon as Coop opened the door, Atlas trampled over him to jump from the truck and bound toward Winston. Coop walked over to them, grumbling under his breath at the dog. Then Atlas and Winston each latched on to one of Coop's legs and humped.

"Hey!" Coop scolded both dogs.

"Oh, my God." Ella's hands went to her eyes, and she covered them. "Some things just can't be unseen."

"A little help here," Coop said, kind of desperate. Kind of cute.

Ella peeked through her fanned fingers and laughed so hard a tear slid down her cheek.

"Yeah, thanks." Coop shook Atlas loose and then tried to dislodge Winston. "Seriously, Dennings, can you get your dog off me?"

Ella shrugged. "He does seem to prefer men."

Coop growled.

"Okay, okay." She walked over and grabbed Winston's collar, hauling him off her grumpy cabinmate. Her sexy, grumpy cabinmate. "Bad boy, Winston," she admonished the dog. "Winston and I were just going for a walk." She gave Winston a scratch under the chin. "Um, you could come." She stood and looked at Coop. Creases formed between his eyes. "Or not." Bad idea. Being friendly to Coop just never seemed to work. "Maybe just Atlas could—"

"Okay."

"Um. Okay then." She nodded upstream. "This way?"

He fell in beside her, his hands shoved in his jeans pockets. The soothing sound of the stream lapping over rocks wound around them, and they walked along in silence. A gentle breeze rustled the cottonwoods, and the piney scent of summer settled over the landscape with the sun sinking to the west.

Winston lagged behind with his tongue wagging almost to the ground. Atlas scampered ahead for a few moments then doubled back to rejoin his buddy.

"Winston," Coop said just that one word.

Ella gave him a curious look.

"He's an English bulldog. You're a history teacher. I didn't make the connection at first, but I get it now."

Ella chuckled. "He was Bradley's dog, but Bradley wanted me to name him. It was either Winston or Churchill. Bradley liked the name Winston better."

She waited for the smart-aleck remark about her being an anal-retentive, nerdy history teacher.

"Well I suppose it was better than naming him Adolf," Coop teased.

And there it was. But she had to laugh, because amusement danced in his eyes instead of grouchiness. Those moments were rare with Coop, especially when he spoke to her. She liked it. A little too much, actually.

Coop stopped and turned to look at their dogs. Winston had thrown himself against a fallen log and refused to get up. Atlas sat at his side like a loyal companion.

"Uh, Ella, I don't think he can make it any farther. Should I back my truck up and load him in the bed?"

She laughed. "Let him stay here. We can walk Atlas a little farther. Maybe Winston will have caught his breath by the time we get back."

They ambled along at a slow pace, and the thrum Ella had been trying to ignore every time she and Coop were within fifty feet of each other revved into a steady cadence. It started in her belly and spread to her fingers and toes. Turned to a pulse and an ache by the time it reached the spot between her thighs. Progressed into a pull in her breasts and lodged in her chest where it made her yearn for something more with Coop. Something that was unimaginable and stupid because . . . well, this was *Coop.*

But what if . . . ?

Ella cleared her throat.

"So how's your case?" she blurted. *Stupid, stupid, stupid.*

Coop's expression darkened. "The same I guess." He kicked at a stick in his path. "Where are you planning to settle when you leave New Mexico?"

Her chest tightened. Of course he wanted to know when she'd be out of his way. Out of his life. Precisely why she didn't need to be wondering *what if.*

She shrugged. "Don't know exactly."

"*You* don't have a plan?"

She bristled. "As a matter of fact, I don't." *Oh, Lord. She really didn't.* "What about you? What will you do if things don't . . . work out?"

He hissed in a breath. "It'll work out. It has to." Stopping, he turned his back to her and looked out over the meadow. He picked up a stick and threw it, whistling to Atlas. Atlas promptly ignored his master and sat by Winston's side, licking his face.

Coop grumbled under his breath again and turned back to the cabin. "I'm heading back," he said over his shoulder, and didn't wait for her to catch up.

Avoiding Ella was his best course of action. He'd been doing a good job of it, just because she usually seemed to be annoyed by his mere presence. Until last week, after the firefighters' dance. After that night, he had a whole different reason to avoid her. Just the sensual way she'd touched his chest made him crazy, and the way she put his hands on her breast, he couldn't get the feel of her out of his mind. Hadn't been able to think straight. So he stayed away as much as possible, finding anything, any reason at all to make himself scarce.

Coop pulled into his dad's drive and followed it as it curved around a grove of aspens that ended in front of the small cabin. Pulling in between Butch's and Cal's trucks, Coop parked, grabbed the sodas he'd picked up on the way out of town, and got out.

He circled around to the back of the cabin and stopped dead in his tracks. Ella and Cal sat at the picnic table, their backs to him. They huddled over an open textbook. She was helping his little brother, the same way Bradley used to help him. Ella, who acted fairly aloof, at least when she was around Coop.

Ella's finger moved across the page, and Cal's eyes followed, his lips moving at the same pace. When Cal was finished, Ella clapped, throwing one arm around him for a hug. She tousled his hair and they laughed together. Coop's heart softened.

Before Coop could sneak away, Butch came barreling out of the shed with a bag of charcoal slung over one shoulder and lighter fluid in one hand. "Hey, son. I was just about to fire up the grill."

Ella's stare swiveled over her shoulder, and Cal waved to his brother. Drawing in a deep breath, Coop walked over to them.

Butch doused the charcoal with lighter fluid and tossed in a match. Flames billowed into the air while his dad joined them at the table.

"Hey, Coop. Ella's teaching me reading strategies for my dyslexia."

Coop stopped a few feet behind them, his stare wandering from Cal's glowing expression to Ella's. She stared down at Cal's book. Hair up in a messy knot, her slender neck exposed. Stray wisps of auburn hair fluttered in the soft breeze, and the back of her shirt was hiked up just enough to expose a petite waist and velvet skin that he'd very much like to touch.

"That's great, Cal." Coop tore his gaze away from Ella. "That'll come in handy when you go to college." Cal shot a look at Ella, who gave him a sympathetic smile.

"Just like Bradley used to help you," Butch blurted.

Ella's gaze darted to Coop again. He'd begged Bradley never to tell anyone about his dyslexia. People thought he was stupid when they found out, but he never thought Bradley would keep it from Ella. Apparently, he was wrong, because from the look on her face, she didn't know.

"Yep, Coop was always smart, but that reading thing held him back. If it hadn't been for Bradley's help, Coop wouldn't have become a chiropractor. Right, Coop?"

Walking around the table, Coop set the soda down slowly and with purpose. And mowed down his dad with a sharp-ass glare.

Ella cleared her throat. "Without you two, I don't think Bradley would've become a chiropractor either. So, it was a fair trade."

Coop's fury turned to confusion. Did Ella just give him some credit? It wasn't the first time she sort of complimented him lately, and he was beginning to like it.

She closed the textbook. "I think that's enough for today, Cal, but you need to read on your own every night. Eventually, the strategies I'm teaching you will become a habit, and you won't even have to think about it. But it takes practice, practice, and more practice. Okay?"

"Sure, Ella. Thanks." Cal thumped his fingers against the book like drumsticks. "Hey, why don't you do the raft race with us to raise money for the Red River Library?"

She gave the back of her neck an uneasy rub. "I don't know how to raft, and I'm not a great swimmer."

Ella doesn't excel at something? Pfft. But uncertainty washed over her face, and she tucked a wispy lock of hair behind one ear with a shaky hand.

"Maybe I could make a donation to the library instead," Ella offered.

"It's easy. Right, Coop?"

"Cal, if Ella's scared, then leave her alone." Coop shoved his hands in his pockets, and Ella's eyes narrowed at him.

What had he said wrong? He was trying to help her out after the almost-compliment she'd just paid him about Bradley becoming a chiropractor.

Cal's face fell in disappointment.

"Well, if it's for the library, then I'm in," she said, a challenging look in her eye.

Cal perked up like a little kid being offered a prize at the fair.

"I'm starting on Ella's bathroom in the loft day after tomorrow." Butch walked up and grabbed a soda from the table. "You boys are helping, right?" Butch shot a warning stare at Coop.

Okay. He guessed he knew what he'd be doing in his free time the next few weeks.

"I've rounded up a few more fellas to help, too," Butch said, and he and Ella proceeded to argue over who was paying. She seemed soft and at ease in cutoff denim shorts, flip-flops, and some sort of white gypsy-looking top that gathered at the waist. Every time she moved, it rode up her torso, exposing a swatch of creamy skin and a perfectly round belly button. No piercing. No tattoos. Coop wasn't surprised. She wasn't the type, and he liked it that way. Her skin seemed almost untouched, unconquered. Like it was calling for him to do the touching and the conquering.

Coop's cell phone vibrated in his pocket, and he jumped. Digging it out, he looked at the number and his heart stuttered. His attorney, Angelique Barbetta. It could be good news. Then again,

Angelique, one of Albuquerque's most ferocious criminal defense attorneys, could be calling to warn him that the police were on their way with a warrant for his arrest.

He ran a hand over his stubbled jaw and turned away to face whatever waited on the other end of the call. Walking to the other side of the yard for privacy, he pressed the green button on his phone and raised it to his ear.

"Hey, Angelique. What's the news?" He turned back to watch his family laugh with Ella while they worked together to prepare the table. Ella fit with the Wells men like an olive fit with a martini.

"You want the good or the bad first?" Angelique cut to the chase with her usual alpha-female tone.

Coop ran a hand through his hair. "I need to hear something good right now." He looked at Ella, who poured lemonade into glasses from a jug. Cal said something to her and she flashed a dazzling smile.

"Kim's story is unraveling. We're not out of the woods yet, but she gave another statement, and it didn't exactly match up to the statement she made for the criminal lawsuit. It's a small crack in the dam that we can capitalize on."

"Does that mean this might all go away soon?" Coop tried not to get his hopes up, but looking across the yard at Ella, his chest squeezed with the prospect of starting over with a clean slate.

"The mismatched statements, plus the fact that there's no physical evidence to support her claim, weakens her allegations even more. If she doesn't drop the complaint soon and you actually do get arrested, I'll request a deposition and break her when she's under oath. When I'm done, her attorney would be crazy to let this thing go to trial."

Angelique would do just that. They'd known each other since high school and gone through four years at UNM together. They'd been friends and never dated, which was one of the reasons he'd hired her. That and the fact that he'd watched her grind up her opponents on the volleyball court in high school. And she'd hammered the opposing debate team into dust, sinking her teeth in like a pit bull with no mercy until she'd claimed victory and had at least one of the girls in tears. It was an awesome sight to behold. And scary.

She'd won his respect, so he never entertained the idea of dating her. Plus, he was a little intimidated by her himself, and she was on *his* side.

"And *why* did she give another statement?"

Angelique hesitated. "Well, that's the bad news."

Coop pinched the bridge of his nose. "Go ahead, Ang. I'm ready." Did he have a choice?

"Miss Arrington filed a civil suit against you seeking monetary damages."

He closed his eyes. When would Kim take her fangs out of him and let him live his life again? All because he broke up with her?

"Her attorney already approached me with an offer, which I turned down. If he thought Kim had a snowball's chance in hell of winning, he wouldn't have even suggested a settlement this soon."

"I hope you told Kim and her attorney to shove it in a very uncomfortable spot where the sun rarely shines."

Angelique laughed. "Not in those words, but yes. Their case is so weak, it would be foolish for you to agree to any kind of settlement. It's just a matter of being patient and not doing anything stupid that would be incriminating."

Coop went still and glanced at Ella. He squeezed his eyes shut for a second. "Listen, Ang, there's a new development that you should know about."

She let out an exasperated sigh. "I can already tell I'm not going to like this."

"You know how I owned the cabin fifty-fifty with Bradley?"

"*Yeeees,*" she drew out. "Something tells me you're about to ruin my day."

"His wife moved in for the summer." He braced himself for the storm.

"What's wrong with you, Coop?" Angelique erupted. "Are you *sleeping* with her? Because I told you to avoid getting involved with women on *any* level until this is over."

"Calm down, and no, of course we're not sleeping together. I'm the last person on earth Ella would get involved with."

Ella'd said so herself at Joe's, but he conveniently left out how her hands had roamed all over his torso and how she'd encouraged him to do the same to her while under the influence of one Mr. J. Daniels. Angelique's fuse was already burning low. She'd blow a gasket if he told her everything.

"Interesting how you said *she* wouldn't get involved with *you.* Are you *thinking* about sleeping with her?"

Yes, almost tumbled out of his mouth. "No!" *Not until recently.* His eyes clamped shut. Angelique was right—what *was* wrong with him? He was an idiot. An idiot who wanted to shag his best friend's widow.

"If she misinterprets just one of your actions, do you know how bad it would look for you?"

"I wasn't happy about it either, but it's done. And Ella isn't a threat to my case. She's . . ." *Freaking gorgeous.* "She's a teacher and kind of a goody-goody." *Except when she wasn't.*

Angelique exhaled. Loudly, to make her displeasure known. "If that's true, then it might work to our advantage. We could always call her as a character witness."

"Try not to worry too much, okay?" Coop said.

"I'm supposed to say that to you. Just keep it in your pants, Wells, you hear me?"

Sure. No problem.

"I'll get back to you with an update soon," Angelique promised. "For now, sit tight and don't do anything stupid."

Like sleep with my best buddy's wife?

He stared at Ella, laughing and talking with his dad and brother across the yard. Happy in the breezy June evening against the green mountains and blue sky of the Red River Valley, not one of the three doubted his innocence.

A startling thought crossed his mind. Maybe he belonged here year-round with family. With friends who didn't jump to the wrong conclusions about him. With people he could lean on through tough times, like now, and who believed him because they *knew* the kind of man he really was, deep inside. With someone like Ella.

Jesus, where did that come from?

"Coop, are you listening?" Angelique blasted through the phone.

"Yeah, yeah. I'm listening." Only he wasn't, because his entire world was tilting off balance right now, and not just because of his legal problems.

He stared across the yard at his best friend's widow, the cold hollowness of guilt creeping into his chest. He wanted her. Wanted to get to know her better the way Bradley had. Wanted her to stop looking at him with such deep disapproval. Instead, he wanted to see acceptance in her eyes when she looked at him.

And desire.

Chapter Twelve

Wanton Publishing loved *Rio Grande Romp*. Success had a price, though. Cyn Caldwell was after her like a fire-breathing dragon to produce that excerpt for book four.

Ouch. Ella hadn't even started it yet.

Dressed and ready for the raft race, Ella sat at the table in front of her laptop, trying to get a little work done before she left for the river. She tapped her nails against her lips and tried to force her brain to engage. A blank white page glared at her. Had been glaring at her since early that morning. Maybe if she could think of a title first, she could find inspiration.

High Country Heat. High Country Hottie.

Ella dropped her head in her hands.

She'd thought Red River would provide a peaceful getaway for her to do some serious writing. But with Butch's troop of tool-carrying helpers milling around her the last few days delivering supplies and taking measurements for her new bathroom, the creative juices just weren't flowing.

The memory of Coop's touch didn't help her attention span,

either. After the firefighters' dance when his hands had closed over her and caressed, the smoky look in his eyes nearly made her forget how much he really disliked her. At that moment his expression hadn't communicated his usual distaste for her. He'd clearly wanted her, but his eyes didn't look at her like she was a mere object of physical pleasure. They looked into her soul.

She wished she could erase that precise look from her memory, because every time they stepped into the same room, her pulse shot up like a thermometer in the middle of a Texas summer.

Finally, Ella held both palms up facing the laptop. "I surrender." She rolled her eyes and flipped the lid down. Jeez, she really needed to get a life.

An hour later, she showed up to the eighth annual Fourth of July Red River Raft Race for Literacy clad in spandex leggings with a pair of running shorts over them, water shoes, a spandex long-sleeved shirt to protect her fair complexion from the blazing New Mexico sun, and a baseball cap that said *I have a black belt in history.*

She pulled her shoulder-length hair through the back of the cap and doused her hands, neck, and face with sunscreen. She locked her car and crossed NM Highway 68 to the rally point. A veritable county fair was already in full swing.

"Hey, Ella!" Cal waved her over to the first aid booth. Cal and two volunteer firefighters wore first aid vests.

"Hi, guys." Ella smiled and joined them. "You guys look great. I feel safe already." She tried to squelch the fear that stung her stomach like a nest of angry bumblebees. Yeah, she was safe. Of course she was. *Don't be a wuss, Dennings.*

Cal's boyish grin lit his eyes. "I took the fire department's first aid and safety training, so I'm official now." He positively glowed.

During one of their tutoring sessions, Cal had shared with Ella that he didn't want to become a chiropractor. He wanted to be a fire-fighter. He just hadn't shared that decision with his dad and brother yet because of the firestorm it was likely to spark.

Ella could relate. Her parents had her ranching profession and entire life planned out for her since she was old enough to remember.

Two boys darted past, one chasing the other using a Steak on a Stick as a weapon.

"Stop that!" Their tall, blond, early-thirties mother yelled after them as she walked up to the first aid booth. "Or I'll make you take two baths tonight instead of just one." They both stopped running, and the pursuer hid the Steak on a Stick behind his back. She shook her head and turned to the first aid volunteers behind the booth. "They'll probably be your first customers of the day."

She stuck out a hand to Ella. "Lorenda Lawson. You must be Ella Dennings."

Ella shook Lorenda's hand with a curious smile. "Nice to meet you."

"I already heard you moved to town." She shrugged. "Small town and all. News travels fast."

"Well, nice to meet you, Lorenda. Are you rafting today?" Ella asked her.

"Not me. No one to watch the kids for that long. My mom and dad are showing property to clients in Angel Fire today, so I'm here representing our real estate office." Lorenda shook her head. "Like I'm going to be able to reel in new clients while chasing two kids around." She smiled toward her two boys, who were trying to skim rocks across the river.

"Ella," Cal broke in. "I think Coop's starting the rafting lesson for the beginners." He pointed to the river where a small crowd had gathered around Coop for Rafting 101.

"It looks like he could use some help," Lorenda drawled. They all looked toward the riverbank, where a voluptuous pupil in a skimpy bikini rubbed all over Coop. Her lower back bowed so far it made her scantily clad chest jut toward him. She tossed her curly locks over one shoulder, revealing her yellow string bikini top for Coop's full view. The muscles in Ella's neck went taut, and something prickled over her like a thousand tiny pinpricks. When Coop looked past the eager female student to talk to someone else, Ella relaxed.

"That's Sandra Edwards. She works at one of the ski and souvenir shops," Cal said, in awe.

"I know who she is." Lorenda turned a scolding eye on Cal. "And her name isn't just Sandra. It's also Trouble." She looked back at Coop like a protective mother hen. "Something Coop doesn't need more of right now."

No. No, he didn't. And at the moment, Ella wanted that itty-bitty bikini to stop rubbing all over Coop—because yes, she was a little jealous if she had to be completely honest. And a little catty. And a little hot and bothered by the spandex athletic shorts and tank top that revealed his beautifully sculpted body. The combination of sporty sunglasses and the boyish grin gave him the bad boy look that women went wild for, each believing they could tame him. Of course, they couldn't.

Hence, the trail of broken hearts in Cooper Wells's wake. And the pissed-off girlfriend who was trying to make sure he suffered. And Ella's growing desire to unwrap that "package" she'd admired the first night she arrived at the cabin, to see for herself what all the fuss was really about.

"I think she's only got eyes for Coop," one of the young volunteer firefighters said, and the other one snickered.

"She's got eyes for anyone with a bank account," Lorenda spoke up.

"Seriously, Ella, maybe you should head down there." Cal nodded toward his big brother.

Ella squared her shoulders and tried to calm her thudding heart. *It's no big deal, Dennings.* A few kids were even in the beginners group.

Like a kid headed to the principal's office, Ella dragged her feet toward the crowd. Coop had already passed out life jackets and explained how to tighten them. The water flowing around his muscled calves and his white sleeveless undershirt accentuated his bronzed skin.

"Have fun," Lorenda called after her. "You look thrilled."

"Positively elated," Ella said with a dreary tone.

"We'll be patrolling up and down the river if you need help." Cal assured her. "And Coop will be in the water watching out for the racers."

Great. That would relieve her stress.

She walked to the riverbank where Coop's rafting lesson was already in full swing. Coop demonstrated paddling with alternate strokes, the movements causing toned muscles in his arms to ripple and harden. Her tongue darted out to wet parched lips, and her entire body grew warm.

The sun. It was the sun. She cleared her throat. *Definitely the sun.*

His head turned in her direction. Behind a pair of polarized sunglasses, it was impossible to see if his eyes were on her, but Ella knew they were because his fun, flirtatious expression faded.

"Glad you could join us, Ms. Dennings," Coop said dryly. The sexy, De Niroesque mole under his left eye was visible just below his sunglasses, and it elicited a tingle from Ella in a certain place where it shouldn't. "I figured you must be an expert rafter, since you chose to miss most of the lesson."

She folded her arms across her chest and jutted out a hip with attitude, but she didn't say anything. Not with her body humming and her mouth turning to gravel just from looking at him.

Coop finished the lesson with general directions about how to maneuver the small one-person craft with the paddle, and Ella didn't understand a word he said.

Ella had joined the lesson wearing something that looked like a second skin, and Coop stopped talking to the class midsentence. He willed himself to stop staring but couldn't tear his gaze off of her. The woman could put on a flour sack and make it look good.

Guilt coursed through him. *She was Bradley's.*

Ross walked up and grabbed two life vests. He handed one to Ella and tried to help her into it. Ella accepted graciously.

"Sandra," Coop unwound her catlike grip from his bicep. "Wait here." She hissed when he stepped away.

He approached Ross and Ella, Ross fumbling with the fasteners on her vest. "Hey, Ross. Could you do me a favor?"

"Sure, Coop. What's up?"

"See that pretty little thing over there?" He hitched his chin toward Sandra I'm-Looking-For-A-Sugar-Daddy Edwards. "She needs some assistance. Could you help her tighten the vest and watch out for her on the river?"

"Uh." Ross looked in Sandra's direction, his mouth opening and closing several times. "Sure, man."

"Thanks, dude. I'll have my hands full with the other newbies." He gave Ross a fist bump. "Sandra will need your undivided attention."

Ross gave Ella a torn look. "You'll be okay without me?"

"I'll be fine, Ross. Go have fun." Ella still struggled with the buckles.

"I owe you one, big guy." Coop slapped him on the back.

"No problem. I'll take one for the team." Ross headed over to

Sandra, and she latched on to his arm like a slot machine that was guaranteed to spit out coins with every pull of the handle.

Coop stepped into Ella's space and tugged at the shoulders of her vest. It nearly lifted straight over her head. "This has to be tighter. If you end up in the water, it'll pop up over your head, and you won't be able to see where the current is taking you." He inserted his fingers into the front of the vest and tugged toward him. She lost her footing and landed against his chest. Her breath caught, and so did his when she turned those big green eyes up at him. He set her away from him and tugged on the nylon strap under her right arm, cinching it up all the way. She gasped.

"That's kind of tight," she said uncomfortably.

He yanked the other side just as tight, and she made a face.

"It has to be to save your life."

Ella blanched. "I didn't realize my life would need to be saved when I signed up for this. Or that I'd be required to wear a corset from the 1700s."

He tugged the front strap, trying not to picture her in a corset. The night of the firefighters' dance, when the wet fabric of her dress had revealed lacy bikini panties, he'd been surprised. He'd expected her to wear parachute panties or something completely boring.

"It's like a torture device." She let out a groan. "Seriously, will my life really be in danger?"

"The little bit of risk involved is the whole point. The adrenaline rush is part of the fun." He secured the straps over her shoulders. "You do know how to have fun, right?" he teased.

She glared at him.

He sighed. "I'll be on the river in case you need help."

"I'm not like you, Coop. I don't need an adrenaline rush to have fun. I like to take things slow and easy."

"Is that why you're wearing your grandma's swimsuit?" He snapped one of the buckles together and secured it. Needling her was the only thing that kept his mind off of the zing he felt inside every time he stepped into her presence lately.

"I beg your pardon?" she sputtered. "I have to cover my arms and legs. Sunscreen doesn't work as well on my complexion. If you haven't noticed, I'm a redhead."

Oh, he'd noticed.

"Really? I hadn't noticed." He crinkled his brow and stared at the hair protruding from her baseball cap. Studied it for a second for dramatic effect. "Hmm. I guess you're right."

Her eyes narrowed. "Love the wifebeater tank top, Coop. It suits you."

He bristled. Considering he'd been unjustly accused of a crime against a woman, that was a cheap shot. "Are you stereotyping me, Ella?"

"Yep."

He pulled the last strap tight, and she lost her balance again. When she grabbed his bicep for balance, his skin tingled under her fingers. He hadn't felt that sensation when Sandra wrapped her cat claws around his arm. Sandra hadn't interested him in the least. Coop couldn't get away from her quickly enough. It was Ella who tugged at his attention and made his pulse sing like the engine of a brand-new luxury car.

"Try not to fall behind, Dennings." He finished adjusting the vest. "I'll have to tow you in if you can't make it to the finish line on your own." He gave the life jacket one last tug. Her knees dipped a little, and her grip tightened around his arm. He steadied her, his heart softening when fear flashed in her eyes and her brow furrowed. Okay, enough of his razzing her. She really seemed scared. "Are you sure you want to do this?"

"If you can do it, then I can certainly do it."

He studied her for a second, then gave his head a quick shake. He looped a nylon cord around her neck and tucked the whistle dangling from it inside the vest. "If you get in trouble, use this."

"Don't worry about me, Coop. I can take care of myself."

"Is that so? Then when we go through the Eye of the Needle, you won't need my help."

She frowned. "The Eye of the Needle? What's that?"

"The only class-four rapid on the course," he said as he turned toward his raft.

Chapter Thirteen

Ella held the double-bladed paddle in her hands, not entirely sure why rafting was considered fun. Nothing about it looked fun to her. She'd watched Coop give another demonstration, watched the first, second, and third waves get in the water and practice before taking off. Not a darned thing about it looked fun to her. When he talked about rolling a capsized raft back into its upright position, her stomach tossed for a second or two.

She tried to stop the trembling in her hands and looked across the river at Coop. He sat in his single-person raft, treading in the same spot like an expert Olympian rafter.

"Okay, last wave. Get into your raft. When you see the orange flag waving," he pointed to Dylan fifty yards downriver, "use your paddle to push off. Remember—don't crowd the person ahead of you, especially when we get to the rapids. If you get thrown out of your raft—"

Ella's ears started to ring.

"—and you can't reach it, roll over onto your back, cross your ankles, and float down the river feetfirst. Your life vest will keep you afloat until we can get to you."

Both hands went numb, and Ella looked down. Her fists were wrapped so tightly around the shaft of the paddle that her knuckles had turned a sick-looking white.

Ella glanced at Coop. He pointed toward her vessel of doom, his eyebrows rose high above his dark sunglasses.

"Everything all right over there?" he yelled.

Releasing her paddle, she gave him the thumbs-up and smiled. No way was she giving him the satisfaction by backing out.

He got out of his raft and waded over to her with a skeptical look.

"I'm good." She waved him off. "I've taught history to teenagers at one of the roughest high schools in New Mexico. I can handle paddling down a river for an hour and a half."

He leaned in and spoke softly so the other rafters couldn't hear. "This really is supposed to be for fun."

"It will be. Just as soon as it's over," Ella said dryly.

One of the kids in the raft next to Ella asked his dad impatiently, "When are we starting?" He couldn't have been more than ten years old, and he glared at Ella. She had a sudden urge to stick her tongue out at him.

"You don't have to do this, Ella," Coop said. "You can drag your raft over to the parking lot and be done with it."

She shook her head. "In front of all these people? No way am I taking the walk of shame."

He studied her, a hand on his hip. "Then get in," he finally said. "We're holding everyone else up." He waded back to his raft.

She got into her vessel of doom, and Coop paddled over to her. Visibly checking her position, he nodded with a scowl on his face. She couldn't keep her raft steady.

Stupid way to raise money. Who the hell came up with the idea, anyway? Writing a check would've been so much easier. Quicker. *Safer.*

"You're looking a little pale, Ella. Sure you can handle this?"

"I'm ready, Dr. Disaster." Seemed appropriate. She smiled at him.

His lips curled up into a half smile. He back-paddled upstream.

Show-off.

Dylan yelled, "Everybody ready?" After a few moments, he waved his large orange flag.

"Jeez, this isn't the Indy 500," Ella muttered. She reluctantly used her paddle to push off the riverbank, watching dry land slip farther away.

"Ella," Coop shouted at her, and she jumped. "Use your paddle." He lifted his high in the air. "This thing in your hands."

Smart-ass.

Ross and Sandra were already a few hundred yards ahead of her, and they disappeared around a bend in the river.

The bow of her raft was pointed to the right, or the starboard side. Right? Er, correct? Ella was already confused. When she dipped her paddle into the water off the starboard side of the boat, it turned more to the right and she was going sideways down the river.

Coop yelled at her, "Opposite side!"

The current took her and swept her to the right again. Now she was facing backward.

The dad of the two young boys called to his sons to stay on the opposite side of the river. Ella wanted to scream at him. Really, what kind of manners was that to teach kids? He might as well have told them to steer clear of the crazy lady.

Coop rotated his paddle from one side to the other, digging into the water with long, swift strokes. He quickly caught up to her. "If you want to turn starboard, paddle on the port side."

"Really? We're in blow-up rafts. These aren't battleships off the coast of Normandy." Ella rolled her eyes. Boys and their fantasies.

"Just paddle, Ella. You're already way behind everyone else."

She dipped her paddle off the left side of her craft, and it drifted to the right. "I didn't do this to win. I just wanted to support literacy in the community." Ella tried not to sound sulky.

"How noble of you. Always the Girl Scout."

Always with the Girl Scout barbs. "This is a charity event, so why are *you* here, Coop?"

A sly smile curled the corners of his mouth. "To watch out for people like you, Dennings."

Coop kept glancing to his left. Ella struggled with the paddle. She was in good physical shape and seemed to be relatively coordinated; that wasn't the problem. She just looked scared. With her acting so vulnerable, a look of terror on her face, and that silly hat announcing she was a nerdy history teacher, he really should have insisted she bow out of the race. But the hardheaded woman probably wouldn't have listened, especially to him.

He refocused on the river ahead.

His raft cut through the water, and he rounded a bend in the river just ahead of Ella. Looking back, he lost sight of her. Up ahead, the first class-two rapid came into view. Easy, even for a novice.

He stabbed his paddle into the water on the left side of his craft and pulled up to the right bank. When Ella rounded the corner, still looking shaky and awkward with the paddle, Coop pushed off and treaded in place by rotating his paddling back and forth.

When she got close to him, he shouted to her, "Class-two rapid ahead. Veer left around that large rock." He pointed to the right side of the river. "As soon as you clear it, paddle on the left side and it'll swing you right so you'll hit the rapid in just the right spot."

She nodded, her green eyes wide and glassy.

The hair on the back of Coop's neck prickled. If he could guide her through the first few rapids with no problems, it might build her confidence. Maneuvering the river was easier than it looked, but fear could cloud a beginner's judgment and slow their reflex time.

He fell in behind her. Her strokes were uneven and apprehensive. She hesitated, still as uncomfortable with the paddle as when she first got in the raft. Most people got a feel for it after a little while, but she looked like a scared child on a roller coaster. She paddled on the right side first and veered to the left just like Coop had told her to do. But unsure of herself, she switched sides too quickly and it turned her to the right before she cleared the rock, setting her on a collision course with it.

"Paddle on the right!" Coop yelled.

Apparently, she heard him and plunged her paddle over the right side of the raft. The move corrected her, but not quite enough, and the right side of her raft banked onto the rock.

"Lean right, Ella," Coop yelled over the din of rushing water.

She did and used her paddle to push off the rock. She cleared the first rapid.

"Good girl," Coop said even though she couldn't hear him. The small knot in his stomach eased.

He went through right after her and lengthened his strokes to catch up.

"Good job, Dennings." Coop tried to hide the concern in his voice. "I didn't think you had it in you."

Her smile was uncertain, the fear still apparent on her wary expression. "I still don't see how this is fun."

"That's because your type doesn't know *how* to have fun," he teased.

"I most certainly do."

"This might come as a surprise, Ella, but most people don't define fun as sitting in a lecture about the pilgrims."

"For your information, I wouldn't either. I'd call it . . . interesting."

Coop laughed. "My point exactly."

Letting her concentrate and acclimate to the ebb and flow of the raft, he paddled alongside her a ways in silence, until a light roar came from up ahead.

"Hear that?" Coop asked her, presenting the very picture of calm for her benefit.

She nodded, her eyes widening again.

"That's a class three up ahead. Enter on the left side of the river. Once you clear the first level, the current will kick you to the right. It's easy for your raft to spin too far. If that happens, just enter the next rapid backward. You'll be fine."

"Backward?" The pitch of her voice rose in alarm.

"Experienced rafters go in backward on purpose. Don't worry, it's more fun that way."

Ella gulped, and Coop's eyes followed the muscle movement down her slender throat. Sympathy pinched his stomach.

He slowed and let her go first. She cleared the first level and maneuvered the second level like a pro. Coop went through and caught up with her again.

"You did great. You feeling more confident?"

She nodded.

"Good, because I couldn't have done any better on that one myself."

A few clearings appeared at intervals along the riverbank. River patrols and onlookers gathered to cheer the racers on. Coop waved to a group on the left. Several of the women issued catcalls. Coop smiled and kept paddling in sync with Ella.

"You're always asking for it, aren't you?"

"What?" Coop's brow wrinkled.

Ella threw her head in a backward direction toward the women.

"Those women?" he asked.

"Don't you know them? You must, for them to react that way."

"I've probably seen a few of them around at Joe's, but I don't *know them* know them."

"Right."

On this long strip of glassy water, Ella seemed a little more at ease. "Did you see me do anything to provoke them?"

"Not exactly. It's just . . ." She stopped talking.

"Just what?"

"The way you carry yourself. You seem to like it, like it feeds your ego or something."

Coop's pulse kicked. His ego had never been his reason for not committing to a long-term relationship. He just didn't want to get on the marital roller coaster that his dad had lived on.

"And does pointing out my flaws feed *your* ego?" Their paddles cut easily into the smooth water, as they stayed side by side.

She shot a glare at him, until he gave her a teasing smile. She laughed and nodded. "*Touché.* I'll give you that one, Dr. Disaster. You've earned it."

The sound of rushing water sounded in the distance ahead and got louder until it became a light roar.

The Eye of the Needle.

He'd maneuvered this rafting course a hundred times, at least. It was an adrenaline rush. Nothing too dangerous, especially with the water so slow this season, but just risky enough to set his blood pumping. This time, a prickle of fear slithered up his spine.

He glanced at Ella and the blood in his veins turned to ice. Obviously, she heard the rapids up ahead, too, and she'd stopped paddling, staring ahead with a blank expression.

And at that moment, he wanted to reach out and gather her into his arms.

Chapter Fourteen

"Let me go through this one first so you can see the easiest path to take," he yelled over the rushing water.

She shook her head vigorously. "Don't leave me here alone."

"I'll be just up ahead." He pointed to the giant three-story boulder that had broken off the top of the mountain in the early nineties and tumbled down into the river, creating a whole new rapid. The narrow entrance into the rapid between several smaller boulders was the reason it was dubbed "The Eye of the Needle." After shooting through that, you had to paddle hard right to clear the boulder, then hard left through the last of the jagged rocks and fast water.

"Watch what I do and follow my lead exactly. I'll pull over on the far side and wait for you to come through."

He waited for a response, but Ella just stared straight ahead and paddled gently to keep her raft going in the right direction.

"You'll be fine," he shouted.

She nodded, her face a chalky white.

"If you get in trouble, use your whistle."

Coop entered the first rapid through the two tall, jagged rocks. The current took him, and he paddled hard right and managed to clear the boulder without even grazing the side of his raft. As he rounded it, he took one last look at Ella, who was paddling toward the entrance, eyes round and hollow. He glided through the second half of the rapid with ease and banked his raft on the right in a small inlet that was outside the current. He waited.

And waited.

A chill crept up Coop's spine until it tickled the back of his neck. The roar of the water melted away. Coop stared at the gap in the rapids where Ella should be coming through any second, but it was empty. Just water rushing over jagged rocks.

The seconds ticked by like hours. *Come on, Ella.* His blood pressure spiked.

It had been too long. She wasn't coming through. Another minute crawled by, and a speck of blue and yellow caught his eye. A wave of panic swept through him like the cold rushing water of the rapids. Ella's paddle rushed through the Eye of the Needle, drumming against each rock as it tumbled through the class-four rapid.

Coop looked up at the jagged edge of the cliff above him. No way to traverse it. Looking across the river, he figured if he could get across to the other side at a sharp diagonal, then he could walk back upstream on the rocky bank until he found a clearing.

Pushing off, he darted across the river at a steep slant and landed on the opposite bank. The bow of his raft rammed onto the rocky shore, and Coop jumped out. With the water up to his crotch, he pulled the rubber craft onto the bank, stumbling under the current. He grabbed the rocky edge and pulled himself out. Dragging his raft far enough onto the rocks to secure it, he grabbed the first aid kit that was secured, along with a flare gun, in a waterproof bag, and unhooked the survival rope from a ring in the back of the raft. He slung both over his shoulder.

Carefully, he picked his way upstream, looking to the left for any sign of Ella. Every second that passed with no glimpse of her made his stomach pitch harder. He increased his pace, still trying to keep his footing and not fall back into the water himself.

Finally, he made his way even with the giant boulder, and as he moved just past it, he saw the red-and-white raft.

The capsized rubber boat beat against the big boulder, and the sick thudding sound caused Coop's breathing to seize. Ella was nowhere in sight.

"Ella!" Coop shouted, a searing burn slicing straight through his heart.

No answer. The raft continued to thud against the rock in a hollow rhythm.

He traversed a little farther upstream and craned his neck. He had to reach her. What if she was badly hurt? Or worse?

"Ella!" he yelled again, his voice growing more frantic. A faint trill wafted across the breeze, and Coop strained to hear. It went off again, a little louder this time.

A whistle.

"Ella, hang on! I'm coming for you." *Thank God.*

Coop's mind zinged as he tried to figure out the best way to get to her. If he entered the river here, the current would shoot him through the rapids again before he could reach her. He waded farther upstream.

Removing the waterproof sack from across his shoulder, he unzipped it and pulled out the flare gun. He flipped the safety switch and raised it into the air. With a pull of the trigger, a flash of orange rose high in the sky. He tucked the gun back into the pouch and secured the strap across his chest again.

Jesus, he should've talked her out of doing the race. She'd been so obviously scared, but there were little kids in this race. No way did he think Ella, of all people, would be so paralyzed with fear. But, if she was hurt, or worse . . . Coop's jaw tightened. He couldn't let that happen.

And suddenly, miraculously, how much Ella meant to him, how important she'd become, spread through him like warm liquid. He liked having her in his life. She sharpened him. Like iron against iron, her stubborn will kept him in line like no other woman had ever been able to, and it made him a better man. Made him want to be a better person.

He had to get to her before it was too late.

He moved farther upstream and unwound the lifeline that was slung over his shoulder. Before leaving the safety of the rocky bank, he tied the rope around a sturdy boulder, first testing it to make sure it could hold him and Ella both. He hooked the other end to his vest and waded in. His shoes, designed for water activities, gave him more traction against the slippery river rocks. When he was up to his waist and the river current started to overpower him, he plunged into the water and stroked toward the other side, angling his body at forty-five degrees.

Halfway across, the current strengthened and fought him with each stroke. His endurance started to wane. His knee banged against a rock, and pain shot through it, but he kept swimming. Finally, a rock that jutted out of the water just shy of Ella's raft came within reach and Coop grabbed it. Holding on to it like a buoy, Coop tried to catch his breath.

Ella's whistle sounded again.

"Ella," he called out. "I'm almost there."

When his breathing leveled off again, Coop pushed off and the current grabbed him. He latched on to another large rock and managed to hang on. If he let go on the left side, it would take him through the first level of the rapids and sweep him past Ella, so he used his hands to maneuver to the right, where the current eased. When he got to the right edge of the rock, Coop pushed off and kicked violently, propelling to the right against the current. He swept toward the giant boulder and reached out and grabbed it, latching on by his fingertips. The jagged edge cut into his fingers, but he refused to let go.

With both hands, he felt his way to the left until he reached the raft. He grabbed on to one of the rope handles and pulled it up. Ella was underneath, her head just above water, her back to him. She'd managed to find a small crevice and burrowed into it, out of the grasp of the current.

Relief surged through him. *Smart girl.*

Coop pushed the raft over her head. As soon as he pulled it free, the river took it, and it swept through the rapids. It jetted through the Eye of the Needle and beat against the rocks with a series of sick thuds.

Ella's head hung forward, and he swam up behind her. "Ella," he whispered gently. "Sweetheart, I'm here." He gripped her right upper arm, and she screamed.

He looked closer. Her shoulder was partially covered by the life vest, but he could see that it hung limp at her side.

"Ella, can you raise your right arm?" he asked against her ear.

She shook her head in jerking movements.

"Okay, I'm going to look under your vest. Ready?"

She didn't respond.

Gently, he lifted the edge of her vest. Her body was contorted where the arm connected to the shoulder.

He slid one arm around her waist while still gripping the boulder with the other. "I've got you, baby."

She leaned back against him, and her head fell back on his shoulder. He was cheek to cheek with her. Her eyes closed and her lips blue, she was in shock, and hypothermia had clearly set in.

"Coop, my . . . my arm . . . can't move it."

"Your shoulder's dislocated. Does it hurt anywhere else?"

"I . . . I don't think so." Her eyes closed. "But I can't feel my feet anymore. Do you think they're still attached to my legs?"

He chuckled. "Of course they are. You're just cold. The feeling will come back when you warm up. I'm going to tie this rope around you, okay?" He unhooked it from his vest and secured it to hers. "Help will be here in just a minute."

"I'm cold." Her entire body shook against him.

"I know, sweetheart." He held her close against him, but between their two life vests and the freezing water, his body heat couldn't reach her. There wasn't much he could do to warm her up, so he anchored her against his chest and wrapped one of his legs around hers. "You'll be outta here soon, and I'll build you a fire when we get back to the cabin."

"That's . . . nice," she whispered through chattering teeth.

Coop placed a delicate kiss on her temple. "I should've taken better care of you. I'm sorry."

"You're here now." Her voice grew more faint. "In living color."

Yeah, he was here in the flesh. Alive and well. And Bradley wasn't, the one who really deserved Ella because he'd been such a top-shelf guy. Coop didn't deserve a woman like her. She'd been right the other night after the dance. He was terrified of everything she represented because he didn't think he could be worthy of a woman of her caliber. And even if he stood a chance with someone like her, he'd probably find a way to mess it up.

Coop heard sirens. Help was here.

In Red River, Coop paced the waiting room of Doc Holloway's office, half of the local residents waiting with him. That was the great thing about a small town. The people might all be in your business, but they were also there to help and support you when you needed it.

The door to the exam room opened, and Doc stuck his head out. About the same age as Coop, Blake Holloway's nickname didn't fit his tall, athletic build, but that's what the townspeople had labeled him, and it stuck.

"She won't let me touch her until she talks to you."

Coop was in the room and by her side like a man with superpower speed. The bed was in an upright position, but reclined slightly, and Ella looked at him from under long lashes.

Doc Holloway pointed to the backlit X-ray that was mounted to a view box on the wall. "There's no broken bone, but the X-ray shows the ball-and-socket joint has dropped anterior and inferior. It needs to be relocated."

"Okay, speak English." Ella's voice was cagey, the pain evident in her expression.

Coop tried to soothe her with a soft look. "Your shoulder just needs to be reset."

Her magnificent green eyes pleaded with him. "Can you do it, Coop? Bradley used to reset dislocated shoulders."

Coop speared fingers through his damp hair. "I can do it, but I can't." He closed his eyes and pulled in a breath. "I mean, I know how, and have done it many times, but legally I can't do it now. My license is suspended."

"But I'm scared. Bradley told me once how painful it is."

Coop exchanged a look with Doc Holloway. Ella reached for Coop's hand and he engulfed it in his. Her hand looked so small, so fragile. Small wrinkles from the water still gathered the skin around her fingertips.

"It's very fast. A split second and it's over. And the pain you're experiencing now will disappear instantly. I'll be right here with you."

The creamy skin between her shimmering green eyes wrinkled. "Doc, can you give her something?"

Doc Holloway nodded. "I can give you a small dose of diazepam, Ella. That will take the edge off, but you'll still feel it. Coop's right, though, it's over fast, and you'll feel much better than you do now."

Damn it. She shouldn't have gotten hurt, and it was his fault.

She nodded hesitantly. "Okay." Her voice was small, almost childlike, and something inside Coop's chest thudded.

Doc gave her the pain meds. "I'm going to step out and give the medication a few minutes to take effect."

Coop nodded, but Ella stared down at Coop's hand clasped with hers.

In a few minutes, the meds took effect, her emerald greens dilating into black marbles. Her head fell back against the white-papered bed, and Coop stroked an auburn lock away from her face.

"You really know how to crash a party, don't you?" he teased.

Her head rolled to the side, and she smiled at him, her eyelids closing and lifting in slow, rhythmic motions so that long, silky lashes brushed her cheeks with each sluggish blink.

"Sorry." Her words slurred a little. "So much for living dangerously. I guess I'm just not cut out for it. You're right. I'm boring and predictable."

Coop caressed the length of her good arm. "That's all right. You're good at other things."

"I'm a good writer." She was dozing now, her eyes completely closed. "Did you know that I'm a writer?"

"I can picture that." A thought occurred to him. "Is that what you're doing on your laptop all the time? Writing?"

"Ummmm-hmmmm. You're a beautiful man, Cooper Wells," she said, her eyes closed. "And the mole under your eye is very sexy. Has anyone ever told you that?" She giggled. "Oh, yeah. Lots of women."

Coop didn't know what to say, but a grin formed at the corners of his mouth.

"I like you. More than I thought. *A lot* more." She giggled again. Then her forehead crinkled again, and she licked her lips, her head gently rolling from one side to the other. "I *really* like you," she managed before giving in to a medication-induced doze.

Well, hell.

Doc Holloway stepped back into the room. "How's our girl doing?" he asked, and Coop's chest swelled.

"She just dozed off."

Doc leaned over her. "Ella, wake up."

Her eyelids drifted open.

He adjusted the bed and positioned her to get just the right leverage. With her arm bent upward at the elbow, Doc gave her a soothing look. "Ready?"

Before she could answer, he thrust his weight against her elbow, shifting it up and back. A loud pop echoed through the treatment room as her shoulder slid back into the socket.

Ella's scream ripped through the clinic.

Chapter Fifteen

Ella slept all the way back to the cabin. Her arm in a sling, she cradled it against her midsection. Coop let the truck roll softly to a stop under a large cottonwood tree, the last rays of evening sun filtering through leafy branches to dance across the metallic hood. The yard faded to a dull gray.

A wrist thrown over the steering wheel, Coop cut the engine and looked at her. The seat tilted back, she was deep in a medicated sleep, her head rolled to one side. He pulled in a weighty breath. This was his fault. He shouldn't have let her do the race. And his teasing had made the situation worse.

Gently, he brushed a few messy strands of hair away from her face. "Ella." He leaned over and whispered into her ear. She didn't move. He gave her good shoulder a light squeeze. "Ella."

"Hmm?" Licking her lips, she rolled her head into an upright position and opened her eyes.

"We're home."

We're home. His tongue tied for a second.

"'Kay," she said, her voice weak from the sedative. She reached for the door handle.

"No, sit tight." He unlatched his seat belt and jumped out of the truck. "I'll come around and help you."

He jogged around to her side and opened the passenger door. Leaning across her, he unhooked her seat belt and took her good arm. She grimaced. "I know you're sore, but it'll only last a few days."

With his help, she got out of the truck and into the cabin, where Coop shooed Winston and Atlas outside before they could jump on her and cause more pain.

He led her toward the hallway.

"My neck hurts more than my shoulder," she said, rubbing the back of her neck.

Coop chuckled. "Now, that I can cure." No, he couldn't. He wasn't a licensed chiropractor at the moment. A muscle in his jaw jumped. "I'll have Dad come over in the morning and give you an adjustment."

She tried to walk down the hall, but Coop stopped her at his bedroom door. "You sleep in here tonight. I bought an orthopedic mattress a few months ago. You'll get a better night's sleep."

He led her to the bed, and stood there. *Well, hell.* What was he supposed to do now?

"Coop," her words came slow and lazy. "I need help getting out of this hoodie."

"Maybe you could sleep in it." That was the only solution that popped into his racing mind, because Doc Holloway had cut off her fitted shirt at his office. Coop had dug around in his truck and found this hoodie for her to put on, but he didn't know what, if anything, she had on underneath. And, Jesus, he didn't want to think about it too much, or he'd never get to sleep tonight.

She shook her head. "I want it off." She sat on the bed, cradling the injured arm against her chest, and kicked off her water shoes.

"Okay," Coop said, raking a hand over his jaw. *Okay, what?* He wasn't actually sure. "I . . . I . . ." He stuttered.

"Coop, I've got an athletic bra on under it." She tried to pull the sling over her head and grimaced. Coop placed a gentle hand on the sling, stopping her movement.

"Not like that. Just stay still." He loosened the buckle on the back of the sling and pulled the strap free. With careful, disciplined movements, he slid the sling off and freed her arm. "Keep it pulled in close to your body as much as you can."

She fumbled with the zipper on the hoodie, but the meds had stolen the dexterity from her fingers. He swiped her hand away and grasped the zipper.

"You're sure?"

She nodded and let her head fall back, eyes closed.

The zipper descended, whizzing along its downward trajectory. And inch by glorious inch the gray hoodie fell away and fair skin appeared. When the black sports bra that held her breasts firmly in place was fully exposed, he swallowed and tugged the sleeves off each of her arms.

"Hold on a second." He got up and pulled the covers back. Under the comforter was an old quilt, worn with use and soft from age. Coop kept it on the bed because it was so smooth and comfortable to sleep under. "Okay, let's get you in bed."

She let him take her arm, and she stood. "I need help with my shorts and leggings." She grabbed the waistbands and pulled one side down.

He swallowed. Hard. "Ella, maybe you should just sleep in them."

"For God's sake, Coop." Her voice was heavy with sleep. "You've seen a woman in her panties before." She leaned against him. "Am I really that repulsive to you?"

Hell no. That was the problem. He clamped his eyes shut and sank two fingers into the waistband of her clothes. Together, they worked them down until the skintight leggings were completely off, and Coop tossed them aside.

He tried not to look at the silky panties that covered just enough to make him wonder what was underneath, yet revealed enough so there was no doubt that it was all good. Desperately, he tried to avoid looking at her flat stomach and slender waist that dipped in just below her ribs. But it was impossible.

She slid into bed. His bed. Ella was in *his* bed.

He pulled the covers up over her beautifully formed body with feminine curves in all the right places. How, he wasn't sure. She didn't get that figure from eating Cap'n Crunch. Her injured arm lay across her stomach, and she dozed.

The setting sun cast a dark shadow over the room as he stared down at her. He reached for the lamp to flick it off.

"Cooper?" Ella said. Her voice was husky with sleep and pain medication.

"Yeah, it's me. I'm right here."

She rolled toward him. "Will you stay with me for a little while?"

He hesitated.

"Please?"

He dragged in a breath. How could he say no to that? "Sure." He turned to pull the chair over.

"No." She patted the bed next to her. "Here next to me."

"I don't think—" Coop tried to protest, but her eyes opened wider, a silent plea flashing through them.

She held back the covers, and he lay down next to her on the side of her good arm. She scooted closer to him.

"Can you put your arm around me?" she asked softly.

"Ella, I don't think that's a good idea."

"Cooper, it's times like this when I miss him the most. I'm not as strong as I pretend to be."

Definitely the meds talking. She always acted as strong and sturdy as a brick house. Built like one, too. But he knew how she felt. Bradley had been his go-to guy just like he'd been Ella's. And when times got tough, Coop missed him too.

Gently, Coop threaded his arm under her neck and rested his palm against the injured shoulder.

"You sure?" Because, God Almighty, he wasn't sure at all. This was *Ella*. Ella Dennings. His best buddy's widow.

She nestled into the crook of his arm and nodded. Her cheek resting against his chest, she said, "I'm sure." An inexplicable contentment blossomed in his chest and spread through him like hot chocolate does on a cold winter day.

He looked down at her.

She seemed so vulnerable, so soft, so desirable. And Coop thought he could stay there, just like this—holding his best friend's widow—for the rest of his days.

"I'm so cold," she mumbled.

And she was. Ice-cold, in fact. She molded her body against him and entwined her feet with his. "I'll stay until you fall asleep." He tucked the covers up around her neck and rubbed her back to keep the circulation going.

"Thank you." She snuggled against him, her speech slurred from the tranquilizers. "And Coop," she whispered, all drowsy. "Why are you smiling?"

Huh. "How do you know I'm smiling? Your eyes are closed."

"I can hear it in your voice." Her eyes never opened. "Tell me why."

"Because you called me Cooper. You've never called me that before."

His mother used to call him Cooper, the only person who ever did besides his dad. And Butch only called him that when he was mad at his son. Cooper had been his mom's maiden name.

"You called me 'baby' and 'sweetheart,' if I remember correctly." She sighed and snuggled deeper into the notch of his shoulder. "And I always remember correctly."

Busted again.

"You remember strange things," Coop teased.

"Yeah, but not in a creepy stalker kind of way. I just have a photographic memory, and I listen well."

Bradley had said as much in excruciating detail, in fact. He'd been amazed at Ella's sharp mind when they first met and how she kept him on his toes intellectually. A trait Coop found annoying at the time, but now he was beginning to see the value in it and why it was so attractive.

"Does this mean we're finally friends?" She yawned.

"Yeah, I suppose we can finally be friends."

"Miracles really do happen." She snuggled in closer, and Coop wanted her to stay there forever. "I wish Bradley could see us. He'd be so happy that we like each other."

Coop's heart twisted. He was definitely glad his best friend couldn't see him groping his wife. He looked heavenward and wondered. Sighing, he closed his eyes and exhaled.

"Ella." Coop stroked her shoulder.

"Hmm?" She smacked her lips, drifting between sleep and consciousness.

"I should've talked you out of doing the race. I knew you were scared. I'm sor—"

"Shh." She snuggled deeper into the notch of his shoulder. "You were there when I needed you. That's what counts."

He adjusted the covers around her shoulder and stared at the ceiling. "Get some sleep, Ella. We both need it."

But she was already far off in la-la land, a soft snore convinced him of that.

Ella woke to a dark room, the warmth of a masculine body encapsulating her. His heartbeat thrummed against her cheek, his soft sleepy breaths caressing the top of her head.

She rolled her head into the fabric of his T-shirt and breathed in his heady scent. Ah, she loved waking up next to him. It was positively intoxicating.

Ella moved her hand to rest on his chest. Her shoulder was stiff and didn't move as freely as it usually did. Gently, her fingers began to stroke the cotton fabric, then moved down his stomach to find the hem. When her hand touched bare skin and traced the defined muscles with her fingertips, he stirred.

"Ella," came his urgent whisper.

She lifted her face to his and found his mouth, her hand dropping lower to the waistband of his shorts. He sucked in a breath and held it. When she deepened the kiss, his fingers threaded through her hair.

Her hand dipped inside his shorts and his breath quickened. She found the generous flesh underneath, and it throbbed and grew thick with each of her loving strokes. He moaned, brushing fingers across her jaw. He angled her head and his kiss grew more intense, his tongue searching out hers, brushing it, caressing it.

"Touch me," she nipped at his lower lip.

He rolled her gently, lovingly, onto her back.

"You're sure?" Desire laced his husky voice.

"Yes." Her own voice was just as urgent because she wanted him so much. Had wanted him for so long. Oh, God, yes, she wanted this. Wanted to feel his weight on her, his pulsating thickness inside of her. "Yes, I want you."

His hand found her breast and cupped it, kneading and massaging until her head turned on the pillow, and she nearly sobbed with need. He found her earlobe with his teeth and tugged.

"God, I've wanted to do this for weeks. I knew they'd taste sweet." He nibbled on it, then he trailed soft butterfly kisses down her neck. Pulling on her athletic bra, he captured an already-taut nipple with his mouth, and she arched into him, a small sensual cry sounding out into the darkness. When his teeth tugged at her peaked flesh, she screamed out. He released it and she felt a void, a loneliness like she'd never experienced before, until he did the same with the other.

She speared one set of fingers through his hair, and raised his mouth to hers. He captured it with a possessiveness that she'd never known, and she wanted him more than she wanted to breathe.

His hand traversed lower and skimmed across her abdomen. His fingers explored with expert marksmanship, and when they dropped to the apex of her thighs, she opened for him. He caressed her through the silky panties, the soft fabric creating just enough friction to make her writhe, make her want more.

"Make love to me," she commanded, and he tugged her panties down. "Yes, I have to have you, Bradley."

He went still.

At that moment, Ella's foggy brain began to clear.

"Coop?" She swallowed, and tried to catch her breath. "Coop, I'm sorry."

He pulled her panties back into place.

"I just got confused for a second."

Coop didn't utter a word. He just rolled out of bed and adjusted his shorts.

"Coop, you can stay." Ella reached for his hand. "I want you to."

And she did. She'd started to see a side of Coop that she didn't know existed. Imagined them eating dinner together every evening. Wondered what it would be like to go to sleep with him at night and wake up with him in the morning. Silly, she knew.

The dark room obscured her vision, and she couldn't see his face. She could only make out his silhouette, but she heard him breathe in deeply.

"Not like this, sweetheart," he said, his voice soft as a whisper. "I can't be a stand-in for Bradley."

He whistled for the dogs as he left the room. A few seconds later the front door opened and closed.

Chapter Sixteen

The gloom of a dreary winter day settled over the cabin, even though it was early July and the weather was beautiful. Ella carried a mug of fresh, steaming coffee in each hand. Pushing through the screen door, it slammed behind her.

She walked toward Coop; Atlas and Winston bounded over to playfully nip at her feet. He glanced over a shoulder, his expression unreadable, then reeled in his line to add more bait to the empty hook.

She stood beside the old fallen log that served as a bench, clumps of grass growing up around it so that it had become a permanent part of the natural landscape. The stream gurgled past at a lazy pace and smoothed the tension in Ella's shoulders. And in her heart.

"Good morning," she said to Coop's back.

"Hey," he answered, giving her a brief glance. "How's the arm?"

"A little sore, but not that bad."

He threw his line in the water again and released the reel to let it float downstream. "That type of injury heals pretty quick. The worst part is popping it back into place."

"I made you coffee." She didn't mind making him coffee. When she woke each morning, his presence in the cabin was the first thing that popped into her mind. Making enough coffee for him and her both had become a comfortable routine. A routine she didn't look forward to giving up at the end of the summer when it was time for her to move on.

"Thanks. Just set it there." He motioned to a smooth clearing of dirt near the bank. "You didn't have to do that." He flicked the short stream rod to jiggle the line, then started to turn the reel slowly, rotating the flick and turn in a methodical pattern.

"I was hoping we could talk," she said.

He gave his head a shake. "Nothing to talk about. Last night was a mistake. It shouldn't have happened." An empty hook emerged from the stream again, and Coop reeled it the rest of the way in. "Won't happen again," he said as he reached for the round container of worms. His frosty disposition chilled her even more than the cool morning air. She shivered even though she wore the long-sleeved hoodie he had loaned her yesterday.

Ella put his mug on the ground and sat on the log, cradling her warm cup in both hands. "Coop, please."

He left the bait on the ground and stood up with a hand on his hip. Looking down, he sighed.

"Let me tell you I'm sorry."

Staring out over the stream, he still didn't turn to face her. Levi's hung low on his hips, an indigo-blue T-shirt hugged his shoulders and biceps. He kicked at a small rock with black hiking boots. "Apology accepted. It's over."

"Is it?" Because hells bells, she didn't think it was over. Calling him the wrong name, especially *Bradley's* name, had to be an explosive kick in the gut.

He dropped his rod and picked up the coffee mug. Blowing on it first, he took a sip. "Forget about it. I know I will."

Of course he would. She'd rubbed all over him when he was

asleep. Probably the only reason he reacted to her at all was because his mind had been fogged over with sleep.

"Okay. Well." She cleared her throat. "I also wanted to say thank you."

His forehead crinkled. "For what?"

"For coming for me yesterday. I don't know how much longer I could've held on."

His eyes darkened, and he glanced away. "It was nothing. I would've done it for any one of the rafters."

"And they would've thanked you, too," she said, and her mouth turned up in a smile. "I was scared, and you were very kind. You took care of me and made me feel like everything would be okay."

He studied her for a second and then sat next to her on the log. "Can I ask why you're so scared of the water?"

She shrugged. "I'm not a great swimmer."

"But you had a life jacket on."

"I've just never been much of a risk taker. You know that; it's one of the many things you don't like about me."

He shot a cloudy look at her, and she gave him a teasing smile. The darkness eased from his hazel eyes, and he laughed softly.

"Did someone drown, or did you have an accident in the water when you were young?" he asked, sipping at the coffee.

She shook her head. "Nope. Just a chicken, I guess. So you're right about me, I'm boring." The few times she'd taken a risk it had backfired. Like kissing Coop in the basement all those years ago. Like asking him to get in bed with her, rubbing all over him, and then calling him Bradley.

She looked away.

Like wanting to make love to her late husband's best friend, even though she and Coop had no future together whatsoever. Because, yeah, she couldn't stop the tingling in unmentionable places every time Coop stepped into the same room. And if she hadn't called him, Bradley last night, she'd probably still be in his bed right this minute, exploring every inch of his beautiful body.

She swallowed when her nipples hardened. She tucked her hair behind one ear. "So, next weekend I may be gone for a few days. Do you mind if Winston stays here?"

He shook his head, but a frown appeared on his lips. "Atlas would love it."

"I need some retail therapy. Red River isn't exactly a shopping mecca."

His frown deepened. "Are you going back to Albuquerque?"

"Denver," she said, and swirled coffee around in the mug.

"Albuquerque's a lot closer, so why drive all the way to Denver just to go shopping?"

"There's no memories in Denver."

They sat in silence for a few minutes, staring at the peaceful stream. His oaky scent and warmth drifted around her like a vise, squeezing out the memories of Bradley until Coop was the only one left.

Her eyes moistened. "Well, thanks again." She stood and turned to the cabin.

"Stay gone as long as you like," Coop said, hauling himself off the log to retrieve his reel.

Ella halted at the brusqueness of his tone.

He cast his line into the stream. "I could use some space. We both could."

On Tuesday, Ella went to Doc Holloway's for a follow-up appointment, then walked a few blocks along Red River's Main Street to Lorenda's real estate office.

said, looking up when Ella opened the office
nt off. She sat behind a massive desk, custom-
rustic. Cedar paneling gave the office an earthy scent.

"Working hard?" Ella asked. She closed the door behind her.

"Nah, the cabins around here sell themselves."

"Then how about some lunch?" Ella plopped into a chair in front of Lorenda's desk like they'd known each other forever. Funny how easily she settled into friendships here in Red River. It'd taken her months to make friends in Albuquerque.

"Sure thing." Lorenda glanced at her watch.

Ella pulled out her phone. "I'll text Brianna and Donna to see if they want to join us. My treat since you guys brought food over three nights in a row after my accident." She tapped on the keys and hit Send. "Which was completely unnecessary, by the way."

"Because you love to cook for yourself so much?" Lorenda arched a brow.

"Coop has a big mouth about my lack of skills in the kitchen."

"Honey, when you shop at the Market, everyone knows what you eat. When I need to buy tampons, I make the forty-minute drive all the way into Taos. Otherwise, the entire town knows it's my time of the month."

Within the minute, Ella's phone dinged with two replies. "The Gold Miner's Café in fifteen." She tucked her phone back into her purse.

"The benefit of living in a small town." Lorenda stapled a few papers. "You can gather a posse and be anywhere in town within minutes."

"So I keep hearing," Ella laughed. She fingered her wedding ring, twisting it around in a full circle. Looked out the window at Main Street. Wheeler Peak's white cap loomed over Red River, stark against the cloudless blue sky. The rest of the Sangre de Cristos were dense with green foliage. People meandered down the main drag, and a Suburban topped with a luggage rack tooled past. "There's some good folks here."

"And is Cooper Wells, DC, one of those folks?"

Ella's attention whipped back to Lorenda. *"What?"*

Lorenda's brow arched again. "I'm a salesperson, so I'm pretty observant with people, and there's definitely something between you two."

Ella surrendered and shook her head. What was the use in trying to hide it? She was a terrible liar, anyway. Bradley always said she was the type to tell on herself if she did something wrong.

Boring. Predictable.

If Bradley and Coop knew about Violet Vixen, wouldn't the joke be on them?

Ella jammed both hands into the pockets of her jean jacket. "I don't know, to tell you the truth." She searched for words that eluded her. "One minute we're enemies, the next we're . . ." Ella didn't know what to say next, because she wasn't sure what they were, exactly.

"Doing it on the kitchen table?" Lorenda offered.

"No! *No*, we've never . . ." Ella looked around as if someone might be listening. That small-town thing, again. "We've never done 'it.'"

"After the accident, I've never seen Coop so protective."

"It was sort of his job. He was just being helpful."

"Sweetie, the paramedics were there. He looked at you like you were the love of his life, and you wouldn't let go of his hand."

Others could see what she and Coop had been dancing around, refusing to admit to themselves? Ella's eyes clamped shut. "What good would sleeping together do? We'd probably still dislike each other when it was over."

Lorenda got up and grabbed her jacket off the coatrack in the corner. Sliding into it, she motioned Ella toward the door. "You sure you guys really dislike each other?"

No, Ella didn't dislike Coop. If the tenderness and concern he'd shown her after the rafting accident and the way he'd touched her in bed was any indication, he didn't seem to dislike her anymore, either.

"We're the opposite of what we each want in a partner." *Of what we each need.*

"Opposites attract," Lorenda said.

Yes, they did. And that scared the heck out of Ella.

She followed Lorenda out the door. Coop did scare the heck out of her. She wanted a long-term relationship. And she couldn't afford to have her heart broken again when it was finally healing from loss and grief. She wanted someone secure like Bradley, someone who was solid and safe. No risk, no heartbreak, no surprises. And no guilt over dating Bradley's best friend.

Coop was nothing but risk. And the loyalty they both still carried inside for Bradley seemed like a wall neither of them could tear down. Even if she and Coop gave it a go, a black cloud of guilt would surely crush any chance of success.

So, why did she want him so much? And not just physically. He'd surprised her and turned out to be far less self-absorbed than she'd always thought. Embarrassingly enough, she was getting attached to him and even found herself wondering if she could make a *life* with Coop.

They walked toward the Gold Miner's Café, both propping sunglasses onto their noses.

Ella took her left hand out of her pocket and looked at her wedding ring. She came here to close a very painful chapter of her life and open a new one. When she headed to Red River for the summer, she had no idea what that meant or where she'd end up. She still didn't, but she'd never find out for sure unless she started living again. Really living, without Bradley's shadow following her and his memory haunting her every move. Without feeling like she was cheating on her dead husband.

Without becoming another notch on Cooper Wells's belt.

"Coop isn't my type, and I'm definitely not his. But it *is* time for me to get back in the saddle and start dating again. That's kind of what I wanted to talk to you girls about today."

They waited for a car to clear the intersection, then crossed over to the other side of Main Street.

"I need some prep work *before* I start dating. Like a makeover at Brianna's salon and a few days of marathon shopping for a new wardrobe in Denver."

That sounded like a plan. She'd get herself "date ready," then she could figure out where to relocate. Preferably somewhere with a large dating pool.

Coop, Cal, and Butch hammered away at the new cabinets in Ella's bathroom. Coop had to admit, it was turning out nice. Probably an upgrade he should've made a long time ago. Then again, he'd never shared the cabin with a woman before, so the need for another bathroom hadn't registered in his alpha-male brain.

He'd spent so much time trying to avoid Ella the past month that he didn't know when he started to *like* her presence at the cabin. Didn't recall when her being there every night and every morning when he woke had filled him with contentedness and satisfaction. It brought him security and comfort. Warmth spread through his chest every time he walked through the front door and smelled her shampoo or that gourmet coffee that she fussed over several times a day. Apparently, it was the only thing the confounded woman knew how to make in the kitchen besides a bowl of sugar-laden cereal.

He placed a nail against a stud and aimed the hammer at it.

Unfortunately, the summer was almost half over, and Ella wouldn't have the chance to use her new space for very long because she'd be moving to destinations unknown.

The hammer connected with his thumb instead of the nail. He howled, dropping the hammer to grab his purpling thumb.

"Go put some ice on it," Butch said. "We'll finish up."

Coop descended the spiral wrought-iron staircase two steps at a time, holding the throbbing thumb. At the bottom, he came to a halt, his feet rooted to the floor.

Ella's suitcase sat at the door, handle up, ready to be wheeled out to the car. Away from him. Only for the weekend, but eventually, she'd roll that same suitcase out to the car and never return.

The same scene played through his mind from his childhood. The arguing between his mom and dad; her tears. A lot of tears. And her begging Coop to move to California with her.

He'd stayed with Butch. Listened when Butch gave her updates on their son's baseball games, schoolwork, friends. But Coop wouldn't get on the phone and speak to her himself. When she came back to Albuquerque just to see him, he sat sullen on the sofa, refusing to speak or look at her. And he never accepted her invitations to visit her in California, especially not after she remarried.

He tore his gaze away from the luggage when Ella walked down the hall and into the den.

"What happened?" Her voice pitched high, green eyes rounded.

"Apparently, you have to be coordinated to use a hammer." Coop glowered at his hand.

"You need ice." She ran to the freezer and scooped up a handful of ice. He followed her into the kitchen as she threw the cubes into a baggy, added a little water, and grabbed a kitchen towel.

He leaned against the counter, still holding his pulsing thumb. It *hurt*.

She stood in front of him in slim-cut jeans that hugged her long legs, and a T-shirt that said *I teach history. What's your superpower?* When she reached for his hand, he let her have it. With a gentle touch, she placed the ice pack over his thumb and molded the cubes around his swelling digit. She wrapped his hand with the towel and held it between hers.

"You'll probably lose the fingernail," she said, looking up at him, and her warm breath washed over his cheeks. He stared down at her, his eyes raking her soft complexion and anchoring to her lips. On cue, the tip of her pink tongue slipped out and traced her plump bottom lip.

His pulse seemed to pound in unison with his thumb. "Fingernails are overrated," he said. "I don't need it." But he was beginning to think he needed her. *No, I don't. She still loves Bradley, she's leaving eventually, and I'm . . . screwed.* He was stuck in a holding pattern until his name was cleared and he could go back to his life in Albuquerque. "It'll be fine. I should get back upstairs."

"Your thumb is the size of a sausage," she said, and then turned a very sexy shade of pink.

Coop's mouth quirked up.

Still cradling his wrapped hand in between hers, their eyes locked for what seemed an eternity. Their breath mingled, pulses quickened, and at the same moment, they swayed into each other.

The landline rang. Ella released his hand and stepped back.

He let out a ragged breath and snatched the phone off the bar. Ella grabbed a dishcloth and started wiping down the already-spotless counter.

He pressed the green button. "Hello?"

"Coop," his attorney's voice came through the line.

The ice taking effect, the throbbing started to numb, and he rested his wrapped hand on the counter. "Hey, Ang."

Ella's shoulders bristled, and she rubbed furiously at the imaginary dirt on the counter.

"I've got a positive update for you, buddy," Angelique said.

Coop's heart skipped, and his eyes stayed firmly on Ella. "I'm listening, Angelique." Ella's profile dimmed when he said Angelique's name.

Huh. Was Ella jealous?

She tossed the rag on the counter, ignoring his stare. With quick strides, Ella hurried to the door and grabbed the suitcase. She threw her purse over one shoulder; found her car keys on the table, pink pepper spray bottle still dangling from them; and pushed through the screen door. The bag thudded against the worn wood planks as she wheeled it down the steps.

"Kim called my office and insinuated that she might be willing to drop the lawsuit if you're still interested in her."

"She's crazy," Coop said, going to the window to watch Ella drag the suitcase to her car. "How is that good news for me?"

"Dude, it makes her look really, *really* bad. I'm about to call her attorney and fill him in on her little innuendo. She'll deny it, of course, but what she doesn't know is my firm records calls if they're flagged by the receptionist. And Kim Arrington's name raised a flag the size of Texas."

He didn't want Ella to leave. Not yet. So he opened the screen door and let Winston and Atlas out. They ran to Ella, and she bent over to give them a good-bye scratch.

"That's great, Ang. Listen, I gotta go. Keep me posted?"

"Will do, buddy."

They clicked off, and Coop went outside, his hand resting against his chest.

"That was my attorney," he said, walking over to Ella and their odd canine couple.

Her shoulders relaxed, and she gave him a nervous smile. She hugged both dogs while they licked at her cheeks.

"Hope it was good news," she said, keeping her attention on the dogs.

He nodded. "I went to high school with Angelique. We never . . . she's just a friend."

"Coop, you don't owe me any explanations." Ella stood up, brushing off her clothes.

"I didn't want you to think . . . ." Why did it matter what she thought? Only, it did. It mattered very much to him, even though it shouldn't. He scrubbed a hand over his jaw and nodded. "It was good news." He looked over the expansive, wooded property, the early afternoon sun heating the air enough for short sleeves.

"You'll be okay without me?" she asked, and then her cheeks glowed pink again. "I mean because of your hand. I can stay in Red River if you need me."

Yes, I need you. To stay. His gaze dropped to her lips and they parted just a fraction, rounding into a tiny O.

That was all it took to crush the small sliver of self-control he'd been hanging on to since she'd been in his bed with her hands wandering all over him. What the hell? He didn't have much left to lose. He closed the space between them, laced his towel-wrapped hand around her waist, and anchored his other hand at the back of her head.

Her mouth fell open, and her shimmering eyes rounded. He pulled her into a kiss. Urgent. Almost punishingly so. And she responded to it in kind, rising to the challenge, grabbing for him.

Kissing him with feminine power until she softened against him and moaned her approval.

He tore his mouth from hers and looked down into her eyes, glittering with desire. The back of his index finger smoothed down her flushed cheek.

"I'll see you when you get home." He whistled for the dogs and strode to the cabin without looking back.

———

Ella looked at herself in the mirror, a little impressed by the transformation.

After two days of highlighting, waxing, plucking, polishing, and several other "-ings" that weren't all that comfortable to talk about, the result had been well worth it. Her bedroom light danced off the new coppery flecks in her hair. New makeup shimmered across her eyelids and cheeks, and new lipstick made her lips look more plump.

She chose a new black fitted dress that wrapped around her like a sarong and tied at the waist. It showed off all of her curves. Toenails shimmering with red metallic polish, she further adorned her feet with a pair of bling-covered platform flip-flops. Long silver earrings dangled from her ears and a set of bangle bracelets made a chic, sassy sound when her arm moved. At Donna's insistence, she'd even bought several sets of matching lingerie, and that was the best purchase of all.

The new purple-and-black lace panties and bra that were hidden under her stylish new dress made her secretly feel a little like the vixen she wrote about in her book. The widowed schoolteacher that had let her appearance go was gone, and someone new stared back at her. Someone who might have just enough sex appeal to get a date. Or at least a few dances tonight at Joe's.

But the real objective was for Ella to make her debut as a single woman again. Get out there. Mingle. Forget the hot, searing kiss Coop had laid on her before she'd stumbled to her car and left for Denver. She had to forget it, because Coop just wasn't an option, no matter how much chemistry sizzled around them. No matter how much she'd grown to like his presence. Who was she kidding? She'd grown to *want* him.

Ella spun in front of the mirror. "Not bad for an old widow, huh?" She looked at Winston.

He burped, his tongue hanging out one side of his mouth like a limp noodle. Atlas curled next to him. Well, at least one of them was capable of attracting a male.

Fanning out her left hand, Ella looked at the sizeable diamond engagement ring and the matching band of diamonds. They glistened under the light.

Her eyes moistened, and a nugget of sadness lodged in her throat when she slid the set of rings off her finger. She held them to her lips and kissed them gently. "I love you, Bradley. I always will." She put them in her jewelry pouch, tucked the pouch into her lingerie drawer, and left the cabin for Joe's.

Chapter Seventeen

When Ella walked into Joe's and joined her table of friends, Donna purred. Literally purred. Like a cat. Well, more like a mountain lion in heat. "Mission accomplished. You look like a cover girl. Or Aphrodite. Every person in the room with chest hair turned to look at you when you walked in."

Including Coop. Their eyes had locked for a brief moment when she stood in the entrance and glanced around the room, looking for her friends. Her cheeks had burned hot at the look of admiration and approval in his eyes. He'd stopped what he was doing behind the bar, and stared. Just stared. At her.

Her heart skittered and she caught her lip between her teeth, lifting a hand in an uncertain wave. Just as he looked away and refocused on filling drink orders. So, she'd squared her shoulders and found Butch sitting with the rest of her new circle of friends.

Brianna surveyed the room. "Several women look like they want to bitch slap you, Ella, 'cause their husbands won't stop staring."

Ella's cheeks burned hot. "Come on, you guys. You make me sound like a floozy."

"You look pretty, Ella. No one thinks you're a floozy, and if anybody does try to . . . whatever-slap you," Butch rolled his eyes and mumbled something about young people's slang these days, "they'll have to answer to me."

"Me too, darlin'," Orland agreed.

A Kenny Chesney song came on and Ross scooted by with Sandra in his arms. Well, there was somebody for everyone.

"Have a seat, Ella," Butch said.

Before Ella could pull out a chair, a burly fellow dressed like a lumberjack came over and put his hand on her arm. "Care to dance, ma'am?"

His firm grip startled her. "Uh, no. No, thank you."

His grip tightened. "Why not? You're not doing anything else." His words ran together in a drunken slur.

She tried to wrench her arm out of his grasp, but he clamped down harder.

"Come on. A purty little thing like you shouthaaan't go wit'out attention." Only "thing" came out like "thang," and Ella caught a whiff of the heavy scent of whiskey on his breath.

"I said no," she hissed and tried to pull her arm free.

"Hey, take your hands off her," Lorenda thundered, and Butch and Orland rose from their chairs.

Ella's free hand fell to the side pocket of her purse and she eased down the zipper.

"The li'l lady can speak for herthelf," Whiskey Breath slurred, barely coherent.

Orland and Butch headed toward him.

"And she said no." Coop grabbed the guy by the back of the collar and pulled him backward.

Whiskey Breath stumbled but regained his footing and swung

at Coop. Coop ducked, but the brute's fist connected just under Coop's eye and he stumbled back. An entire table of lumberjacks scattered and lurched in their direction. Ella and Coop's friends did the same.

Ella looked at Coop and blanched. He was red-faced like a raging bull ready to charge. For her. The last thing he needed was to be arrested for a barroom brawl, especially on her account. Before anyone could make another move, Ella moved in behind Whiskey Breath, held her Taser to his neck, and pulled the trigger.

The 240-pound drunken swine hit the dance floor with a thud.

"Holy cow." Andy, always the quiet one, walked up.

"No kidding," said Lorenda, knocking over her chair when she shot to her feet. "You are one bad-ass redhead." A sly smile of admiration slid across her lips.

"I'm from Texas," explained Ella, still staring at Whiskey Breath sprawled on the floor. "If my dad had anything to say about it, I would've been packing a loaded Glock." She pointed to Whiskey Breath. "Lucky for him, I don't like guns."

The entire room stared open-mouthed as Whiskey Breath twitched on the floor.

"Remind me to stay on your good side," said Donna. "I'm a little scared of you now. And in awe." She looked at Hank. "That's it. I'm gettin' a Taser."

Hank rolled his eyes and crammed his Stetson back on his head. "As long as you don't use it on me along with all that other kinky stuff you're learning from Violet Vixen's books, I'm good with it."

Donna slid her arms around Hank. "Awww. That's so sweet."

Joe barreled out of the back room, all 285 pounds of him, and stomped toward them. "What's going on here?" He looked at the lump of plaid and dirty jeans on the floor, the Taser-induced seizing starting to slow. "You got two choices." He stared down the band of lumberjack onlookers.

"You can either take your friend and leave, or I'll call the sheriff and they can carry him off. Your call."

The skull-capped lumberjacks looked at each other and then picked up their buddy and carried him out.

Coop signaled to Dylan, who notched up his chin.

"Ella, you're coming home with me, just in case they try to follow you." Coop wasn't asking her.

"Really, I don't need you to hold my hand." Actually, she would've liked that and a whole lot more. Heat crept up her neck and settled in her cheeks. "I just took out a guy twice your size, I'll be fine."

"Not if they catch you off guard, Rambo," Coop argued.

"I seem to remember my pepper spray trumping your baseball bat not too long ago, even though I totally wasn't expecting you to swing it at my head," Ella said to remind him of who won their showdown the first night she arrived at the cabin.

She turned off her Taser and slid it back into her purse on the table.

"Ella, listen to what Coop says. He's thinking smart. Guys like that don't take 'no' lightly. They like having the last word." The concern in Butch's voice was apparent. "Coop and I will drive your car back to the cabin tomorrow."

All of her friends added their approval of Coop driving her home. Coop's lips moved, and she swore she heard something about a damned stubborn woman.

She nodded at Butch, outgunned by people who obviously cared about her. "If you insist. I've kind of had enough for tonight."

"Get your purse." Coop gave her a flippant look. "And whatever weapons you're carrying, and we'll go now."

Andy snorted. "Who's really protecting who?"

Ella couldn't help it. She snorted, too. Until she looked in Coop's direction and saw his searing glare. Ouch. Her unladylike laughter came to an abrupt halt, and she cleared her throat. "But you're in the middle of a shift."

"Dylan's covering for me."

"I just need to get my machete and sword, and I'll be ready." Coop's eyes rounded.

"Just kidding." She gave him a hopeful smile, but Coop didn't seem to think she was in the least bit funny.

They drove back to the cabin in silence, emotion simmered in the air around them. A primal tension had settled over Coop. He'd nearly had an out-of-body experience when he saw that freak grab Ella's arm. If she'd refused to ride home with him, he would've carried her out over his shoulder.

No way was he letting her out of his sight after seeing the looks on the Lumberjack Club's faces. They were mean bruisers who didn't appreciate a 120-pound redhead, who'd just had her nails done, felling one of their own as easily as a chainsaw cutting down a sapling. They tended to take that kind of thing personally. Especially when they landed face-first at rhinestone-clad feet that had dainty little flowers painted on the big toenails.

The funny thing was, Ella didn't seem in the least bit scared. She'd been so terrified of the river that she'd completely frozen and nearly gotten herself killed. But there'd been no fear in her eyes when she dropped a mean imbecile more than twice her size.

"Where'd you learn to defend yourself like that?" Coop finally broke the strained silence.

"My dad insisted on it. I wasn't joking about the gun. When I refused to carry a concealed weapon, I pacified my dad by taking a very intensive self-defense course. He finally settled for pepper spray and a Taser, as long as I learned to use them aggressively." She chuckled. "He's a Texan. He means well."

"He's a dad looking out for his daughter the best way he knows how," Coop clarified.

Ella's stare turned toward him, and she studied him.

"Thanks," she finally said.

"For what?"

"For looking out for me. Again." Her voice turned a little wistful. "That's what I like about you. You keep showing up when I need you."

He swallowed. She needed him? "I didn't do much. You handled the situation pretty well all by yourself."

"I wasn't trying to start a fight. I've never been the type that likes men fighting over me."

He stared at the road in silence for a minute. Finally, he said, "Is that why you never told Bradley?"

She inhaled a sharp breath. Coop glanced at her, her soft features illuminated by the glow of the dashboard. A surge of desire ignited in him, and he had a sudden urge to pull over and taste those lips that were so perfectly and seductively parted ever so slightly.

"I guess. I don't know," she stumbled over her words. "I didn't want to hurt him. And, yes, I didn't want him to be angry with his best friend over something that I started." She looked ahead into the darkness. "I was embarrassed and ashamed, and not just because it had happened." She paused. "But also because I liked it so much."

Coop swerved; he grabbed the steering wheel with both hands to keep from veering off the road and tumbling down the side of a mountain that would probably kill them both.

Ella clutched the dash, her breathing quick and heavy. When he'd corrected the truck, they both relaxed.

Really? He'd never guessed.

"Sorry," was all he could think to say about nearly getting them killed on a deserted road. *Lame.* He raked a hand over his jaw.

"Why didn't *you* ever tell Bradley?" she asked.

He thought on that a minute, measuring his words. He'd asked himself the same question a hundred times since that night in the cabin basement so many years ago. He'd certainly felt guilty enough over it, for the same reason Ella had. He liked it. A lot. And he hadn't exactly pushed her away, so he couldn't totally blame her. He had been an eager participant and might not have stopped if she hadn't been smart enough to end it before it went any further.

"After that kiss, I figured maybe you just wanted to marry him because he was a doctor. I'd seen it many times with my dad. Five, to be exact. Seen it myself once I started practicing." He tapped a thumb against the steering wheel. "To be perfectly honest, I warned him not to get married at all."

Ella looked at him and nodded. "I knew you didn't want Bradley to marry me. It was obvious how much you disliked me. But why didn't you tell him the truth?"

"He loved you." Coop exhaled. "No sense in making waves." No, Coop hadn't really liked Ella, but Bradley had been bent on marrying her. And Coop was too afraid of Bradley knowing the truth. He'd been too chicken to tell him that he'd lusted after Bradley's girl, even if it was only for a few wayward minutes in a cold and dank basement.

Then she'd gone and surprised Coop by being a loyal and devoted wife. There was no point in telling Bradley after that. Coop had seen too many divorces, been through too many of them with his dad's five failed marriages. He wasn't going to be the cause of that for Bradley. "I chalked it up to poor judgment and a little too much wine. Mistakes happen." He shrugged. "That particular mistake never happened again, so who was I to judge. I've made enough of my own."

And he had. The mess his life had become was proof enough of that. Kim Arrington still had her teeth sunk into him because he was such a screwup.

Coop pulled into the winding driveway of the cabin and followed it around to the back. He pushed the gearshift into park and killed the engine. With one arm over the steering wheel and the other on the console, he leaned into Ella and raked her face with an appraising look. He saw desire there and felt the same. Not just below the waist the way he usually felt it—cool and detached because it was just about sex in the moment. With Ella, he felt it in his chest, in his limbs, deep in his heart, and far into the future. It was unfamiliar and foreign, and so, so good.

"And I was embarrassed to tell my best friend that I had kissed his girlfriend when he'd asked me to watch out for you. Ashamed to tell him how much I wanted you and didn't want to stop that night in the basement."

He reached out and caressed her cheek with his thumb. His fingers feathered across her neck, and his thumb found her lips, traced them, taunted them, and they opened for him. She took the tip between them and suckled, gentle and slow. Her tongue flicked over the tip, and he couldn't help himself. He wanted her, more than he'd ever wanted any woman.

Coop covered her mouth with his and drank her in. She tasted so good, so sweet, like one of her fancy gourmet coffees mixed with coconut lip gloss.

With both hands, he framed her face and deepened the kiss with an intensity that almost consumed him. He'd never wanted a woman more than he wanted her right now. It wasn't wise. Stupid, even, but he didn't just want her. He needed her.

He pulled away just enough to graze her nose with his. Nipping at her bottom lip with his teeth, he stared at those plump lips, swollen from his kiss.

"Jesus, you're beautiful."

Her big green eyes searched his. "Let's go inside," Ella whispered, inviting, offering.

Oh, yeah. But he had to be sure. And he wanted her to be rock-solid certain, too. His life was already a hot mess; he wasn't about to screw it up even more with misguided assumptions.

"Are you sure this is what you want?"

Staring up at him with a lusty gaze, she nodded. "Yes, I want this."

"I'm not Bradley." He cupped her cheek with a flushed palm and ran his thumb across that plump bottom lip of hers. It parted for him, calling him, drawing him in with a magnetic pull. "Not even close."

She nodded, just one gentle dip of her head. "And I've never been a one-night stand."

His gaze swept over her pretty face, and he breathed in deeply, because that was the fly in the lip-glossy ointment. "I know."

Chapter Eighteen

Coop led Ella up the stairs, his fingers laced with hers. He let go to unlock the door, her impatience growing without his touch. Her flesh tingling for the warm feel of him. Pushing the door open, he let her go in first. When she turned to face him, his expression darkened with hunger, his stare devoured her. He pushed the door closed and locked it, his smoky gaze staying locked with hers.

He walked toward her, his eyes caressing the length of her body. Burning a trail of hungry need all the way to her toes, which curled against her bedazzled flip-flops. "I've been wondering something all night." His voice was husky with desire. He stopped a breath away from her, but didn't lift his hand to touch her.

"Wondering what?" Ella tried to control her quickened breaths, but the butterflies in her stomach . . . well, there was nothing she could do about it. And the throb between her legs—she hoped very much Coop was about to do something about *that*.

His gaze dropped to the sash at her waist and he reached up, taking the narrow strip of fabric between two fingers. "What would happen if I did this?" He tugged the sash until the knotted bow released.

Oh, yeah. That was a good thing to wonder.

As he dropped the strip, half her dress fell away with a swish, and his potent stare lowered to her purple-and-black lace bra. He swallowed, his gaze growing thunderous with want. Her skin sizzled under his stare.

Mouth dry and thighs wet, Ella found the smaller bow at her hip and pulled at one of the strings. It slid from its knot and freed the other half of her dress. With a slight wiggle of each shoulder, the black garment descended to the floor. Two quick little kicks and her fashionable flip-flops skittered across the room. Ella stood in front of Coop wearing nothing but a matching pair of expensive lacy undergarments, an ankle bracelet, and a toe ring.

Grandma's swimsuit, my ass.

A thought came out of left field and knocked the air out of her lungs. She hadn't been naked with anyone but Bradley in nearly a decade. And since Bradley, there'd been no one. *No. One.*

Oh. My. God.

For a fleeting moment Ella wanted to bolt from the room. Until she looked deep into Coop's hazel eyes and saw a depth of emotion she'd never expected. Not just carnal lust, but something deeper, something real.

Coop slid a hand around her waist and pulled her to him.

Before she lost her last nerve, she stepped into his arms and grabbed for him. His mouth found hers, and she opened to him, tasted him, melted into him. One hand traced up her spine, and she shuddered under his touch, his fingers finding a home at the back of her head. The other hand dropped to the top of her bikini panties, and he inserted the tips of his fingers under the elastic, flexing them into her flesh. Those magical, beautiful fingertips stroked her skin, soft and gentle. Then his entire hand dived beneath the black lace and her bottom filled his warm palm. He kneaded and caressed until she couldn't breathe for wanting more.

Ella wanted to see him, touch his bare skin, feel his muscular body pressed against hers with no barriers in between. She gathered his shirt in her fist until it pulled free of his jeans, then she set to work on the buttons. Finally she slid her hands onto his ripped torso, the muscles dancing underneath her touch. Hot and sleek and utterly, wonderfully male.

She sighed. As girls back in Texas would say, "daaaayum."

"Ella, I want you," he breathed against her ear, and shock waves lanced through her entire body, the epicenter between her legs threatening to erupt.

Oh, yeah, the gears of her nether regions sprang to life. No worries there. A little rusty maybe, but they were turning and churning nonetheless. Still, it had been so long.

"Coop, it's been a long time," Ella panted. "I'm not on birth control."

"Maybe," he panted even harder. "Maybe, I have something." He pulled his wallet from his back pocket and fumbled through it, his breath heavy.

Please, please, please let him have something.

"Yeah, I have a few." He pulled three gold squares from his wallet. *Thank you, thank you, thank you.*

"Three will do for now." Ella reached for him again, and he smiled at her, a lazy, sexy quirk that lifted one side of his mouth.

"I've heard nothing but good ideas out of you all night." He lowered his head, but she pulled her head back.

"I . . . I just hope you're not disappointed."

His brows knit together and his eyes darkened.

"I haven't . . ." Ella bit her lip.

"How long's it been, Ella?"

Ella looked toward the ceiling, trying to mentally count the months, which quickly mounted into years.

"Ah." One corner of his mouth turned up into a satisfied smile. "Has there been anyone since Bradley?"

She shook her head and leaned her forehead against his chest.

He circled her shoulders with one arm, and the weight made Ella feel safe.

"Hey, hey." He placed a finger under her chin and angled her face upward so she could look into his eyes. "It's a lot easier than rafting."

She laughed.

"And I'll make sure you enjoy it a whole lot more."

He brushed a soft kiss across her lips, and angled her head so his mouth fit in the curve of her neck. He suckled and feathered kisses up to her ear, and her knees gave way a little.

Coop caught her and held her weight against him.

"Your bedroom or mine?" she managed to ask.

He lifted her off the floor. "We'll get to that later. Wrap your legs around me."

When she complied, he carried her to the bar and sat her on the edge, shoving a bar stool out of the way.

"I'm too close to the edge. I'm going to fall." Her voice held a note of panic.

"No, you won't. I'm not going to let you." He tugged at her panties. "These need to go." He found her mouth again and kissed her fear away. Clinging to him, she lifted her bottom, and he pulled the panties off, tossing them in a corner.

For the first time since they arrived, the dogs made themselves known. Her panties dangled off one side of Winston's head, and he growled.

Ella and Coop both laughed.

"They've been having all the fun. It's our turn." He stepped between her legs, and she wrapped herself around him.

Slowly, she traversed the hard angles and planes of his arms, his chest, over his rib cage. Exploring his beautiful body with her fingertips, his muscles twitched and warmed under her touch. A body she'd admired for so, so long. She found his button and zipper and relieved him of his pants and boxer briefs. He sprang toward her, pulsing and searching, while he kicked his clothes and boots to the side.

Oh, yeah. Definitely more fun than rafting.

Coop's weight shifted, and he slid hot, flexing hands up both her thighs, then around to grasp her bottom. With a quick, firm tug, he pulled her to the edge of the counter against him. She grasped the edge of the counter with one hand, the other digging into his back.

"You need to trust me." Coop nipped at her earlobe.

And unbelievably she did. Slowly she let go of the counter, giving Coop full control over her body, and a chunk of her heart went with it. She found his pulsing member with one hand. While she stroked his length with slow, methodical sweeps, she threaded the other hand through his hair and guided his mouth back to hers.

His hands smoothed up her back to the clasp of her bra. With a quick flick of his skilled fingers, it came loose, the straps sagging at her shoulders. His palms came around to mold over the mounds of aching flesh, and he massaged. The silk fabric and lace trim of the bra created enough friction over her taut nipples to drive her insane as he worked her breasts into two smoldering peaks. Her insides coiled like a clock wound too tight and ready to unfurl. She made an indiscernible sex sound as he pulled her bra off and found a pink and throbbing nipple with his teeth, tugging gently.

She panted out his name, and he smiled against her flesh. Then devoured the peaked bud with his wet lips and flicking tongue.

"Where's the condoms?" she asked in an incoherent pant, both hands buried in his hair.

"Not yet," he breathed against her throbbing nipple, then covered it with a hot, wet kiss, suckling her into a whimper. Releasing it, he moved to the other side and showed that the same attention.

Ella flexed her searching fingers across his muscled back and swallowed.

"Oh, God," she panted. "You're . . . you're so good at this."

His response was a splayed hand against her chest that pushed her gently back until she rested on both elbows. He tugged her aching nipple between his teeth, and she nearly sobbed. When his expert mouth started to descend, indulging her pebbled skin with slow, moist kisses, she squirmed.

"Coop," she rasped out. "I want you in me."

"No," he said and circled her navel with his tongue.

She tugged at his hair, too self-conscious to let him go any further. It'd been so long. So very, very long.

A sensual sound just below a scream ripped from her when he sank to his knees and buried his tongue between her thighs. He hooked one of her thighs over his shoulder and laved at her swollen cleft.

She arched and writhed and begged until he inserted two fingers into her, and she fell to pieces.

A climax rolled over her like waves pounding the shore in a storm. When the convulsions wracking her body started to subside, Coop trailed hot kisses up to her neck and gathered her into his arms, laying a soft but deep kiss on her lips.

Her brain still foggy from the aftershocks of orgasm, Ella swallowed, her throat dry and gravelly. "Now can we get a condom?" she asked, cocooning him inside her arms and legs.

He produced one out of nowhere like a magician pulling a coin from behind her ear.

Her gaze ate him up. "Put it on."

With his teeth, he ripped open the gold square and rolled it on fast and sure.

Curling one set of fingers under her bottom, he pulled her to him, anchoring her against the impressive package she'd admired so shamelessly since the first night she arrived at the cabin. He nudged her legs farther apart, his magnificent erection pulsing at her slick entrance. He pulled back a little and rubbed the tip of his nose with hers.

"Ready?" he asked and nipped at her lip.

He was giving her an out, but she didn't want it. She just wanted him. All of him.

"*Yes.*" The raw desire in her voice made Coop chuckle with satisfaction.

He drove into her with one fluid movement, and a husky sex sound that communicated her approval wrenched from the back of her throat. And oh, his package was even more impressive then. He moved inside her, reaching between them with one hand to stroke the small point of ecstasy that'd been ignored for far too long. His expert fingers circled that small throbbing spot until her body tightened around him, and she arched into a cataclysmic orgasm that had her calling his name through the euphoric fog of sated desire.

When she could breathe again, he rested his forehead against hers. "Keep your legs around me. I'm going to lift you again."

"But what about you?" she panted out. "You haven't . . ."

He laughed. "We're just getting started," he said, lifting her off the counter and carrying her to the sofa still buried deep inside her. True to his word, they *were* just getting started.

After laying her on her back, he sank into her so deep, the fit so perfect that she arched against him and her body inconceivably started to tighten around him again. A hiss swooshed out of him.

"Jesus, Ella." His words were strained with almost painful self-control. "It's like you're made for me."

Ella gave herself to him fully and completely. On the sofa, in his bed, in the shower—until all the condoms were gone. With all three gold packages of bliss used up, Ella trailed kisses down his stomach and took care of him in a whole different way. Her technique must have inspired him, because he did the same to her again until she whispered his name.

She might've even heard herself beg him to do that thing with his thumb again, but she really wasn't sure. And when their hunger had finally been sated in the early hours before dawn, they drifted off into a peaceful sleep entwined under the soft quilts on Coop's bed.

Something nuzzled Ella's neck, and she turned onto her side, swatting it away. Soft kisses feathered down her neck, and a gentle moan came from the back of her throat, rousing her from an otherworldly sleep. Coop leaned over her, fully dressed.

"Hey, sleepyhead," he whispered into her ear.

Just the sound of Coop's voice ignited a burgeoning need deep in her belly. She reached for him. "Come back to bed."

"Can't." He kissed her. "Dad's on his way. We're going to get your car."

Ella tried to pull him down on top of her. "You and I can get it later."

Coop laughed. "I need to make a stop on the way home."

"Where?" Ella found the hem of his T-shirt and traced up his firm chest. Roped muscles danced under her fingertips, and his breath caught.

"The drugstore," he said, his voice husky with need, his eyes shut.

"Mmm. In that case, go ahead. Buy two boxes." Her hand fell to the stiffness in his pants.

"I was thinking three," he ground out.

"Now you're the one with the good ideas." Ella laughed and pushed him away.

"I'll be back soon." He studied her for a minute, and Butch's truck roared into the drive.

"I'll have coffee ready when you get back." She pulled him down for another kiss.

He groaned. "I gotta get out of here. If I can walk now."

Ella laughed. "See you in a bit." She pushed at his chest, and he left.

Ella rubbed her eyes and yawned as she heard Butch's passenger door slam and the truck pull away. Wandering into the kitchen, she made a cup of coffee in the French press. She smiled and sipped her coffee, the hot liquid and thoughts of Coop spreading through her, soothing her.

She sat down at the table and flipped on her laptop.

Cyn Caldwell was still hounding her about the excerpt from book four. Ella had drawn a blank since her rafting accident. After spending a night with Coop, though, she had plenty of inspiration for the teaser that would be inserted at the end of the third book.

Ella banged away at the keyboard, the words flowing like honey onto the page. She'd never felt so fresh, so revitalized, so sensual—like the lead character in her book. That woman had been just a fantasy, an invention of her imagination. Last night Coop made her feel every bit the erotic lover that she wrote about in her books.

An hour later, she e-mailed the excerpt to Cyn, who promptly sent a response that read, "About damn time. This is good, BTW."

Ella brewed another pot of coffee and grabbed her cell phone to check messages while sipping at a cup. Her sister's number popped up and Ella cringed. Charlene's calls were always tense and left Ella wondering what she'd done wrong. She couldn't deal with it today, not when she finally felt alive again for the first time in two years. The Delete key was an ingenious invention. Almost as clever as the condom. She pushed the button and tossed the cell onto the counter.

She brushed her teeth and climbed back into Coop's bed, ready to make sure his early morning trip to the pharmacy wasn't for nothing.

———

An hour later, Ella woke up from her snooze and smacked her lips together, yawning and stretching. She looked around the empty room and felt a surge of disappointment that the spot beside her was still empty. Coop hadn't made it back yet.

Odd.

Maybe he was buying out every pharmacy in the county. She sighed and tossed the covers back. A girl could dream, couldn't she?

Ella padded into the den and let the dogs out. She poured a bowl of cereal and found herself whistling. Would she ever be able to wipe the smile off her face? Probably not, especially if Coop made a regular habit of . . . well, doing the things that made her smile. A tingling sensation zipped through her. Her night with Coop had been sweet and tender and urgent and unbridled all at the same time.

A shrill ring startled her. She reached for the landline.

"Hello?"

"You're on speaker phone," Marilyn announced, and Carissa and Becca squealed out a greeting.

"Hi! What's up?" Ella's voice had a singsong tone to it, eager and happy and practically ADD. She tried to dial it down.

Too late.

"Cut the crap," Marilyn's voice was as hard as marble. "Why are you so happy?"

"Uh, no reason. I'm just, you know . . ." *Crap.*

"Oh!" Becca cut in. "You met someone?"

Ella pulled in her bottom lip.

"So, you met someone," Carissa probed, always the lawyer.

"Uh, you could say that."

"You did Coop, didn't you?" Marilyn sounded pissed, and Ella heard simultaneous gasps from Carissa and Becca. "I knew it was a mistake to let you stay at the cabin with him. He was just too convenient, his ass was just too cute to resist, and you were just too desperate."

"Gee, thanks," Ella drawled.

"I knew I should've bought you an assortment of girl toys. They really are like the real thing. Maybe better, depending on your selection of men," said Becca. "Of course, I was married to a gay man, so a refrigerated cucumber would've known better how to please a woman."

Yeah, that one had taken them all by surprise.

Marilyn sighed. "So, how long has this been going on?"

Ella glanced at the clock. "Well, let's see. Almost twelve hours. I mean, it started twelve hours ago and we finished about four hours ago, give or take."

"OMG. He can go that long?" Becca said, totally impressed. "I so need to get married again to a straight guy."

Longer, actually, if they hadn't run out of condoms. And, yeah, Ella had been very impressed, too.

"Were you drunk? Because you totally can't hold your alcohol, and if Coop took advantage of you while your judgment was impaired—" Carissa was already building a case.

"I wasn't drinking, unless you count soft drinks. I sort of initiated it."

She almost always had with Coop.

Becca giggled. "You're such a slut. Maybe I should move to Red River."

A beep sounded in Ella's ear, and she looked at the screen on her handset. Caller ID showed Butch's number. Ah, Coop was probably calling to tell her he had to drive all the way to Taos to find enough condoms for the next few days. She smiled.

"Listen, guys. I know you're worried, but don't be. Really. I'm not going to let this get out of hand." Unless you considered her and Coop getting crazy on the kitchen counter out of hand, then yeah, it was already way out of hand. Totally. But then she really didn't care to compare definitions of "out of hand" with her friends at that moment. She cleared her throat. "Someone's calling in. But, I promise I'll call you guys in a few days, okay?"

Marilyn grumbled something about sending her a toy catalog.

"Okay?" Ella insisted. The phone beeped again. "I'm hanging up now."

"All right, but if I don't hear all the details in the next few days, I'm driving up there. For real this time."

Ella smooched into the phone. "Love you guys."

She pressed the green button and switched to the incoming call. "Hello?"

"Ella, this is Butch." His voice was grave, and Ella's stomach did an instinctive flip. "A deputy is on his way to the cabin to get you."

Her heart kicked against her chest. "Butch, what's wrong?" Afraid of the answer, her eyes squeezed shut.

"It's Coop." Butch's voice shook. "He had an accident in your car."

Chapter Nineteen

On the way into town, they approached the crash site, and the deputy slowed to pass with caution. Ella's throat closed around a sob. Her hand went to her mouth, and she fought for a breath. A tow truck lifted the Beamer onto a flatbed trailer. It was barely recognizable. A huge indentation in the center of the hood left no doubt that Coop had hit a tree head-on at full speed. The windshield shattered, the driver's window completely gone, the deployed airbags still fluttering in the wind—it was a mangled remnant of Bradley's one self-indulgence.

And Coop . . . Ella choked on another sob. If the car looked this bad, how bad was he hurt?

"Is Coop . . . ?" She couldn't say it. Couldn't go through it again, couldn't lose another man that she cared about.

They crept past the crushed car and the debris scattered along the road. Ella's tears flowed.

No! No, he was fine. But what if Coop wasn't okay? What if one night was all she'd ever have with him?

The deputy glanced at her, a worried look on his face. "Maybe we should discuss it when we get to the urgent care clinic. His family is waiting for you."

Ella's stomach turned a cartwheel and bile rose, burning her throat.

"Please," Ella donned the sternest teacher voice she could muster. "Tell me right now. I've been through the horror of losing a husband, I don't want any surprises when I get there." It was imperative to be strong for the victim and their family. God knows she'd needed the strength given her by her own family and friends, because Bradley's parents rarely made an appearance until they found out the size of his life insurance policy.

The deputy inhaled. "He's pretty banged up. That's all I know."

———

Fear etched Ella's delicate features, her eyes swollen and red from crying, when she moved the curtain aside and looked in at Coop. Relief washed over her face and her grim expression eased.

Coop had never seen such a beautiful face. God, he was glad she hadn't been with him. She hurried to his side. Her emerald eyes shimmered with wetness, and he tried to lift onto an elbow to greet her.

He grimaced and hissed in a breath, pain lancing through his upper body.

His forearm—stitched up where shattered glass had torn out a chunk of his flesh—was wrapped with an ACE bandage, so she took his other hand. "Lay down." She ran a hand up his arm and onto his bare chest, the paramedics having cut his shirt off in the ambulance. The red marks that spattered his torso were already turning purple around the scratches from the airbag.

"Hey." She gave him a shaky smile.

"Hey, yourself." The grapefruit-size knot over his eye wasn't the only thing throbbing now that Ella had arrived. Even with his head pounding from the impact, he still wanted her. Not only had last night been the best sex of his life, but Ella had touched his heart in a way that made life seem impossible without her. She wasn't as boring and predictable as he'd once thought. She was full of life and sass, and when she told him she hadn't been with anybody in such a long time, he'd felt a strange gratification. Like she belonged to him. Only him.

"Coop, I was so scared you were—" Her voice cracked, and a dainty hand covered her quivering mouth.

He stroked her hand. "I'm okay. Stop worrying."

"You don't look okay." She let out a shaky laugh and ran gentle fingertips over his battered and bruised chest again. "You look awful."

"You look gorgeous." His eyes went to her rosy lips, and he thought of what she'd done with them just a few hours ago. He looked down at her hand clasped in his. Her left hand.

His breath caught in his chest for a moment. Caressing the empty space where her wedding ring used to sit, he stared at the long, slender finger. Bared. For him.

Last night he hadn't noticed if it was on her finger or not because he had more pressing things on his mind. But now his chest expanded with a satisfied breath. When he could get out of this hospital bed, he bet he'd be a little taller, a little stronger. And a little sad, too, because it must've been a hard step for her to take.

"You took off your wedding ring." He almost whispered.

Her lush lips lifted into a soft smile. "It was time." Lines appeared between her eyebrows. "What happened? No one would tell me. I had a good mind to pepper spray a few folks just to get answers, but you had my keys."

He laughed, but pain lanced through his chest and head, so his smile turned to a scowl.

"It was your admirer from Joe's the other night," he managed to say while the stab of throbbing eased a bit. "He and a couple of his

Neanderthal buddies must've waited outside Joe's, watching for me. I got a good look at them before they ran me off the road."

"Oh, Coop." Her eyes grew wet again. "They could've . . . hurt you even worse."

"I'm sorry about Bradley's car," he said, tightening his grip on her hand.

Ella shook her head. "It was just a car. This is my fault, not yours. Those guys were mad at me."

"It's not your fault they're assholes." He lifted her empty ring finger to his mouth and kissed it. She shivered, goose bumps racing up her arm, and Coop's chin lifted a little with pride at how she reacted to him.

Ella was here. For him. Without her wedding ring and wearing the same worried look she'd had when Bradley was dying. He'd just spent the night with his best friend's wife, then destroyed Bradley's car, all within a twenty-four-hour span of time. That had to be a record for being the crummiest friend in the history of crummy friends.

But Ella was different than any other woman he'd ever been with. By this point in a relationship he was already looking for an exit strategy. This time, he kept thinking about how much he didn't want it to end. The muscle in Coop's jaw flexed, and pain shot through his neck.

The door opened and Butch walked in. Ella jerked her hand out of Coop's and stepped away from him. Her expression clouded over. Coop looked at her, but she refused to meet his eyes. She fidgeted, and a light blush colored her cheeks.

Huh.

"I called your mother, Coop."

Coop's attention snapped to his dad. "Why?" Coop blurted, annoyed.

"Because she's your mother," Butch said, deadpan. "She wanted to talk, but I told her you weren't up to it."

"Good." The only woman Coop wanted to talk to right now was Ella, who was rubbing the back of her neck and avoiding his stare. Why wouldn't she want his dad to know they were together? Because they *were* together now, right?

"You should consider calling her when you feel like talking."

The doctor walked in, thank God, because Coop had no intention of discussing the subject of his mother.

"Doc, when can I get out of here?" He was ready to go home. Where Ella didn't have to pretend she didn't care about him.

Ella fussed over Coop for two days, and it was kind of nice. Fantastic, actually. Especially when she helped him shower. Being injured had its perks. *Two* kissable perks that brushed against his chest when she lifted her arms to wash his hair and rinse it out.

He'd walked around the yard some each day to work out the stiffness, but his body had taken a beating and still ached from head to toe. The stitches across his forearm still throbbed. So when he wasn't stretching his legs with a leisurely stroll around the property, Ella had insisted on a *Walking Dead* marathon on Cal's recommendation. Nothing like a little zombie gore to make a guy feel better, especially with an attractive redhead curled up next to him, peeking through her fingers.

Thank you, little brother. No more siphoning off his gas.

Propped against big, fluffy pillows that Ella had bought for him, he ate from the tray she'd positioned over his lap. Ella climbed onto the bed and clicked off the television just as a zombie took one through the head with a sword like a live game of Fruit Ninja. The lamp cast a yellow hue over the room; the sun had long since gone down. He looked up to find Ella's gaze roaming his bare chest, and the spoon stopped midway to his mouth.

"Joe sent the stew over for dinner," she said, licking her lips. "I think every person in Red River has called and offered to bring over food."

"You accepted, right?" Because as much as he'd grown to like Ella, the woman couldn't boil water without burning it. He'd moved the fire extinguisher from the hall closet to the pantry, just in case she set the kitchen on fire while making coffee.

"Of course," she grinned.

"You're not eating? Aren't you hungry?" he asked.

A naughty smile spread across her lips. "Oh, I'm hungry."

His mouth went dry.

Her brow arched, and she nodded to the tray. "Are you done with that?"

"So done with it." The spoon clattered onto the tray.

She moved the tray to the nightstand and slid back onto the bed facing him. Her fingertips feathered over the bruises on his chest. The muscles twitched and shifted at her touch. "I picked up a few extra items yesterday when I went into town to get you more ibuprofen."

"More condoms?" *Please say more condoms.* Because the two boxes he'd bought the day of the accident had been scattered in the wreckage somewhere along Highway 578.

Her index finger explored the crevice between his pecs, which flexed involuntarily. Then her finger trailed along the faint line of hair, over his belly button, and disappeared beneath the quilt that covered him from the waist down.

"Uh-huh, but if you're too sore—"

His fingers closed around her wrist, stilling those magical fingers. "I'll manage," he said, his voice heavy with lust. He pulled her to him until she straddled him. Fisting her auburn hair in his good hand, he tugged her mouth to his. She sighed and melted into his kiss.

Running both hands over his chest, her hips circled against his. He groaned and whispered his desire against her hot mouth.

She broke the kiss and locked gazes with him, her arms draped around his shoulders. "I don't want to hurt you."

"Baby, right now, the only thing that hurts is the thing you're sitting on because it wants you so bad."

"But you're still injured, and I'm kind of . . . aggressive."

No kidding. When their clothes came off, she transformed from a conservative history teacher into a sex kitten. She'd been hesitant for about thirty seconds, until he'd loved her with his tongue. After that first orgasm, she'd let go of her inhibitions and let him taste and touch every inch of her body, then she'd done the same to him.

"Then go easy on me," he teased her.

A silky brow arched high. Lowering her head, she nipped at his lip. Then she blazed a trail of hot, wet kisses to his ear and whispered something that almost made him lose it right then.

He swallowed hard. "Jesus, Ella."

"What?" She looked at him. "You want me to stop?"

"Hell, no. I just wasn't expecting anything that . . ." *Erotic.* ". . . sexy from you."

She frowned. "You don't expect me to be sexy? Is that what you just said?"

"Uh," he said, because that was the most intelligent thing that came to mind after sticking his foot so far into his mouth that his toes tickled the back of his throat.

"Is that sort of like your Girl Scout comment? Because you already know how wrong you were about that."

Wrong as a tornado hitting a glass factory. His fist still anchored in her hair, he pulled her lips to his and kissed her hard and deep.

"Forget the Girl Scouts. Whisper that in my ear again," he murmured against her lips.

She smiled and took his bottom lip between her teeth to suckle. Then she did exactly what he asked, and whispered the steamiest, most seductive promises into his ear.

"*Jesus,*" he panted out, his voice dark and rugged. "Get a condom, Ella."

"No," she whispered. "Didn't you say no the first night we were together, and I asked you to make love to me right away?" She scooted backward and nipped a trail of wet, caressing kisses down his chest. Licked at his navel and nudged his legs apart to settle there on her stomach. She pulled back the quilt and lowered her mouth to his boxer briefs, taking the elastic waistband between her teeth for a quick tug. "These have to go. I think you said that to me, too." Her hot breath against his prick sent shock waves through his body, and he shuddered. "I really want to see that birthmark of yours again. It's in such an inviting location."

She tugged the boxers down enough to have access, and good God, Coop's fingers stayed entangled in her hair for a good long while. And hell, she could explore his birthmark anytime she wanted, because she was good at it.

Ella controlled his body and hers, giving them both pleasure, until several empty gold wrappers lay strewn across the nightstand. Her cheek rested gently against his shoulder, and he stroked her long, flowing hair to its tip, then started at the top of her head and did it again. And again. And again.

He loved to touch her.

"Am I hurting you?" she murmured against his chest, her voice laden with satisfaction and sleep.

"Uh-uh. Nothing you do to me hurts, sweetheart."

She smiled against his skin.

"What?"

She shrugged. "I like sweetheart and baby a lot better than Cinderella."

His hand stilled against her head. "You knew?"

"I'm not stupid, Coop."

No, Ella definitely wasn't stupid. "I'm sorry."

She feathered soft kisses over his chest. "So am I. It takes two, and I wasn't very nice to you, either."

"I'm still a screwup," he said, because it was true. With any luck, his legal problems might go away soon, but his situation was still in shambles. His life back in Albuquerque was gone. No business left, no condo, and no friends. So why was he so anxious to get back there when everything he needed was right here?

"Coop." Her body tensed and went rigid against him. "Maybe we should share our secrets. You know, so we both know what we're getting into."

Right. How bad could Ella's secrets be? Cheating on a college exam? Skipping to the end of one of her nonfiction history books to read the ending first? No way was he walking into that open field of land mines. What happened in his past could stay in his past.

He grasped her chin and angled her mouth up to his. Kissed her rough and hard, until her breath quickened and she whimpered. He broke the kiss. "I don't want to hear about the past." He bit at her lower lip just firmly enough to elicit a tiny moan. "Right now, I just want to hear you whispering into my ear again."

His mouth covered hers with a deep, urgent kiss, and she did what he asked. Until late into the night.

Coop rode in the passenger seat of his dad's truck on the way to Doc Holloway's office. He flexed his hand and looked at the stitches that'd held a six-inch jagged gash together. "I'm glad these are coming out today. Thanks for taking me to the doctor."

"I figured Ella could use a break. Besides, I wanted to talk to you about the situation."

"Don't worry about it, Dad. The Lumberjack Brigade got their revenge. I doubt they'll be back."

"You're probably right, but that's not what I'm worried about." Butch scratched his chin. He tossed one wrist over the steering wheel of his Ford F-150. "It's none of my business, but you know, son, Ella's not the casual relationship type."

Coop stared straight ahead. "You're right. It's not your business."

"Then humor me. I'm your old man, that should count for something."

"What gave us away?" Coop asked.

"You mean besides the half dozen boxes of condoms Ella bought at the pharmacy this week?" Butch's forehead wrinkled.

"She tried to be discreet." Coop was actually a little embarrassed. *Wow.*

"Right, in Red River?"

Coop laughed.

"It wasn't just that. It's the way you two look at each other and the vortex that swirls around you when you're within a mile of each other." Butch shook his head and smiled. "Never seen anything like it."

Coop inhaled. "Ella's . . . different."

Butch nodded. "Exactly. That's why I'm worried about her getting hurt."

Coop turned to study his father. "You're worried about *her*? Thanks, Dad." His dad had no idea. No freaking idea of how much Coop cared about her. How much he'd tried not to. How scared he was that she'd eventually leave him. And how much it hurt when she'd recoiled in the urgent care emergency center, not wanting anyone to know they were sleeping together.

"Shouldn't I be? Your track record isn't the greatest where women are concerned."

Coop just sat and stewed, because his dad just hit the target at a hundred paces.

"Look, I don't want to be a jerk—"

"Too late," Coop inserted, and Butch looked annoyed.

"I'm your father, and I love you. But, I loved Bradley, too, just like he was my son. Ella was loyal, and she loved him."

"I know, Dad," Coop said, because Christ, he was terrified that he could never fill Bradley's shoes, that he'd always be an alternate who won by default because the better man died. That she'd never love him as much as she loved Bradley.

"She was a good wife to him."

"You should know, Dad, you had enough wives of your own."

"Don't be a smart-ass. Ella's been through enough. She's still vulnerable."

Coop raised an eyebrow at his dad. "Are we talking about the same woman? You did see her drop a guy twice her size without breaking a nail, right?"

"She doesn't need more heartbreak and bad memories to carry around. That's all I'm saying."

Coop studied his dad. Nope. Not a clue that Ella had complete power over him and his happiness. If Butch had looked out for any one of his extensive collection of wives the way he was looking out for Ella, maybe he'd still be married to one of them.

Coop pinched the bridge of his nose. Butch had no freaking idea that Ella's heart wasn't the one in danger of being broken. Coop had to give his dad credit, though. He was concerned for Ella. Coop wasn't one of Albuquerque's most eligible bachelors anymore, and Ella could do a whole lot better.

"If it makes you feel any better, I really care about her. Much more than any other woman I've been with." He inhaled. "It's different with her."

They drove in silence until the Red River city limits sign came into view.

"It was the strangest thing, you know, when the car started to spin. Like it was happening in slow motion." Coop stared out the window at Wheeler Peak. "The sky and clouds reflected off the hood, moving when the car spun, and it seemed so slow, like I had all day to just sit and stare at it." He paused.

"Were you scared?" Butch finally asked.

He nodded. "Yeah, but not for the reasons you might think. Later when I thought about it, the reasons surprised even me." He inhaled, deep and ragged. "I was scared I wouldn't see Ella again. Most of all, I was scared of leaving her behind, of putting her through that kind of grief again."

His dad chuckled, and Coop shot him a disgusted look.

"You think that's funny, Dad?"

Butch shook his head. "Nope. I think you're in love."

Chapter Twenty

"Get on the bed, and lie on your stomach."

Coop lifted a coy brow. Ella got more interesting with each passing day, revealing a new unexpected layer like an onion. He liked onions. Sweet and spicy at the same time. And tasty.

"Really?" He snaked an arm around her waist and pulled her close. "I've fantasized about this since I saw you in that soaking wet white sundress."

"Very funny." Ella pushed at his chest and held up a bottle of therapeutic massage oil. "Your dad says you need this for your shoulders and neck every day to relieve the muscle spasms from the accident."

"But you're not a massage therapist. Maybe you should lie down and I'll give the massage." He tugged at the fitted V-neck T-shirt that clung to every one of her curves.

"Take off your shirt," Ella commanded, swatting his hand away from her.

He sighed with resignation. "Alright. I can think of worse things than you rubbing massage oil all over me while I'm half-naked." Pulling his T-shirt over his head, he tossed it toward Atlas and Winston, who cuddled over a floor vent. "You're not trained in the art of massage therapy, and you're not exactly a bodybuilder." He squeezed one of her slender biceps. "So I doubt it'll be very effective."

"Excuse me?"

The galled tone of her voice startled him, and his eyes snapped to hers. "Uh, I mean deep tissue massage takes a lot of upper body strength. You're petite. And beautiful." She still glared at him. "And *perfect?*"

"Face. Down." Ella pointed to the bed. "Now."

With a sigh of resignation, Coop fell onto the bed and turned onto his stomach. Ella climbed onto the bed after him. "Your dad said you might say something stupid like that, so he gave me a few pointers." Throwing one leg over his buttocks, she straddled him, anchoring him into the mattress with her weight.

"I like this already," he said, his words muffled against the bed quilt.

"And he gave me this." From under the pillow, Ella produced a four-pronged massage tool. "He said it's very . . . effective on trigger point muscle spasms."

Lifting his head as much as Ella's weight would allow, he saw the torture device in her hand. "Oh, no you don't." He tried to flip over, but she clamped him between her legs. "Come on, Ella, that thing hurts."

"I'll be gentle. I promise." Under her breath she added, "Unless you insult my biceps again." She flipped open the bottle and poured warm oil onto his back. It seeped across his skin like liquid velvet.

After smoothing the oil across every inch of his exposed skin, she set to work on his neck and shoulders. Her touch wasn't as novice as he'd thought it would be, and she used her index fingers and thumbs to work along each gravelly muscle. One by one, they released, the tension ebbing like an ocean tide going out.

"You okay?" Ella asked as her two thumbs pressed into the flesh on each side of his spine, inching downward at a pace that might take her a month to finally reach the last vertebra. Which was fine by him, because he couldn't remember ever getting a massage this good.

"I'm excellent, actually," he murmured, his words lazy, and his eyes closed. "You're much better at this than I thought you'd be. How'd you learn?"

"You don't live with a chiropractor without learning a few tricks of the trade."

Of course. Bradley had taught her. An onslaught of guilt washed through him, because Coop was now the lucky recipient of those talented hands in more ways than one.

Her fingers reached the top of his jeans, and he really wished he'd disposed of those along with the T-shirt. Her thumbs began to spiral outward in circular motions across his back and rib cage.

"Damn, woman, that feels good," Coop managed to groan out.

Ella laughed that deep, hearty laugh that made his chest fill with contentment every time he heard it.

"Are you ready for the trigger point work?" She reached for the torture device his dad loved so much.

Still pinned facedown on the bed, Coop managed to reach behind him and grab her wrist. "Later." Before she knew what he was doing, he pulled her down next to him and rolled her onto her back. "Right now I have a chronic spasm in a whole different location that needs attention."

Her eyelashes brushed her cheeks as she blinked bashfully. "Oh, really? Where would that be?"

Grabbing one of those very talented hands of hers, Coop lowered it to the mound of pulsating flesh below his waist. Her eyes flared.

"Oh! That is quite a spasm you have there. But we're not finished with the treatment your dad prescribed."

"Consider it a therapeutic massage of a different nature." He tugged on the V-neck of her T-shirt, and a rosy peak greeted him. He took it between two fingers and worked it.

A shudder rolled through Ella's petite frame, and she arched against him.

"You're . . . definitely better at this kind of therapy than I am." Her words were almost a gasp.

He leaned forward so his warm breath caressed the sensitive skin of her breast. "Oh, I wouldn't say that." Grabbing the neckline with his teeth, he pulled it down until both nipples strained eagerly toward him.

He ground his hips against her. "As I'm sure you can feel, you've done more than an adequate job for a novice."

She swallowed, the rise and fall of her chest rapid and urgent.

When he captured one hardened nipple with his mouth and suckled, she bucked against him, a small cry rolling off her lips. He tugged on her Nike running shorts, easing them down over her hips until they were gone. Flexing and releasing his fingers down her thigh and up again, her skin felt like soft cashmere under his touch. Soft, pliant, rich, and unattainable. Yet she was his, and his alone. Somehow the mountain gods had decided to smile on him, even though he didn't deserve it.

He ran a flattened palm under her T-shirt and up her torso, but her bra obstructed his mission. "Take this off," he said, biting at her lip. "Or would you prefer I tear it off?"

Her lush eyelashes fluttered down, and she teased him with a come-hither smile. "You wouldn't."

Arching a brow, he grasped the V neckline with both fists.

"Wait!" She grabbed at his hands. "This shirt is brand-new."

"Then lose it. Now," he commanded, but his mouth twitched. She raised to pull the shirt and sports bra over her head.

After discarding his own jeans, he moved on top of her, and a quake of lustful anticipation shimmied through her from the top of that auburn head all the way down to her pretty little painted toes. He felt her tremor of ecstasy against his skin as it washed down her length like a gentle ocean wave, and a sudden urge to follow the same path forced his mouth on a downward path.

He explored each lush breast and the valley between with expert precision, and the taste of her was utterly exquisite, like drinking fine brandy in front of a fire. Smooth and satisfying as its warmth spread through him, reaching every bit of tissue in his body.

Her breaths became urgent as his hands and mouth explored her body; her hands clutching, grabbing, lacing through his hair. Soft moans of pleasure escaped her every time his tongue touched a new spot.

He descended lower, his lips and tongue and teeth nipping at the quivering flesh that molded to his touch. Each rib was visible under her creamy white skin, and he traced every one with care and loving attention as her breaths grew more rapid.

Ella clawed at his shoulder, trying to pull him up. "Make love to me." Her voice was an urgent plea, disoriented. Desperate.

Oh, he planned to make love to her, but first he wanted to please her in a different way. He sank lower, finding that perfect spot with his warm kiss that made her utter incoherent words, disjointed sounds, and syllables that begged him to take her.

When Ella clutched the bed quilt in both hands and arched toward him, a violent climax rolling through her, he pulled himself up and looked into her eyes, dark and glazed with lust. There was so much he wanted to say to her, to tell her how he felt, what she meant to him, how she was amazing, and different than any other woman he'd been with, and that she made him feel different, too. But his throat closed, and his brain whirred like an outdated hard drive, and he could only think to do exactly what she had begged of him a few minutes ago.

And so he did. When he sank into her, she wrapped her legs around his waist, and they rode the wave of bliss together fast and hard until they both lay sated and dewy, wrapped in each other's arms.

The landline jarred Ella from her satisfied slumber. Oh, jeez, was she drooling on Coop's chest? Clamping her mouth shut, she swiped at her chin, and then dabbed at Coop's chest gently so he wouldn't wake. She tried to clear her muddled brain, still dazed from their lovemaking.

Coop snored lightly, his cappuccino-colored hair all mussed and sexy. Man, oh man, he really was good at this sex thing. She'd never experienced so many . . . and such savage org—

The landline sneered at her again.

She unwound Coop's arms from around her shoulder and waist, and he stirred.

"I'll get it." Ella brushed a light kiss across his lips.

"Tell whoever it is we're busy." Coop never opened his eyes.

Ella chuckled.

Rolling onto his side, Coop snuggled into the pillow, his gentle snore returning instantly.

She fumbled around for her clothes while the phone continued to ring. Finally she pulled on her pink lace panties and Coop's T-shirt, because her shirt was lost in the melee of clothes Coop kept scattered around his room. If she was going to keep sleeping in here, she was really going to have to clean it for him, whether he liked it or not.

Her bare feet skittered across the cool floor, and she grabbed the receiver.

"Hello?"

"What took so long, Isabella?" Her sister's snappish tone clawed at her ear like nails on a chalkboard.

"Charlene? Is something wrong?"

"No," Charlene said, clearly annoyed. "Can't I call my little sister once in a while?"

"Um, sure. What's up?" Okay. *Awkwaaaaard.* Because Charlene wasn't the Chatty Cathy type, especially with Ella.

"Same ol', same ol'." Charlene yawned like she was bored. "The ranch is bustling right now, so we're either workin' or sleepin' all day, every day."

"How are the kids?" asked Ella. She loved to hear about her nieces and nephews.

"Royce is doing two-a-days to get ready for football season. This is his last year of high school, ya know. And Kendra's got cheer practice nearly every day, so I hardly see either of them anymore." Charlene's voice shook a little. "Kendra says she's serious about movin' away to go to college."

And for the first time . . . well, ever . . . Charlene didn't mention Ella moving back to East Texas.

Ella softened her voice. "Then let her go, Charlene."

"I can make her stay here to go to college the way mom and dad did us. I can refuse to pay for it if she moves away."

"And look how well that worked out. I moved anyway."

"But why, Isabella? That's what I can't understand. Why would you want to leave your home and your family? Why aren't we good enough?"

Dragging in a breath, Ella's heart squeezed a little. "Oh, Char. That has nothing to do with it. I love you, and I miss you every single day. But I wanted a little adventure, something different. I wanted to experience just a little sliver of the world outside of the ranch."

"But you never came back. Not even now that Bradley's gone. You know you could visit once in a while." Charlene coughed, probably trying to mask the continuous sniffles that flowed over the phone line.

"Did you ever think that maybe it's because you guys won't stop hounding me about moving back? I have a life out here, Char. Friends, hobbies, this cabin." Well, the cabin wouldn't be hers much longer, but that was beside the point. "I *like* my life here. Why can't y'all accept that? Maybe even show an interest in it?"

And it dawned on Ella that she really did like her life in Red River.

Charlene sniffed again. "Well, I suppose you have a point. But where does that leave me with my daughter? I've already lost you, I don't want to lose her, too."

"You haven't lost me, Charlene, and you're not going to lose Kendra, either. But you do need to accept her choice if she wants something different than you did. Don't nag her, and for God's sake, don't hound her about moving back *every single time* you talk to her."

Charlene was silent except for a small sniffle.

"She'll love you all the more for it, Charlene, and you'll have a better relationship with her in the end if you respect her decisions."

"Well, are you *ever* coming back to visit?" Charlene huffed.

"Of course I will, but my home isn't in East Texas anymore."

Maybe her new home was right here in Red River. With Coop.

Chapter Twenty-One

"We're in Red River," Marilyn announced several days after the accident.

Ella nearly dropped the phone. "Wh . . . what? You're not here."

"Sitting on Main Street right now outside of the Hummingbird Souvenir Shop."

They were totally here.

"Why did you guys drive all the way up here?" Ella tried not to sound frantic.

"I warned you if we didn't hear from you, we would drive up. And we didn't hear from you."

Ella's palm went to her forehead, and she closed her eyes. She couldn't tell them how far she'd actually fallen for Coop. They'd hog-tie her and drag her back to Albuquerque. And, oh God, she absolutely didn't want them involved in her rather interesting situation with Coop. Because, really, she didn't know what else to call it except a "situation."

They'd had the hottest sex she'd ever experienced, even with him all sore and bruised. He was pretty amazing in bed. And on the floor. And in the shower. And any number of other locations, come to think of it. Her mouth went dry just thinking about him. But she didn't want to explain any of this to Marilyn, Carissa, and Becca, because she wasn't even sure what it was herself. Except really, really good sex. The best. With the man she had begun to lose her heart to.

She'd have to Google the person who invented the condom and build them a personal memorial in the backyard. Genius, really. Massage oil was a pretty brilliant invention, too.

And her friends might expect her to be reasonable and give it up since it was Coop, for God's sake. That's probably why they went to the trouble of driving all the way to Red River. To tell her to give up the man she'd grown to care very deeply for. Which she didn't want to do just yet, even though he hadn't indicated wanting a future with her beyond the summer.

"I spaced calling you guys, we . . . I had a lot going on the last few days." Did she ever. A. Lot. "But, driving up here was kind of extreme, don't you think? You should've called first and I could've told you it was unnecessary."

"We didn't mind the drive, and we wanted to see you. Give me directions to your place and we'll drive out there."

"No! No, I'll meet you in town." Her mind raced. "There's a place around the corner from where you're at called the Rio Grande Bistro. It's got an outdoor patio that's great this time of year." And secluded from the inquiring minds of Red River's locals with sharp ears and hearing that reached into the next county. "Give me a few minutes to get ready, and I'll see you there."

Ella hung up and chewed her lip.

"Who was that?" Coop came in from taking Atlas and Winston for a stroll along the stream, one side of his face still a fading purplish blue.

"Um, it was my friends from Albuquerque. They just drove into Red River. Do you remember Marilyn, Carissa, and Becca?"

He nodded. "I'm pretty sure I met them at a party or two at your house. Are they on their way to the cabin?" He refilled the dog bowl with fresh water and set it back on the floor. Atlas and Winston lapped at it like they'd been wandering the desert.

Ella chewed her lip harder. "No, I'm meeting them in town for lunch."

"I'll drive you." Coop pulled two large dog bones from a box in the pantry. Atlas spun in a circle, and Winston barked.

"No! No, you don't need to do that. You're still mending. I could just borrow your truck."

He shrugged, passing out the canine treats. "I could stand to get out of the cabin for a little while." He walked to her and slid an arm around her waist. "You've kept me occupied for days now. I've barely seen the sunshine." He nipped at her neck.

She sighed, melting into his hard chest. This wasn't going well. He placed a gentle kiss in the hollow of her neck, making her skin pebble against his hot, breathy mouth. Yes, actually it was going really well. It just wasn't going as she planned.

"I could go by the pharmacy while you're having lunch with your friends." He chuckled. "You know, stock up and all, since you're so insatiable."

"Me?" She swatted his shoulder.

"I didn't say I minded." Coop brushed a gentle kiss against her forehead and rested his chin on top of her head.

"You definitely don't mind. It's been kind of hard not to notice how much you don't mind."

"Let's get ready then. Your friends are waiting."

"Park here," Ella commanded him, two blocks from the Rio Grande Bistro.

"I can bring you all the way to the restaurant."

"That's not necessary. This is a good distance from both the pharmacy and the Rio Grande. I can walk. It's a nice day. I'll call you later when I'm done. It might be a while." She blathered on, her rattled nerves showing.

WTF? Coop looked at her.

"Sure." He pecked her on the lips, trying not to smudge her lip gloss. She fidgeted with the strap of her yellow sundress, and her breasts bounced a little. He really wanted to pull the clip from her hair and mess up that perfect upswept twist that rested at the back of her head, but she'd put a lot of effort into getting ready to see her girlfriends. A few stray curls had escaped and cascaded around her face. He plucked one that lay against her neck and twisted it around his finger. "You look pretty."

Her lips parted, and he had a sudden desire to see those lips wrapped around his—

"Thanks," she whispered, and he could see a spark of desire in her eyes, too. Yeah, she wanted him as much as he wanted her.

"So, I was wondering if you wanted to do something later?" he asked.

Her mouth twitched into a wicked smile. "Seriously?"

He laughed. "Besides that. Do you want to do something before *that?*"

"You mean like a date?" She looked a little surprised, like the idea hadn't crossed her mind. When it sank in, a smile spread across her lips.

"Isn't that what people do when they want to spend time together?"

She nodded. "Yeah. That'd be nice."

"I'll see you in a few hours." With a quick peck, Ella slid out of the passenger seat and shut the door. She walked down the street in a summery yellow sundress that made her look like a lemon drop. Delicious enough to eat.

She wore a very high pair of spiked heels with all kinds of straps going in every direction, and her polished toes peeked out the front. Oh, yeah. He'd love to see her in nothing but those.

Her outfit may have been a tad overdressed for Red River, but he guessed she wanted to look nice for her friends.

His gaze followed her down the street, his jaw tensing. Her friends. That must be the problem. She didn't want her friends to see them together, the same way she hadn't wanted his dad to see them holding hands.

His gaze didn't leave her until she disappeared around the corner wearing those bedroom heels. Then he tried to rub out the muscle spasm that had locked his jaw.

Ella pulled the tissue paper out of the bag and squealed. "Becca! I can't believe you got me this." She jumped from her wicker patio chair, nearly knocking over the umbrella that shaded the four women from the early afternoon sun, and gave Becca a hug. Ella held up the leopard-print handbag, covered in an assortment of bling, for everyone to see, and sat back down. "I've been admiring this for months, but I was too chicken to buy something this edgy." She tossed it over one shoulder and struck a Marilyn Monroe pose. "What do you think?"

"Why do the rest of us bother?" Marilyn nudged Carissa. "Now our gifts are chopped liver."

"Oh, baloney," said Ella. "You guys shouldn't have brought gifts anyway."

"Well, your birthday is right around the corner, isn't it?" said Becca.

"Oh my gosh, you're right. I forgot," Ella gasped.

"You forgot your own birthday?" Carissa raised a brow.

"Jeez, the sex is that good?" Becca said, a little awed.

"See, what would you do without us?" Marilyn said. "You wouldn't even remember your own age."

Ella missed them so much. Since she arrived in Red River, Coop had kept her busy, her mind so boggled. First with trying to avoid him and his foul mood, and now with no ability to keep her hands off him; she hadn't realized how much she'd missed her friends until she rounded the back corner of the bistro and found them sitting on the patio.

"I really don't know what I'm going to do without you three," she said, her voice a little shaky.

"Then come on back to Albuquerque. You can start over there just as easy as anywhere else," said Marilyn.

Ella shook her head. "I wish it were that simple. But, I can't get over Bradley if I stay there. It was just too hard, too painful. That's why I had to sell the house. It was so awful seeing him in that bed day after day."

"Leave her alone," Carissa scolded them. "I want you back in Albuquerque as much as anyone, but I understand your need for space."

Ella sipped her iced tea and studied her friends. She loved these women. They were each so different, like the pieces of a jigsaw puzzle. Together, they made each other whole. Except now she felt another piece was missing. And that piece was shaped like a five-foot-eleven chiropractor by the name of Cooper Wells.

"What?" Marilyn's brows knitted together as she shot the question at Ella. Becca stopped talking in midsentence.

Ella snapped out of her daydream about how well some parts of Coop fit together with some of her parts. A jigsaw puzzle, indeed. "*What*, what?" She lifted a shoulder.

"Okay, spill it," said Carissa. "We want details." Her persistence was what made her such a good attorney. It's also what made her annoying sometimes.

Ella shrugged. "It all happened so fast." She was still stunned by how much she cared about Coop. How different the real Coop was from the playboy persona he'd always hidden behind. "I'm not sure what it means or if it means anything at all. It's hard to tell right now." Right. The way they were going at it every night, it was pretty easy to tell how much they liked each other physically. But beyond that, Ella wasn't sure what Coop wanted.

Coop was nothing like Bradley. But Bradley was gone and Coop wasn't. He was very, very much alive.

"This is probably a stupid question, but I have to ask it anyway. Are you in over your head with Coop?" Marilyn asked.

Ella cringed. It was only a matter of time before these mother hens started to worry over her, and she really, really didn't want to talk about it yet. Because, heck yeah, she was in over her head, and they'd probably spend the rest of the day scolding her for letting it happen. For putting herself and her heart at risk after what she'd gone through with Bradley's illness, especially with a man whose life was currently turned upside down.

Ella sighed and rubbed the back of her neck.

"Oh no," Marilyn said, and Ella's three friends exchanged worried looks. "You're in love with him."

Ella started to protest. Deny it. But what good would that do? She gave her friends a half smile and lifted a shoulder in surrender.

She tensed. Felt Coop's presence before she saw him. His soapy scent spurred her pulse into a gallop just as a masculine arm encircled her shoulders and gave her arm a firm squeeze.

"Hello, sweetheart." Coop's voice oozed charisma and sensuality.

Ella looked up into Coop's oh-so-innocent eyes, which twinkled with wickedness. He leaned down and planted a sultry kiss square on her parted lips. She bit back the "what the hell are you doing here" accusation that teetered on the tip of her tongue. He pulled away just enough so his warm breath caressed her face, locked his eyes with hers, then dropped his gaze to her lips.

"These are for you." He handed her a large bouquet of bright yellow lilies. "They match your dress, so I had to get them for you."

Three simultaneous "awws" sounded from her friends. The very same friends that wanted to find a tree and a rope and make them a wardrobe accessory for Coop just a few weeks ago, and Ella wasn't even sleeping with him then.

She just stared at him, unsure how to respond. One of Coop's caramel-colored brows rose high, coaxing her, provoking her. Their silent battle of wills raged on until Marilyn cleared her throat.

"Hi, Cooper. You may not remember us, but I think we met you once or twice."

"Oh, I remember you ladies. Good to see you again." He greeted each one. Becca's and Carissa's mouths hung open. When he grabbed each one's hand, they almost cooed. Ella suppressed the urge to kick them under the table. Too bad they didn't bring their kids. Ella would buy them double scoops of Blue Bell ice cream and a Red Bull as payback. It would make an interesting ride home.

"And, please, call me Coop. All my friends do," he said smoothly. He beamed a dazzling smile at Marilyn, who looked like she might melt.

So much for Mrs. Hardass. And so much for not wanting to talk about Coop, because here he was in the flesh, making a show of his near supernatural ability to charm intelligent women into slobbering fools.

"Coop, pull up a chair and join us," Marilyn said, all breathy.

"He can't, can you, Coop. Aren't you meeting your dad or something?"

He shook his head. "Nope. No plans at all for the next few hours." He gave Ella another dazzling smile. The kind that had most women eating out of his hand and sucking on his fingertips. The kind that charmed the spandex high-compression pants right off her. Ella licked her lips and tried to refocus.

"Then by all means." Becca motioned to an empty chair at the next table. "Have a seat."

"Well, if I'm not interrupting and if Ella's not embarrassed to be seen with me."

Ella ground her teeth. "No, of course not."

"Don't be silly, Coop, of course you're not interrupting. We're finished eating anyway," Becca said.

When Coop turned to retrieve the chair, Marilyn mouthed a "tsk, tsk" at Ella, who glared and grabbed her iced tea glass off the table. Before she said something she'd regret, she took a long drink.

"So tell us what you two have been up to here in Red River?" Marilyn asked, looking at them intently.

Coop circled her shoulder again and caressed the top of it with his fingertips. "Oh, a little rafting, a little dancing, a little fishing." He gave Ella a sly smile, mischief flickering in his hazel eyes. "Lots of physical activity." He turned a wondrous smile on Marilyn. "Gotta stay fit, ya know?"

Ella choked on her iced tea. Taking her glass, Coop handed her a napkin and rubbed the bare skin between her shoulder blades.

"Are you okay, love?" he asked her affectionately.

Love? Really?

Her three buddies exchanged envious glances, and Ella's face burned so hot her makeup might've melted a little.

"Butch, Coop, and a few others are redoing my bathroom," Ella interjected, and they all looked at her like she was interrupting. *Seriously?* These ballbusters were just lecturing her on the phone about how unwise it was to get involved with him. With just a few smiles, they were already wrapped around his very capable finger.

And, oh, what he could do with those fingers. Her entire body flushed from head to toe.

"What happened, Coop?" Becca asked, gesturing at the colorful bruises on the side of his face.

Ella gave him a pleading look. If he told them about Lumberjack Guy, they'd never leave her alone. Or they'd go after the culprits themselves, vigilante style. These ladies looked out for their own.

He touched the spot with his fingertips. "Oh, I had a little fender bender. Nothing to worry about."

"Sorry to spoil the party, but I have to ask, how's your legal situation?" Carissa said, leaning forward on her elbows. "You know, I'm an attorney. I might be able to help."

"My attorney said there's been a break in the case. The plaintiff just changed her story, which looks bad for her."

Ella's head whipped around to study his profile. That was important news that he'd failed to share with her. Maybe he didn't see a reason to share it with her.

Precisely why she didn't feel comfortable going public with their . . . their . . . their *arrangement* yet.

"Well, what are you going to do until this mess gets settled?" Marilyn asked.

"I'm doing fine right here in Red River." He shrugged. "I've got a job, friends. Family." He looked at Ella.

"And after all this is over? What then?" asked Becca.

Their third degree didn't seem to bother him. He still looked as cool as a summer breeze. "I'm not sure. I was just wondering that myself." Ella's eyes met his, and he didn't look away.

Her heart skittered. But this conversation should've been private, along with the important developments in his legal case.

Damn him and that thing he did so well with his thumb and forefinger.

"Please, let me get lunch for you ladies. It's the least I can do." Coop waved over the waiter and fished several bills out of his wallet.

"Well, Ella, you look like a million bucks," said Marilyn.

"Yep. Haven't seen you look this good in . . . years," said Becca, and an uncomfortable beat of silence went by.

"Besides all the great sex you two are obviously having—" Carissa blurted.

Ella sputtered. Marilyn gave Carissa a scolding look, and Becca elbowed her in the ribs.

"—You went shopping and had your hair done."

Coop caressed Ella's shoulder with his fingers. He raked dark eyes over her face. "Ella's full of all kinds of surprises. You should come by the cabin and see what she's done with the place."

"All I did was clean it," Ella ground out.

Coop ignored her. "It looks like a real home, not the man cave it's always been."

"Uh-huh," Ella said, reaching her breaking point. Placing the fine point of her stiletto sandal into the top of his all-weather hiking boot, she flashed him a wide smile and pressed down with just enough pressure to get his attention. "You're so thoughtful, Coop. Flowers, you bought our lunch, now all these compliments. What else do you have up your sleeve today?" She smelled the bouquet of lilies and toyed with a petal. Gazing into his dark eyes, she plastered on a wicked smile.

He grimaced.

"Oh! I'm so sorry." She dislodged her shoe. "I didn't see your foot there."

Well, it seemed to work. He sat there quiet as a church mouse until they were ready to leave.

"Take care of our girl, Coop," said Marilyn, and Coop tried not to laugh at Ella's thunderous expression.

"You still need to check in with us. We worry about you," Becca said to Ella.

"I will, but you guys need to stop doting on me. I can take care of myself."

"Yeah, and Coop, let me know if your attorney needs any help. I'm staying at home with the kids right now, but I can still prepare briefs and do research, you know, stuff like that."

"Thanks, Carissa. That means more than you know." And it did, because they didn't seem to doubt his innocence when so many of his own friends had cut him off without a second thought. Maybe Ella's friends simply trusted her judgment, but their support choked him up a little, nonetheless. So what was Ella's problem? He'd thought she'd be relieved that her friends accepted him. "Have a safe trip back."

After several tearful good-byes, Coop threaded an arm around Ella's waist, pulled her flush against his side, and guided her to the alley that led to Main Street. As soon as they turned the corner, Ella jerked away and rounded on him.

"What were you doing back there?"

"Me? You almost took off two of my toes with those lethal weapons you call shoes! I'll limp for a week, maybe two."

"You had it coming," she seethed. "How dare you interrupt my private time with my friends. What were you trying to prove? That you own me like one of your other bimbos?"

"And what were you trying to hide? Are you embarrassed for people to know that we're . . ." His words trailed off, and his forehead wrinkled, because he didn't know what exactly they were doing. Besides having mind-boggling sex every night, several times a night, and once or twice each morning. He got a little aroused just thinking about it, because she'd even pulled him into bed a few times in the middle of the day. He was glad the nearest neighbor was at least a mile away. Otherwise, they probably would've gotten arrested for disturbing the peace by now, as loud as Ella was. The way she whispered his name with an urgency that made his soul quake every time she came had caused him to make some noise, too.

She folded her arms under her breasts.

"My point exactly." She glowered at him. "You can't even say it out loud. Do you have any idea how much trouble you've just created for yourself? Those women will be like sharks in the water if you suddenly disappear from my life like you have with all your other girlfriends. There is no possible explanation that will pacify their bloodhound instincts. They'll hunt you down if they think you've hurt me."

He was the one about to get his heart trampled on when she moved from Red River. But he really couldn't blame Ella. He had made a mess out of his life and lost his career, at least for the time being. He didn't have anything to offer her right now. But still, he couldn't let her go without a fight, because he cared so much for her. She'd walked into his life and his cabin and taken him by storm. He hadn't stood a chance.

He took slow, deliberate steps toward her until she was backed against the red brick wall of the bistro. The alley was empty, but every now and again a car passed on Main Street or pedestrians walked by. So far, no one had noticed them.

He wedged one leg in between her thighs, and her breath caught. The hand farthest from the street traced up her outer thigh and up under her dress. Her chest rose and fell in a quickened rhythm, and those lush lips parted.

"Who says I'm disappearing from your life?" he whispered against her lips, which formed a perfect O. Her lips were so good at that. Lip gloss shimmered under the blue afternoon sky, and its cherry blossom scent made him hungry for the sweetness of her lips. "You're the one planning on leaving at the end of the summer." He pressed his hips into hers and she sucked in a breath, her eyes fluttering shut. Pulling away so their noses grazed, Coop whispered against her mouth, "Unless you find a reason to stay."

Emerald-green eyes popped open and stared at him.

"To answer your question, that's what I was trying to prove just now—that you have a reason to stay."

He hoped he really could give her a reason to stay. That his attorney would crack Kim's lies wide open and get him out of this mess, so he could get his life back.

When he covered Ella's mouth with his again, he consumed her, owned her. Kissed the damn sense out of her until a beautiful little sound of ecstasy escaped from somewhere in the back of her throat.

He pulled away panting and looked toward the end of the alley where it emptied onto Main Street. "Let's get out of here before someone sees us. It'll be all over town before dinner, and I know you don't want that."

She swallowed and nodded. He helped her find her footing, and she smoothed her dress.

Coop started for Main Street.

"Coop, wait."

He turned back to her. She looked so pretty, so soft standing there all dressed up with her hair mussed like she'd just taken a tumble in the sack with him.

"I'm not embarrassed to be seen with you. It's just so different . . . so unexpected. I . . . . I mean this wasn't exactly part of my plan."

He took her in, and nodded. "I know. Mine either. I'm willing to take the chance if you are. But I have to be honest, I'm getting the better end of the deal." And he was. He finally saw what Bradley had seen so many years ago. "You're the only woman that's ever made me . . . want more from a relationship. Made me want more from myself as a man. Want more for my life." He held out his hand to her. "I know it's a gamble. *I'm* a gamble. But I think we're worth it. So I'm asking you to roll the dice with me."

"You know I've never been one to take risks." She studied his hand, and then she reached out and took it, threading her fingers into his. "But maybe that is what's missing in my life."

Chapter Twenty-Two

"Where are we going on a date that I need to bring a bathing suit?" Ella asked. They'd been driving for some time, the road winding into a secluded part of the mountains that Ella had never seen.

"You'll see." Coop's mouth twitched at the corners and turned up into a wicked smile.

"I don't like surprises." Ella grew suspicious.

"You'll like this one."

"And I especially don't like the water if it's dangerous. Didn't you get the memo?"

"I did, actually, when we were rafting. But you'll like this water. Promise."

"And if I don't?" Fear bit at her stomach.

He pulled off the main highway onto a secluded dirt road. A large brown sign said "Carson National Forest," a picture of Smokey the Bear carved into it on the left.

"If you don't like it, you can torture me with your Taser or pepper spray." He glanced down at her feet, a worried look in his eyes. "Or those daggers you call shoes."

Her feet were adorned with the platform flip-flops she had bought on her weekend shopping spree with the girls. Relief washed over his face.

"Oh, good. I like these better. Much safer." He flashed another devilish grin at her. "Although, I wouldn't mind if you wore those spiked heels to bed sometime."

She quirked a brow, and he chuckled. "A man can hope, can't he?"

He turned onto a winding drive that led them to an adobe building set on several sprawling acres of land. They pulled to a stop, and he grabbed their bags from the backseat.

They walked to the entrance, a sign—"Aguas Rojas – Mineral Springs"—etched into the thick wall like a petroglyph.

Coop checked in, and a staff member showed them to their private cabana.

It was gorgeous. Aromatherapy filled the room with a scent that seeped into tensed muscles and relaxed Ella more with each breath. A spread of cheeses, crackers, fruit, and antipasto was already ready for them, and a bottle of red wine.

"I had them put bottled water in here for you, since you and alcohol seem to have a love-hate thing going."

"Thanks." She smiled at Coop.

"After we eat," he pointed to the expansive window, "we have our own private hot spring waiting for us. *Shallow* hot spring, and no rapids this time."

She turned to the window. The sun was setting behind the mountains. Purple, pink, and orange streaked the evening sky. A rocky pool of water and a hammock beckoned to them just outside the sliding doors.

"Hence, the bathing suit," she said.

"Uh-huh, but let's eat first." He uncorked the bottle of wine, poured himself a glass, and filled hers with sparking water.

"This is really nice." Surprised, Ella's soft stare slid over him.

"It was either this or the drive-in theater in Questa, where at least half the speakers don't work."

Ella laughed, knowing that Questa was a town about the size of her big toe. Kind of like where she grew up. With Coop, it actually sounded romantic, though.

"Well, this was a good choice. We can save the drive-in theater for a really special occasion," she said and slid into one of the chairs at the quaint table set up for two.

Coop occupied the other chair and dished up a plate of food for her.

"Mmmm, this is so good," Ella said, the flavors of the cheese and salami melting on her tongue.

"Better than Cap'n Crunch?"

She laughed. "My mother tried to teach me to cook when I was in high school. It didn't take."

"You? Miss Overachiever couldn't master something? Say it isn't so," Coop teased her.

"I'll have you know I didn't always get straight A's."

"Oh, really? When did you not get an A?"

"I got a B. Once. In welding class. I took it on a dare."

Coop snorted. "You in a welding hood, brandishing a blow-torch?" He laughed hard. "I can't even picture it." He howled with laughter, a tear appearing at the corner of his eye. Nodding, he snorted between words. "Actually, yes. Yes, I just did picture it."

Ella smirked at him. "Very funny. Glad I could provide tonight's entertainment." She speared another slice of salami.

They ate in silence while Coop regained his composure and wiped his eyes.

"I know from some of the students I've taught that it's hard having a reading disability. Want to talk about it?"

His expression went slack, and he stared down at his plate.

"Maybe I shouldn't have brought it up." She tried to soothe what must've been painful memories probably replaying through his mind. "I'm a teacher, Coop. I know how cruel kids can be, and how hard it is for kids to grow up with challenges beyond their control."

He popped an olive in his mouth, chewed, and swallowed. Then he rolled his wine around in the stemmed glass for a minute.

Her gaze raked over him. The angles of his handsome face were so perfect. So superb. So easy to look at. Sometimes she found herself staring at him. Just staring, because he was simply beautiful to her. The athletic curves of his shoulders and arms were even more fascinating, drawing her attention every time they stepped into the same room. Just looking at him made her mouth water, her limbs quiver, her body go wet in all the right places.

"I always thought I wasn't very smart. I was happy when I got an occasional B. Most of the time I got C's. My dad's dyslexic, too, so he couldn't help me much. When he went to chiropractic school the curriculum was much easier than when Bradley and I went, so he didn't face as many challenges as I did. Then God sent me an angel named Bradley Dennings. Bradley made sure he took all the same classes as me in high school, at UNM, and in chiropractic school. When we studied together, he read out loud, so I could absorb everything that way. I had to listen to every single word of our class lectures. No dozing off, no goofing off, just listening and learning. That's how I passed."

"Bradley never told me any of that," said Ella. Actually, she'd always assumed Coop *was* a goof-off. Her mistake, because he wasn't. Not really. When he cared about something—or someone—he gave it his all. It was obvious how much the people in Red River meant to him. Even his job bartending at Joe's was important to him, and he made a real effort to do his best, never acting as though the job was beneath him.

"I never asked him to keep it from you. I think he knew how embarrassing it was for me, and how people labeled me most of my life. I guess he was respecting my privacy." Coop took another sip of wine. "My test scores were never that great because I struggled with reading the questions, but I knew the material. Still, everyone assumed I was a dunce."

Her heart squeezed, and she slid a hand across the table to grasp his. Just his touch warmed her.

He lifted her hand, holding their palms flat against each other, then he threaded her fingers through his. "And now Cal has you as his angel." He kissed the back of her hand, and her insides melted into hot liquid. "Thank you for that."

And her heart did a happy dance.

———————

"Are you sure about this?" Ella stood on the edge of the rocky pool and dipped her toe into the water. "The bottom isn't going to fall out from under our feet or anything?" He was up to his chest, and when she pointed that dainty toe and tested the water right in front of him, he wondered what it would taste like.

"I'm sure." He pointed to the waterline at his chest. "It doesn't get any deeper than this."

With a wary look, she took his outstretched hand and descended into the water with slow, unsteady steps. Coop was a little disappointed when those curvy hips and full breasts, covered only by a tiny purple bikini, disappeared under the steamy water. Her hair was pulled into a messy knot behind her head, and a few strands fell free.

He pulled her to him. "See? Nice, huh?"

The natural mineral waters and hot springs were soothing, and fabled to contain healing powers. Coop wasn't sure he believed that, but when he was trying to decide on a unique place to take Ella on a date, Aguas Rojas sounded pretty romantic.

She nodded. "Yeah, this is nice." She threaded her arms around his neck and wrapped her legs around his hips.

He groaned. Even in the water, she still had an amazing effect on him.

"So, this is a private spring? We have it all to ourselves?" Her voice sounded naughty. Cinder-Ella had been a misconception all these years. Ella was more of a seductress than he'd ever have thought. Maybe she'd been reading those erotic books that all the ladies in Red River were talking about.

He chuckled. "It's completely private, but I didn't bring you up here for that."

She let out a disgruntled sigh.

"Later," he promised. "For now, I just want you to enjoy the water."

"Do you come up here a lot?" she asked. Her body tensed against his chest.

"Never. This is my first time."

She melted into him again, her warmth amalgamating to his. Their heartbeats mingling, melding, beating as one. *Nice.* The nicest thing he'd ever experienced, actually.

"Then, thank you," she whispered against his ear, her voice faint as the mineral water eased the tension from her body. She became less guarded. "I like being the only one."

He nuzzled her ear. "You're it, baby." A shiver raced over her, and she tightened her legs and arms around him.

He waded around the minipool of hot water, trying to enjoy the view. But really, all he could think of, feel, and taste was Ella's perfect body molded to his. She filled his every sense, her warmth spreading through him until it felt like a burning ember all the way to his core.

"Ella?" he murmured into her ear.

"Hmmm?" she said against his shoulder, her voice sleepy and content.

"Do you want to know why I didn't visit Bradley very much? I want you to know because it must've bothered you." It bothered *him*, and he still carried guilt over it.

She lifted her head off his shoulder and stared into his eyes.

"You don't have to talk about it if you don't want to," she said. "I know you loved him like a brother."

"I want to talk about it with you." He pulled in a gravelly breath. "I care about what you think."

Ella tucked a wet strand of his wavy hair behind his ear and caressed his cheek with the back of her hand. "I wondered at first. I was angry for a long time because I thought you abandoned him. But then, when I came to Red River and got to know you better, I think I figured it out."

His brow wrinkled.

Ella stroked a soft fingertip across his forehead to smooth out the tension. "Coop, I had to sit and watch him wither away in that bed, not even in his right mind toward the end. I was his wife, and I loved him, and even I wanted to get away from seeing him like that. I'd have done anything not to have to watch it. I couldn't stand it. It almost killed me right along with him."

"I'm sorry, Ella." Coop's voice was a plea. "I should've been there for both of you, but when I saw him in that bed the first time, I couldn't handle it. He was the best guy I ever knew, the best friend I ever had, and there was nothing I could do to save him."

Coop choked back the pain that stabbed at his heart.

Ella put a finger over Coop's lips. "Shh. He wouldn't have wanted either of us to keep suffering. It's time for both of us to let him go."

"Is that why you left Albuquerque?"

She inhaled, and nodded. "There were just too many bad memories there. I didn't want to remember him that way. You know, the way he was at the end. I wanted to remember him when he was young and healthy and happy. Like when he came here to Red River."

"You made him happy, Ella."

She rubbed her cheek against his. "Thank you. That means a lot coming from you."

He waded around the pool with her snuggled against his neck, wrapped around him like a second skin. He caressed her back with his fingers, and she brushed soft kisses across his shoulder.

They were silent for a long time, just soaking in the therapeutic waters. Just *being.* Coop loved the way she molded into his arms, against his chest. Yes, the sex was great, but he loved the simple quiet time they spent together, too. It made him aware of how badly broken he'd been. Severed in two, in fact, but Ella was the glue that had put him back together and held him there, allowing him to be whole and content for the first time.

"Coop?"

"Yeah, sweetheart." Sweetheart. He'd never called any girl that before. He purposefully used their real names instead of terms of endearment.

With Ella, it sounded good. Sounded right.

She brushed kisses up his neck to his cheek, and his heart thrummed in his chest.

"Do I make *you* happy?"

He pulled her head up and found her mouth. After a long, deep kiss that involved a lot of sensuous sounds, he pulled away. "Yeah, you make me very happy."

Her face shone like another star in the clear New Mexico sky.

"Let's go home, and I'll show you just how happy you make me." He nuzzled her neck.

"Okay, but let's stop by the drugstore first." She giggled.

"Already taken care of, babe."

Chapter Twenty-Three

When Coop finished his early shift at Joe's, he sat down at a table to talk to Hank and Andy. "What's up with you two?"

Hank swilled his beer. "My wife's turned into a sex fiend because of those darned books."

"Mine, too." Andy shrugged with a smile.

"And that's a bad thing?" Coop asked, a little confused.

"I'm good with it," said Andy.

"Well, I'm not," Hank retorted. "Some of the toys she's been ordering online are just a little too twisted. People will think I'm a sex maniac."

"How will people know?" asked Coop.

"In this town? Are you serious?"

"I see your point." Coop rubbed his jaw. "I've seen several of those books around, so I don't think you're the only husband suffering." He grinned at Andy. "Sounds like a good problem to have."

"Now they're driving into Taos to get the new book next week when it's released. It's been on the news and everything. I drew the line when Donna wanted to get me a C-ring," mumbled Hank.

"TMI, dude," Andy said.

Coop's cell phone rang. "Saved by the ringtone." Cal's picture popped onto the screen, and Coop hit the green button. "Hi, Cal."

"Hey, Big Bro. Dad and I picked up Ella earlier. She's at our house tutoring me. Want to come over for dinner?"

"Sure. I just finished my shift, I'll be there soon." Thank God, because the conversation with Hank and Andy had gone beyond bizarre. "All this tutoring is going to help you get into college. You're going to be a senior this fall. It's time to start thinking about where you want to go."

The line was silent.

"Cal?"

"Yeah, about that."

Coop got an uneasy feeling. "I'm listening."

"I don't think I want to go to college."

"Of course you do. You can't go to chiropractic school unless you go to college first."

More silence.

"Cal?" Coop drew out his brother's name into three syllables.

"I don't think I want to be a chiropractor, either."

"What? Of course you do. We've been planning this for years."

Cal sighed. "No Coop, you and Dad have been planning it. I've got other plans."

"Like what?"

"Like being a firefighter. Look, we can talk about this later. Did you know today is Ella's birthday?"

What? "No, actually, she didn't mention it." Why wouldn't she tell him? That was kind of an important detail to overlook.

"We offered to take her out, but she didn't want us to make a big deal about it. To celebrate, Dad's cooking on the grill and I'm churning ice cream. It's the best we can come up with on such short notice."

"Sounds good. Give me a little bit, I've got to make a stop on the way." Coop hesitated. "And Cal, we're not finished discussing college."

The line went dead, and Coop stared at his cell.

Coop pulled into Butch's drive and parked in front of the house. He got out and walked around to the backyard. Ella and Cal sat at the picnic table again, their favorite tutoring spot, and talked.

"I'm not smart enough to go to college anyway."

The familiar sadness Coop had felt growing up hit him square in the chest like a hammer.

"You *are* smart enough to go to college. Don't use your disability as an excuse."

Coop had to stop himself from applauding Ella's comeback, because that was exactly the right thing to say. Smart *and* wise. And gorgeous to boot.

"The question is, do you *want* to go?" she asked Cal.

Cal shrugged. "I'm not sure. I don't think so. I'm happy here in Red River, and I really want to be a firefighter. That's my dream. I don't want to be a chiropractor."

"My family wanted me to be a veterinarian so I could stay on the ranch and work it, just like they all did. It angered them that I wanted something different. I was the Judas that broke away."

Coop hadn't thought of it that way—Ella's family resenting her just because she wanted something different. Something more.

"I love my family, and I liked where I grew up, but I wanted to experience a little bit more of the world, and I wanted to give back because my life had been so blessed. So, I moved out here and became a teacher."

"Did your family ever forgive you?"

She nodded and patted his arm. "Sure they did. They still miss me and want me to move back to East Texas, but that's just because they love me."

"Did you regret becoming a teacher?"

"Never. I loved my job. Loved teaching kids like you, even if they did act like knuckleheads sometimes." She ruffled his hair. "Being a firefighter is an honorable profession, just like teaching. Just be sure that's what you really want, and you're not giving up on an opportunity to go to college because you're afraid to leave here or because of your reading disability. If you do decide to go to college, you can still be a firefighter, and you could move back here when you're done with school." She elbowed him. "Besides, dyslexia can work to your advantage in college."

"No way." Cal shook his head in disbelief. "Really?"

"Girls will think you're complicated. They'll line up to help you study."

Cal looked stunned, then a mischievous smile spread across his face. "That could work."

"Don't discount college just yet. Just think about it, that's all I'm saying." Ella's schoolteacher voice was so solid. So exactly what Coop's little brother needed to hear right now.

"UNM is only a few hours away, and we'll all be waiting here for you when you come back."

We. Here. Coop liked the sound of those two little words more than he thought possible.

———

They drove home after dark, full from the side of beef ribs Butch had grilled and the homemade ice cream. Infinitely better than Cap'n Crunch. Ella sighed, happy and content.

"You okay?" She reached for Coop's hand. He grabbed hers in return, almost urgently, but he didn't say anything. Just looked ahead at the road.

Her free hand went to her throat, and she fingered the small gold heart he'd given her as a birthday present. How did he find something so quickly? She'd purposely not told anyone about her birthday, especially him, because she didn't want him to feel obligated to buy her a gift. After losing someone she loved, Ella didn't care much about material possessions. It was time, quality time, she craved. And since she didn't know for sure how much time she'd have with Coop, that's all she'd wanted that day.

But the dainty heart that nestled in the hollow of her throat just above her collarbone was perfect. Simple. Elegant. It represented love.

When they got back to the cabin, he hurried her to the door. The dogs barreled past them as soon as Coop opened it. He pulled her inside and kicked the door shut with his foot.

"The dogs—"

"Can wait." His lean body closed around her, enveloping her with need. His desire so obvious, so apparent, it vibrated through him and prickled over her skin like a maestro conducting a concerto. "I need you. Now."

Without warning, he picked her up and carried her into his bedroom.

Placing her on her back, he lay next to her. He didn't kiss her yet. Just ran his warm palm from her neck down her stomach, and massaged her sex through the thick fabric of her shorts. Then, gentle and slow, he undressed her. So carefully, like she was a doll that would break in his hands. When he rubbed the lace strip between her legs, she moaned. A small shudder of a noise escaped from somewhere deep inside him. It cut to her soul and made her ache to her core.

"Coop." She tried to clear the sensual fog from her head, but it gripped her senses and clouded her consciousness. She needed to tell him, say the words, so he would know how she really felt about him.

She loved him. Fully and completely.

And it terrified her.

He was none of the things she'd wanted in a man. Yet she loved him and wanted him just the way he was now. Not the man he'd been before, but the man he'd grown into. The man she never knew existed.

When he slipped his hand under her lace panties, she arched toward him. Under his touch, her body ebbed and flowed, quivered and undulated, until she was begging him to take her. To relieve that violent demand that she felt climbing inside her.

She tore at his shirt, and he didn't seem to mind. When she couldn't get the buttons undone fast enough, she ripped them off, and they popped and flew in every direction. With the barrier gone, Ella ran her palms over the hard planes of his chest. He stared down at her with the look of a conqueror, and she very much wanted to be conquered by him. Only him.

He still hadn't kissed her. Just drank her in with eyes blazing with lust, scorching every inch of her bared body from head to curled toes. And she did the same to him.

Ella couldn't remember how his pants came off, or her panties and bra, nor did she care. He laced one set of fingers through hers and pinned her hand to the pillow over her head. When he entered her, she cried out and buried her face in his shoulder. The ecstasy of him filling her so completely was unbearably sweet.

"Ella," he grunted, going still. "Baby, you're biting me."

And, oh heavens, she was. She released his shoulder from between her teeth and kissed the same spot, running her tongue over the teeth marks.

"Sorry," she murmured against his sinewy neck. "I'll make it up to you."

"I'm counting on it." His voice held a smile, and Ella pulled him deeper inside her.

His strokes were urgent and fast at first, but then he found a slow, sweet rhythm that bespoke pure, tender emotion.

At that moment, Ella knew Coop loved her, too. He hadn't said it in words, but he was communicating it to her now through an unspoken language—with his body, with his touch, with every movement that he so carefully orchestrated. It wasn't just sex. Their bodies, their souls, their hearts were mingled and entwined into one until she wasn't sure where she ended and he began. Because there was no beginning and no end to them as individuals anymore. It was just them. One entity, bound together by something so much bigger than just sex.

Ella shattered into a million tiny pieces as an orgasm overtook her, washing her over the edge of complete and utter bliss. A moment later, Coop found his release and whispered her name as he did.

They lay there for a long time, the sounds of night filtering into their room through the silence. When their breathing returned to normal, Ella caressed down his rib cage, over his hips, gently massaging. Then she traced a circular pattern over to his spine and down to his buttocks.

Swelling inside her again, he moaned. "How do you do that to me?" he ground out. "When you touch me, I go crazy."

A smile spread across her lips, and she nibbled sweet kisses over his shoulder and neck.

His breathing grew ragged, and his cock grew thick and hard again. "When we're in a crowd, sometimes I want you so much I could take you to my truck and make love to you right there. Even in broad daylight."

Ella giggled. "Would you really do that?" she asked, moving her hips into him gently.

"Of course not." His teeth, jaw, and eyes all clenched as she moved harder against him, and he lifted onto his elbows to hover over her. "You deserve better than the backseat of a car."

"What if I were willing?" she asked, her voice taunting and seductive.

His eyes flew wide, and he stared down at her.

She shrugged. "I've never done it in the backseat of a car, but I'd do it with you." She bit her bottom lip. "It might be fun."

His eyes glazed over with desire, he began to move in her with slow and gentle strokes. "So, Miss Straight-Lace wants to live on the edge? With me?"

Her laugh was coupled with a moan of pleasure as his strokes grew more determined.

"Only with you." She stared up at him. Her breath caught when he sank so far into her, her insides began to quiver on the brink of another orgasm.

In a movement so smooth and quick she squeaked, Coop had her on top, guiding and moving her hips in a circular motion with one hand while he stroked her cleft with a thumb.

He lifted her to his tip, then plunged her down on him again. The sexual tension built and roiled inside her with every stroke. Close to the brink, Ella reached up and grabbed the headboard, taking control of the force of her body pounding into his. He murmured her name, one hand clamped to her hip, the other still stroking her sex, and he rose to suckle one breast, then the other.

She came with a desperate cry of his name, which pulled him with her, and she collapsed against his heaving chest.

In sweet silence, Ella slid down his body to cuddle against his side. He bundled her onto his chest and pulled the covers up around them. After feathering sweet kisses across the top of her head, he settled into his pillow, still wrapped around her like a straitjacket.

When Ella heard his soft snore, she murmured against his chest, "I love you, Cooper." Then she drifted off into a peaceful, content sleep, hoping this would last forever.

Chapter Twenty-Four

Coop and Ella pulled into a parking spot in front of the post office and got out. In a town the size of Red River, the post office served as a social gathering point just as much as Joe's did. If the crowded parking lot was any indication, the locals were out in force.

"The gossip must be flowing today," Coop said, nodding to another car that inched into the lot off of Main Street. "Donna's got a full house." He opened the door for Ella.

Ella laughed as she walked through. "She's the best source in town."

Two older women chatted it up about their last visit to Doc Holloway's office, while people milled in and out of the post office buying stamps, mailing vacation postcards, or picking up mail. Ella stopped to talk to Donna behind the front desk, while Coop went to his box and dialed in the combination. He picked a few envelopes from the box and thumbed through them, walking over to the counter.

Sheriff Lawson walked in. "Just the people I wanted to see." He made a beeline for Coop and Ella, tipping his gray cowboy hat to the other ladies. "Just wanted to let you know we picked up that group of troublemakers last night over in Questa. They got into another barroom brawl over there and we caught 'em before they got out of the county."

Ella closed her eyes and sighed her relief.

"Thanks, Sheriff." Coop shook his hand. "I was worried every time I had to leave Ella alone, but she wouldn't stay at my side twenty-four-seven."

The sheriff gave her an appraising glance. "Looked to me like Ella can hold her own."

And that was the problem. Ella didn't need him. She'd said she loved him when she thought he was asleep. No begging him to stay with her, no needy latching on or smothering him. She loved him, but she was willing to let him go if he didn't fit into her plan to move on.

Just like his mother.

Ella's smile was bright and illuminating until she looked at Coop. Her eyes scanned his face, and her smile faded, a wrinkle appearing across her forehead like she'd read his thoughts.

Coop ignored it. "Donna, you left a message that I got a package."

"Sure did." Donna retrieved it from a box at the back of the mail room. "From Amazon." She handed it over. "What you readin'?"

Coop hesitated. "Chiropractic journals. Boring stuff."

"Speaking of books," Donna interjected. "Violet Vixen's new book is coming out next week. Finally! Ella, you up for a trip to Santa Fe with us gals? A few advance reviews are out and it's supposed to be even hotter than the first two books."

Ella rubbed the back of her neck and looked away.

"Uh, I think I've got a call. Or something." Sheriff Lawson tipped his hat. "See y'all later." He made a quick exit, and Coop wished he had a call to take. Or something.

"I, um." Ella's weight shifted in quick, jerky movements. "I download my books."

Donna clucked her tongue. "Lorenda has an e-reader, but she's going anyway just for kicks. You should come, too."

"You *should* go, Ella. Someone has to keep them out of trouble." Coop winked at Ella, and he clamped the unopened package under his arm, jamming his free hand in his pocket. Ella's curious look skimmed the package.

"I just *might* go lookin' for some trouble while I'm there, Mr. Smarty Pants." Donna tossed her curly bob to one side.

"See?" Coop said to Ella. "They need a responsible chaperone."

"Uh, well, there is something I need to do in Santa Fe, so I guess I could go along for the ride."

"Great! What is it you need in Santa Fe?" Donna asked.

"I need to buy another vehicle. Coop's had to drive me everywhere."

Which he didn't mind in the least.

"And I can't keep inconveniencing him."

Why the hell not? He kind of liked being inconvenienced by her, because he didn't see it as an inconvenience. The extra time with Ella had been nice, and they'd settled into a comfortable routine together.

"I need my own car."

Okay. Another car wouldn't hurt.

"I don't like being at the mercy of others."

Coop's jaw clenched so tight he thought he'd have to pry it open if he ever wanted to speak again. Or eat. Or kiss the little sex goddess standing next to him. Because what she really meant was *I need my independence.*

Was she still preparing to move on just in case Coop lived up to his reputation and left her high and dry? Was she preparing herself to cut him loose if necessary? She wasn't the scared little kitten she once thought she was, looking for a savior, a protector like Bradley. She was fully prepared to move on alone and make a new life somewhere else, with someone else, if that's the road she found herself on.

And why wouldn't she? She'd had it all with Bradley. He was twice the man Coop would ever be. Coop was just a poor imitation.

"Sounds like a plan. We'll drop you at the dealership, and you can take care of business while we shop," said Donna.

Coop cleared his throat. "You ready?" he asked Ella.

Before Ella responded, Donna stopped them. "Oh, I almost forgot." She grabbed a letter from behind the counter and handed it to Ella. "This came for you, Ella. It's from Wanton Publishing. Probably some sort of publisher's clearinghouse scam or an order form for magazine subscriptions, but since Coop was coming in for a package, I didn't call."

Ella's rosy cheeks turned white as snow.

"Yeah, junk mail, I'm sure," Ella gushed, a little too fast.

But instead of opening it or tearing it up and throwing it in the trash can that conveniently sat within an arm's reach, she shoved it deep inside her purse.

That evening, Coop stood behind the bar at Joe's, drying glasses. A few tourists dined, and Ella and their gang of misfit friends occupied their usual table.

Joe lumbered out of the back office and sat at the bar.

"How's business?" he asked.

"Slow," Coop and Dylan answered simultaneously.

"If one of you wants to clock out, go ahead."

"Actually, there is something I need to do." Coop looked at Dylan.

Dylan nodded. "I've got this."

"Joe, do you mind if I use your computer for a minute? I don't have one at home."

Coop wasn't up on the latest technology and didn't really care to be. He still used a flip phone, much to Cal's horror, who claimed a real ladies' man would at least have a smartphone and Netflix. Ella had installed Wi-Fi when she first got to the cabin, but he still didn't have his own computer. Didn't see a need for one, since the point of Red River was to rusticate and relax.

"Sure," Joe said. "You know where it is."

Coop found Joe's computer in the back room and Googled Wanton Publishing. "The World's Front-Runner in Erotic Romance," or so the tagline proclaimed. A myriad of racy book covers came up, *New Mexico Naughty* and *Southwest Sizzle* being the most prominent. They were front and center on the website. A *New York Times* bestseller, with the next book, *Rio Grande Romp,* set for release in a week. A must-read, a sure success, another bestseller, according to the website. The author, Violet Vixen, lived in New Mexico with her English bulldog and was a sponsor of several literacy programs.

The skin at the back of Coop's neck prickled. He shook it off.

The website didn't offer a picture of Ms. Vixen, so he searched the net for any information he could find. Nothing more came up than what the website offered. At a dead end, he logged on to Amazon and bought Ms. Vixen's first two books, then preordered the third. He set delivery to his new e-reader, which he still didn't know how to turn on. Tonight was as good a time as any to figure it out.

He logged off Joe's computer and went to find his friends.

"How about Arkansas? The houses are big, the pay is better, and there's lots of eligible men," Donna said to Ella as Coop walked up to their table.

"Seriously, guys. I haven't thought that far ahead. I'm staying in Red River for a while. I've gotten a little attached to you guys," Ella said, and shot a warm smile at Coop.

"So, Ross," Lorenda spoke up. "Where's Sandra?"

He shrugged. "She dumped me for some corporate exec from San Francisco that was vacationing in Taos."

"Told you." Lorenda eyed Ross.

He smiled and took another drink of beer. "It was fun while it lasted."

"Go on, Lorenda, dance with Ross and make his day." Donna tried to shoo them toward the dance floor.

"I'll be happy to dance with Ross, but I'm not making anybody's day. I'm off-limits. Period. At least until my boys are grown, and by then I'll be an old woman." Lorenda's chair scraped across the floor as she stood and pointed to Ross. "You. Come on, let's dance."

"Yes, ma'am. I never argue with a pretty woman." Ross followed her onto the dance floor, and they waltzed to an old Hank Williams, Jr., tune.

Coop stood beside Ella's chair and nudged her. "Want to dance?"

She smiled up at him, warm and affectionate. He held out his hand and she took it, following him onto the dance floor. When he took her into his arms, she melded to him and matched his steps in perfect unison.

"You're a really good dance partner." She rubbed her cheek softly against his.

"So are you," he said, his voice gravelly. "The best."

She nodded against his temple. "I've never partnered with anyone so perfectly."

He pulled her tight against him, and didn't want to let her go. Ever.

"When we dance together," she whispered, her voice gone all breathy, "it's almost as good as our lovemaking. But not quite," she added. "I've never felt anything as good as when you make love to me."

Fire shot through every nerve ending and pooled below his belt. He breathed her in, the scent of flowers and sweet spices dialing up his desire even more and making his mouth water.

"You smell good," he said, exercising an incredible amount of self-control by not sinking his teeth into her delectable earlobe.

"You don't. I think you need a bath." She tightened her grip on him.

"Uh, thanks for the heads-up." He sniffed under his arm, the lust-laden spell broken.

"I have a surprise for you when we get home," she said, the word "home" making Coop's insides go warm and soft.

The corners of her mouth still turned slightly up into a flirtatious smile. Amazing how she could insult him and flirt with him at the same time. Women were an elusive enigma, especially this woman who'd turned out to be so different than he'd once thought.

"A new stick of deodorant?" He raised a brow at her.

"Nope. Much better."

"Mmm, that sounds interesting. Give me a hint?"

"Your dad and Cal have been working on the bathroom while you're at work. They finished today."

"And that's a surprise for me? They were explicit that the bathroom is for you."

Her lashes fluttered down to brush her cheeks. "I had them add a few features that we can both enjoy." She raised both eyebrows. "At the same time." Desire sparked in her green eyes, turning them a deep shade of pine.

He ran his hands down to cup her exquisite ass, not really caring if anybody saw. "You're right. I think I need a bath."

Chapter Twenty-Five

Coop couldn't find enough time with Ella around to actually get out his e-reader and learn to use it. He'd charged it at Joe's last week, but that was about it. He certainly didn't want anyone there to know he'd bought erotic romance novels. If even one person found out, the entire county would know within the hour, and Coop would never live it down.

Finally, when Ella left with the girls to drive to Santa Fe and insisted she didn't need him to buy a car, he had the cabin to himself. He got out the device and turned it on. A colorful screen popped up, and then he was stuck. He touched the screen over a few icons, but nothing happened. Coop still didn't understand what was wrong with a real book, but whatever. Technology. Go figure.

He read a few of the directions, always a struggle with his dyslexia, but it seemed fairly self-explanatory, and before he knew it, Violet Vixen's books were downloaded and ready to go.

And holy hell, Violet Vixen had some imagination. Nothing prepared him for the wordy aphrodisiac that jumped all over him. On every. Single. Page. Hence, the term "erotic romance."

Wow. You learn something new every day.

Now he understood the female craze over these books. Men had been viewing similar material in one form or another for generations. A few Super Bowl commercials had been so provocative they had shocked Coop in the past, all geared toward men. So why should women live by a different standard?

Something bit at Coop's conscience. Hadn't Ella said that very thing at Joe's not too long ago? But she also said she didn't read the books, so how would she know? Why would she even have an opinion on the matter?

Probably just an educated observation, because Ella was very well educated and wicked smart. Way too smart to read erotic romance novels. She probably read encyclopedias just for the fun of it.

He skimmed through several more chapters, steam virtually rising off each page. Seriously? He wondered if Ms. Vixen was married, and if so, how did her husband handle all this? It would have to affect his career negatively. How could he not be embarrassed at work? Maybe that's why she kept her true identity a tightly guarded secret. He'd searched the net for a picture or some sort of hint as to who she was, but couldn't find anything.

Why he was so interested, he wasn't exactly sure. He just had a gut feeling that kept prodding him on.

Coop looked at his watch. He still had several hours, but with his dyslexia, reading was a slow, painful process, so he started to skip over sections of the book. He wanted to finish before Ella got back, because he may not have much time alone once she returned. Three books was a lot of reading to get through in a few hours, especially for him.

He'd promised her he'd meet her at Joe's for dinner when she pulled into town with her new set of wheels, so he needed to get busy.

Ella called Lorenda's cell number. "Hey, I've got a brand-spanking-new Xterra. Have car, can travel. Where are you guys?"

"We're still standing in line at the bookstore," Lorenda huffed. "I swear, I'm buying these three e-readers for Christmas. I've already downloaded my copy of *Rio Grande Romp*, and I'm reading it as we speak. Well, not really, because I can't read and speak at the same time, but you know what I mean. Sheesh, these crazy women are making me crazy, too. Hold on." Lorenda said something stern to Brianna and Miranda, then got back on the phone.

"Sorry, our so-called friends are trying to wrench my reader away, and I almost had to fight them for it. They're lucky I'm not a violent person. Now they're insisting we read it out loud on the way home, so Donna can drive and still hear the story."

Ella laughed. "I'll come suffer along with you, Lor." It'd be interesting to see the crowd in action and eavesdrop on some of the conversations anyway.

Lorenda gasped. "Oh, my God, a catfight just broke out toward the front of the line."

"It's getting violent over there?" Ella asked, a little alarmed, because really, this was sort of her doing.

"Yeah. If the bookstore runs out of print copies, they may have to call out the SWAT team. One rather unstable-looking lady threatened to take hostages."

"Oh, my," Ella murmured into the phone.

"Seriously, get over here with your Taser. We might need it." Lorenda laughed. "I'm thinking of using it on my own friends if this goes on much longer. I've never seen women act so insane. Except the day after Thanksgiving, when large-screen TVs are on sale. And wrapping paper."

Ella laughed. "You're right. My mom and grandma get vicious

when gift wrap and bows go on sale. I've seen them throw down with other women half their ages over half-price gift bags."

"Oh, a security team and Channel Twelve News just arrived," said Lorenda. "Now it's a party."

Ella's anxiety level spiked. "Tell you what. I'll make a coffee run for all of us."

"Throw a little bourbon in mine. I need it," Lorenda joked.

"Be there in twenty. And when we get back to Red River, dinner at Joe's is on me."

It was the least she could do, because the frenzy going on at every bookstore across the country and the exponential downloads that had already occurred around the world equated to dollar signs for Ella. Unbelievable. Who would've thought it? Definitely not her. She was really just goofing around when she opened a blank document and started typing in the first story. She'd just been trying to fill the lonely hours of boredom and trying to get her mind off the lovely man who wasted away in the bed she was sitting next to. The first two books had been her fantasy of Bradley miraculously recovering, and what she'd do with him if he did.

The end of the third book was based on the spark of a new relationship she had imagined *if* she and Coop ever slept together, which they hadn't at the time. The lead characters in both books stayed the same; it was just Ella's muse that changed. The excerpt for the fourth book that was included at the end of book three was her real-life fantasy come true with Cooper Wells; she'd just changed the setting. Instead of their cozy cabin in Red River, the lead characters had multiple encounters in a doctor's office. Her book's heroine was an uptight high school librarian who visited a chiropractor for headaches. What transpired in his office would make Hugh Hefner blush. That's what women seemed to find so exhilarating about the story—the naughtiness of getting it on in an exam room with other patients waiting.

Guilt washed over her.

It had made for a great teaser. It was so good, so sexy, so intimate that women would be foaming at the mouth like rabid dogs for the fourth book, *High Country Heat,* to be released. But it had been a risk. If Coop ever read it, he'd know she was Violet Vixen. He'd have to know because there was no doubt whatsoever about the physical details of the first time they made love. Especially since she mentioned the hero's sexy birthmark located in the most intimate of spots—a distinctly shaped birthmark that the heroine loved to explore up close and personal. If that ever got out, it could hurt his case and his already-damaged reputation.

It wouldn't get out, though. How could it? They hadn't even told anyone that they were sleeping together yet. Oh, some of their close friends and Butch had guessed. It was hard to miss; the way they looked at each other, their body language screamed "We're getting it on all the time, every chance we get." So far, they'd all tiptoed around it, probably guessing that Ella and Coop themselves weren't even sure where it might lead.

So the only other person on earth who knew the steamy details of their incredible sexcapades was Coop, and he didn't read erotic romance novels. From what she could tell, Coop didn't read much at all. A fact she frowned on, until she found out about his dyslexia.

Ella thanked the salesman who had just made a sizeable commission off her, got into her new, paid-for-in-cash four-wheel drive, and headed to the nearest coffee shop.

Life was good.

So why did she feel like a hornet's nest had just been shaken up inside her stomach?

Chapter Twenty-Six

Ella tried the landline again, but Coop still didn't pick up. Strange. She told him she'd call when she was on her way with a more accurate ETA. He said he'd keep the handset at the cabin with him, or she could reach him on his cell if he was already in town, but both went straight to voice mail.

Well, Coop wasn't the greatest at checking messages.

Still. An uncomfortable feeling jabbed at her insides.

Butch and Orland sat at the bar, Dylan working the evening shift. They hadn't seen or heard from Coop either.

Andy and Hank had joined them, and they all gathered around a table, the ladies discussing the first two chapters of *Rio Grande Romp* that they had read out loud on the way back to Red River.

"Told you they'd get back together," Miranda said with a smug laugh.

"They're not exactly back together. They had sex again, but they're not back together," said Brianna.

"They did it in his office on the exam table, with a room full of patients sitting in the waiting room. I'd call that back together," huffed Miranda.

"I'd call it malpractice," Hank said. "What kind of doctor would do something like that to one of his patients when he was just supposed to be adjusting her spine?"

Donna snorted. "I'd say he adjusted her, all right. In several places."

Hank rolled his eyes. "I still don't understand why you ladies read that trash. Seriously, if a doctor did that kind of thing in real life, he'd lose his license. Maybe even go to jail."

Ella's stomach did a flip. *Oh, my God.* What had she done?

The front door of Joe's slammed open, and Coop stormed toward them.

Ella froze.

His look of thunder and anger and hatred was directed solely at her, and she knew. She just knew. A deep, jagged pain crawled from her stomach up into her chest and crushed her heart into dust before Coop could even speak the first word. He didn't have to, because she had already guessed what he was going to say.

"How could you?" Coop stopped short in front of their table, glaring at her as if she were the only person in the cavernous room.

The entire place went quiet, and all heads turned in their direction. The world melted away, and it was just Ella and Coop and his awful stare of contempt. He was so indignant, so scornful, so obviously betrayed, that he wasn't using his head. His emotions had taken over, and his stare was a little crazed.

"It's you. You're Violet Vixen. And you didn't have the decency to tell me."

Every woman at the table gasped except Ella. Probably out of disbelief that Coop could accuse her of something so ridiculous, at least in their minds.

"Coop . . ." Ella stood slowly, cautiously.

"You used me for material for your ridiculous books. You knew what it could do to my case, and you did it anyway."

Ross stood. "Back down, buddy. I think you're out of line." Ross's entire countenance bowed, his fist contracted like he might coldcock Coop.

"Ross, it's okay," Ella said without taking her eyes off Coop. Coop needed to blow off some steam, get it off his chest, and she didn't blame him. But this wasn't the place, and he'd already said too much.

"Why don't we go outside, Coop?" Ella asked, her voice cautious.

Coop's brow wrinkled. "I'm not going anywhere with you."

"Ella's not Violet Vixen." Donna blew out a blustery breath. "What's wrong with you, Coop?"

"Ask her yourself," he challenged Donna without his eyes leaving Ella.

All eyes turned toward her.

"It's true." She looked at Coop. "Not the part about me using you, but the part about me being Violet Vixen."

Gasps rounded the table again, and murmurs rippled through Joe's like a human wave at a major league baseball game.

"*You're* Violet Vixen?" Lorenda said, clearly in shock.

"That's so awesome. My friend is Violet Vixen," said Brianna, more in awe than anything else.

Miranda whistled. "You really are one bad-ass chick."

Ella raised a hand to hold her friends at bay. Now wasn't the time to deal with them and their onslaught of questions. Her first priority, her first concern, was Coop.

"Coop, no one knew." She tried to find words, but they all seemed shallow. His life, his future, his career was hanging in the balance, and she'd just given incriminating intel to the enemy camp that could send him away for a long time for a crime he didn't commit.

The erotic scenes in her book had flowed onto the page after the first seductive dance they'd shared at Joe's. Why had she done it? She'd known it was dangerous, but sex with Coop had been so good. He'd coaxed her out of her shell and made her feel so sensual. She'd acted out a few of her fantasies with him, and tried to live a little dangerously for once in her life.

Her boring and predictable life.

"No one knew? That's all you have to say for yourself? What about my birthmark, Ella? And the mole under my eye? Every woman I've been with will know it's me once they read that excerpt. Didn't you think of that?"

"No one knew until *now*," Hank murmured, crossing his arms over his chest. "And it seems to me that that's on you, Coop. I'm not fond of those books, but you're the one that just announced it to the world."

Coop looked like he wanted to slug someone. Anyone. The muscle in his jaw clenched and released in cadence. "At the post office you said you didn't want to be at the mercy of others, but you sure as hell don't mind me being at yours, do you?"

"No! No, that's not what I meant." Ella took a step toward him, but he backed away. "I, I . . . you don't like needy women, and I didn't want to chase you away. I didn't want it to end." Her voice was an urgent whisper.

"You couldn't come up with more original material on your own? You had to use me as your sex toy to find new material to write about, since Bradley's dead?"

That hurt. A small cry caught in Ella's throat. "Coop, I never did any of those things. Not with anyone but you."

"Is that why you came to Red River to begin with? To get me to fuck you so you could finish your damn books and make a fortune at my expense?"

Ella's eyes filled with tears, and all the air rushed from her lungs. "I'm sorry—" She choked on a strangled cry. "I didn't think anyone would find out."

"I think that's just about enough," Ross said.

Butch walked over to the table. "What's going on here?"

"Wait." Donna was still trying to catch up. "You two are sleeping together?"

Lorenda rolled her eyes. "What planet are you on, Donna?"

Coop's expression turned to repugnance as his eyes stayed locked on to Ella. "Not anymore." Then he turned to Ross. "She's all yours, pal. Maybe you can be her muse for book four. She really likes it on the kitchen table."

Ross took a step toward him, but Butch got between them. He looked at Coop with a deadly stare. "What's this all about, son?"

Coop looked around the table. Every person there wore a horrified expression.

"Nothing, Dad. I'm done here, done with everyone." Cooper Wells turned on his heel and strode out the front door, leaving an ocean of gaping mouths and one heartbroken bestselling author in his wake.

A week later, Ella packed up a few more of her things. She'd allowed herself to get so comfortable at the cabin that her belongings were tucked in drawers and on shelves throughout the place. But most of her things had migrated into Coop's bedroom.

She sighed and ran a hand over the soft, rumpled quilt on his bed. The one she'd grown so fond of sleeping under while wrapped around him like bark on a tree. She couldn't remember when his messy habits had stopped annoying her and gave her a sense of comfort and belonging instead. Their clothes, their belongings, had mingled and mixed until they blurred together. His and hers had become theirs.

It would take some effort to sort through every room and gather up her things, so she started in Coop's bedroom. Maybe it would be easier if she finished with that room first, the room where they'd made so many good memories together. She boxed up everything of hers that she could find, took one last look at the bed they'd so easily and comfortably shared, and closed the door behind her.

In her room, she got down on her hands and knees to search under the bed, just to make sure she didn't overlook any of her possessions. Until a week ago, she hadn't slept in there for a while, not since Coop had insisted she move into his room and share his bed every night. There was something under the bed, but she couldn't see what it was, exactly.

She went looking for something long and slender that could reach that far up under the bed. In the hall closet, she found Coop's baseball bat and returned to her room to fish out whatever was there. When it finally caught on the end of the bat and she was able to pull it out, she sat back on her feet and choked back fresh tears.

In one hand she held the bat that Coop had used to defend himself the night she arrived. In the other, she clutched the shoe he'd dug out of the muddy ditch she'd gotten stuck in that first night. It was clean now, and she tossed it into a suitcase.

She wandered down the hall and returned the bat to its home in the closet.

Coop hadn't come back to the cabin since that day at Joe's. Instead, he sent Cal to pack a few clothes for him. Cal tried to make excuses for his older brother, but Ella told him it was okay. She was fine. Cal left with an apology.

The worst part was Winston. Okay, maybe not the worst, *worst* part, but Winston had been a slobbering sad sack since Coop left and took Atlas with him. *I guess Coop was tired of both him and his dog being sex objects.*

Ella found Winston moping in a corner on top of Atlas's favorite squeaky toy. She bent down to scratch him behind the ears. "I know how you feel, buddy." Winston gave a pathetic whine. "You'll just have to find another companion. Maybe a cute Great Dane next time." She chuckled, but Winston just stared wistfully at the wall.

A knock sounded at the door, and Ella left the packing for later.

"Hi." She let Lorenda in. "What's up?"

"I was elected to see how our favorite author is doing," Lorenda said.

Ella's brow arched.

"Okay, I told the other gals to stay away. They're not exactly the most tactful bunch of ladies I've ever known, and I didn't want you to get upset."

Ella's brow rose higher.

"Okay, *more* upset. They're really worried about you, and they sent comfort food." She held up a sack from the Red River Market and unloaded two pints of Blue Bell on the counter, along with plastic spoons and napkins.

"What flavor do you want?" asked Lorenda.

"Cookies 'n Cream. Is there any other?"

Lorenda took the lids off, shoved a spoon in each one, and handed Ella a container. "Cheers." They bumped pints.

"I'm doing fine. Really." *So not doing fine.* "Do you know how Coop's doing? He won't answer my calls."

"He's kept a low profile. Miranda's seen him at work, of course, but everybody's giving him a wide berth. He's not saying much. He mostly just stews quietly."

Ella sighed. "Well, I'm almost done packing, so I can leave any day now." Ella scooped a chunk of ice cream into her mouth and talked with her mouth full. What the heck? She was guilty of much worse than talking with her mouth full and wallowing in self-pity.

"You sure you have to go?" Lorenda asked. "I mean, maybe you should stay until you and Coop can settle things."

Ella shrugged. "In case you didn't notice at Joe's, Coop settled things right there."

"He's just angry because he cares about you. People lash out when they're hurt. Maybe he'll listen when he cools down."

Ella shook her head. "I don't think so. I mean, can you blame him? I've probably ruined his life."

"People make mistakes, Ella. He's certainly made his, and you didn't hold it against him."

No. No, she didn't, and she could have. But still . . .

Lorenda shrugged, snagging another bite of ice cream. "Well, he didn't seem to mind all the great sex until he read it in print."

"I doubt he thought our sex life would end up in a book for the world to see." She looked at the ice cream label. "Yum, this is good. You're my new BFF. Anyone thoughtful enough to bring me Cookies 'n Cream after a public humiliation is a friendship forged in blood. Like when guys in the movies slice their palms with a knife and then shake on it."

"You said you're sorry," Lorenda said.

And Ella really was sorry. The regret gnawed her to the bone.

"You may be right, but it takes two to work things out. He's made it clear that he doesn't want to accept my apology."

"I know it might not be what you want to hear right now, because you clearly have feelings for him, but you obviously didn't give a second thought to the accusations against him. If he can't find it in his heart to at least listen to you, then maybe you're better off," said Lorenda.

Ella inhaled deeply. "It's my own fault. I shouldn't have written our intimate details into a book without him knowing. Plus, I knew getting involved with him was probably a dead-end road, but for the first time in my life, I wanted to live on the edge. Take a risk, throw caution to the wind and experience life going Mach five with my hair on fire. I rolled the dice and I lost. Now I've got to move on. It's what

I came here to do anyway. It's just going to be a little harder now. I wanted closure with this cabin, and now I have it, just not in the way I thought."

"Any idea where you're going?"

Ella shook her head. "Not permanently. I promised my family I'd come home for a visit, so I think I'll drive to East Texas and stay there for a few weeks. Maybe a month." She laughed. "It might take that long to smooth things over with my Southern Baptist family now that they know about my new profession." She shrugged. "After that, I don't know where I'll end up. My editor wants me to move to California because there's been some chatter about turning the books into screenplays. She says LA is the perfect place for me right now, but I don't know. Maybe. Maybe not."

Ella shoveled another bite into her mouth. "Where do they make this stuff?" She held up her pint. "Maybe I'll move there. That would be convenient."

"Well, we're planning a going-away party for you at Joe's Saturday night."

Ella smiled. "Awww, you guys are so sweet. Thanks, but I'm not really in much of a party mood."

Lorenda tried to cheer her up. "Well now, that's the point of the party. You will be afterward, and just so you know, we asked Joe to give Coop that night off. We're trying to keep our plans quiet."

Ella cocked a brow in you've-got-to-be-kidding-me disbelief. "Good luck with that. You think you can keep it quiet in this town?"

"We're giving it a shot." Lorenda shrugged. "And, we're looking out for Coop, too. Ross might do him bodily harm if he talks to you again the way he did at Joe's the other day."

"I wouldn't worry too much if I were you. I don't think Coop will come within a thousand yards of any place if he knows I'm there."

Chapter Twenty-Seven

Coop wiped down the bar and frowned as two Red River residents walked past him with curious looks and knowing smiles on their way to find a table. Those looks had become the norm since Ella had turned him into a walking freak show in her latest book. The excitement of having a local celebrity in their midst had stirred the town into a buzz of energy. The word had spread like a raging forest fire, and it had even made it into several national magazines. In his rage, he'd blown Ella's cover, and probably ruined himself in the process.

Maybe he'd been a little cruel, his words a little over-the-top when he confronted Ella the other day. But no one could imagine the shock that coursed through him when he'd gotten to the last quarter of *Rio Grande Romp* and the familiarity of those chapters started to sink in. When he'd finished the novel and read the excerpt for book four, Coop had nearly choked.

He'd dropped his new e-reader on the floor, fumbled for it, and flipped back through some of the pages he'd just read. After rereading the excerpt, there was no mistaking whom the author was, but he still couldn't bring himself to believe it. Until he sat in stunned silence, staring down at the backlit text and the author's bio. All the pieces fell into place.

Of course. The author was from New Mexico and lived with an English bulldog. No mention of a husband, because Bradley was gone. Had Bradley known? Coop couldn't imagine that he did.

He thought back to the day at the post office. An envelope from Wanton Publishing had come for her, the same publisher as the books. Probably a royalty check. Judas money. When she'd tucked it under her arm, it should've chinked like thirty pieces of silver.

Now it all made sense. That's what she'd been doing on her laptop. That's why she didn't have to go back to a teaching job. That's why she was here in Red River ruining his life, putting his future in jeopardy. All to make more money off her books.

After Kim, he'd vowed not to get sucked in by another conniving female, but he'd done just that. He probably could've handled the situation a little more discreetly, but still, she had it coming. Ella had lied to him, manipulated him, and then knifed him in the chest. Almost literally. He'd felt the blood drain from his chest like his heart had been ripped out when he realized the extent of her deceit.

He'd been crashing on Butch's sofa the past week and intended to do so until Ella left Red River. He didn't know when that would be; fall was still several weeks away. But he'd have to tough it out, because he wasn't about to share a cabin with her anymore. If she didn't leave soon, he'd see if she would buy him out and he'd rent a place. She obviously had the money.

And he wasn't about to return any of the half dozen calls from her that he'd let go to voice mail.

So why did he feel so crummy about it all? About the way he'd talked to her, about the thought of her leaving and not sharing his bed anymore? Every night when he bedded down on his dad's sofa, he felt a mixture of regret and anger, because no matter how mad he was at her, no matter how badly she'd betrayed him, he wanted her with him. In his bed. Every night.

He dried another glass and slammed it on the shelf.

Butch and Orland sidled up to the bar, and they both ordered the usual. Coop filled two frosty mugs with Budweiser and topped off the foam.

"Still haven't come to your senses?" Orland asked.

"Excuse me?" Coop asked.

"Ella," Orland said, like just mentioning the name was self-explanatory. "You still haven't talked to her?"

"I have nothing to say to Ella Dennings," Coop said flatly.

"Sure you do." Orland drew on his beer. "You got plenty to say to her. Some of it nice, some of it not so much. Either way, get it off your chest and move on, before it's too late."

"After what she did? You think I should just get over it? Talk it out like she forgot to mention breaking an old fishing rod or something?" Coop tried to keep his voice calm but wasn't exactly successful.

Orland thought about it for a moment. "Yeah," he finally said. "I do."

Butch just sat quietly. Coop figured it was because his dad wasn't exactly an expert on getting relationships to work out with a happily-ever-after ending.

"And what if I end up in court with her book being used as evidence against me?"

Orland shrugged. "Maybe she should've asked before she put her . . . uh . . . experiences with you in her book for the entire world to read, but it's not exactly her fault if you end up in court to begin with. That one's on you, buddy."

"I didn't force myself on Kim Arrington," Coop hissed.

"I believe you and so does everybody else in Red River, but that doesn't matter," said Orland.

Coop tossed the bar towel over one shoulder and folded his arms across his chest. "Really? Then what does matter?"

For the first time since the two old geezers sat down, Butch spoke up. "What matters is that Ella gave you the benefit of the doubt when none of your so-called friends back in Albuquerque would even speak to you." Butch set his beer down on the bar and measured his words carefully. "Son, I've never talked much about your mother. Mostly because you didn't want to hear it. But that was the easy way out for me. I'm your father and I should've made you listen. You've blamed your mother all these years, but I could've easily gotten her to stay with me, with us. I was just too selfish at the time to listen to her needs. She didn't ask for much. If I'd thought of her a little more, she would've stayed. I realized that after I got over being angry when she left. It took me about a year, but I drove out to California to get her. It was too late."

Coop's mind raced. "You . . . wait . . . you went to California to get her back?"

"Yes, I did."

"But, when? I don't remember that."

"You and Bradley went to baseball camp the year after she left. You were in El Paso for a week. That's when I drove out there to win her back. I told her I'd start considering what she wanted, what made her happy. Promised her I'd change and start thinking more of her, take her on a vacation besides Red River, maybe even go to one of those romantic movies once in a while."

Coop was still trying to wrap his mind around it. "But she didn't come back with you. What happened?"

"She'd already moved on. Started over. She said if I'd told her that before she left Albuquerque, there might've been a chance for us. But I was too stubborn and selfish and I refused." Butch took another long drink, letting the memories form into words. "Her heart was already too hardened toward me because of what I'd put her through. And because I let you believe it was all her fault. She didn't want me anymore."

"It *was* her fault, Dad."

Butch shook his head. "No, son. You can't dance a two-step alone. But I took the coward's way out and let you believe that. She was the best thing that ever happened to me, and I let her go without trying to get her to stay and work it out. I was a fool. So everything that happened after that was my fault. Getting married again so many times, putting you through all that, that was my desperate attempt to forget that I messed up. The only good thing that came out of all my stupidity was you and Cal."

Coop just stared at his dad, disbelief spiraling around his head like smoke. "Why didn't you ever tell me this?" Coop whispered.

"I tried a few times, but you'd get mad and storm out. I guess I didn't really know how to make you listen, or maybe I just didn't want to. But it's time you hear it anyway, because the best thing that's ever happened to you is packing up her things as we speak to leave town. Probably for good."

Coop tried to wrap his head around *that*. So much wrapping in such a short span of time was making his brain hurt. "Ella's packing? To leave?"

"That's what I hear," Butch said as he downed another drink from his mug.

Orland added, "They're having a going-away party for her right here at Joe's. You're not invited, by the way, since it's supposed to be a happy occasion and all. But you didn't hear that from us."

Coop pulled into his usual parking spot behind the cabin, but Ella's new SUV was gone. His chest tightened, and he stared at the back door. What if he was too late?

Atlas whined, easing his head over the console from the backseat, and licked at Coop. Coop looked at him and chuckled. "You missed home, huh?" He scratched Atlas's head. "So do I," he said and looked at the cabin again.

He should go inside, but he was afraid of what he would find in there. Or not find. If Ella was already gone, he didn't want to face how royally he'd screwed up.

Reluctantly, he got out of the truck and opened the back passenger door for Atlas, who bounded out and made for the cabin like a flash of lightning. As soon as Coop's boot connected with the first step, Winston's deep bark rumbled on the other side of the door.

Relief surged through him. Ella was still in town.

Atlas jumped and barked at the door while Coop unlocked it. When he finally pushed it open, the two dogs tumbled across the floor like two long-lost soul mates that had been separated for an eternity. Coop laughed.

They were inseparable, and Atlas had moped around for days without Winston. Kind of like him without Ella.

Atlas and Winston obviously loved each other. And Coop loved Ella.

The realization hit him square in the chest and knocked the air from his lungs.

He glanced around the cabin and rubbed at his chest, trying hard to catch his breath. When Ella moved into the cabin a few months ago, she didn't have a lot of belongings with her. Several suitcases of clothes, a few small boxes of personal possessions that she didn't want to put in storage, her weapons, which he was well acquainted with, and her laptop. But she'd obviously been packing, giving the cabin an empty, lifeless feel.

He set his keys down on the counter, and an envelope with his name scrawled on it caught his eye. He picked it up and ran his thumb over Ella's looping handwriting. So creative and artsy-looking, the letters so large and flowing that just his four-letter nickname covered the entire front of the white envelope. So her.

She'd left her imprint on his heart the same way she'd scrawled it across the envelope. He lifted it to his nose and breathed in. Her scent wafted around him, and he closed his eyes to let her image dance under his eyelids.

Shaking himself back to reality, he inserted a finger under the lip of the envelope and tore it open.

The deed to the cabin—signed over to him, notarized, and already filed at the Taos County Clerk's Office. Three weeks ago.

Attached was a note in Ella's handwriting.

Dear Coop,

It's yours. Bradley would've wanted you to have it, and so do I. For what it's worth, I didn't use you for material to put in my books. But you did inspire me to love again, something I wasn't sure I could do after losing Bradley. Please don't let my mistake rob you of finding love again either. You have so much of it to give when you find the right person.

Take care of yourself,
Ella

A small lump remained inside the envelope. He turned it over, and the small gold necklace he'd given her for her birthday slid out and dinged against the counter. He hadn't had more than a few minutes to shop when he found out it was her birthday at the very last moment. He'd driven to the nicest gift shop in Red River and picked out this petite charm. The simple gracefulness of it matched her. The shape represented his heart, which she had conquered like it was the spoils of victory.

The landline rang, jarring his thoughts. He grabbed for it.

"Hello."

"Coop, it's Angelique. Got good news for you." Her voice beamed with victory.

"Okay," was all Coop could say.

"Kim Arrington just dropped the criminal complaint and the civil suit against you. It's over, buddy."

Coop stood rooted in place, frozen in time.

"Coop? Are you there?"

"Uh, yeah, yeah, I'm here. That's great news, Angelique, really."

"Okaaaaay. Then why do you sound like you just got a death sentence with no stay of execution?"

Jesus, criminal defense lawyers. So melodramatic. "No, I really am happy. You've done an amazing job for me. I'm just in shock, that's all." He tried to gather his thoughts. "When . . . how did all this happen?"

"I had a little chat with her attorney and reminded him what a weak case they had, especially since she changed her story."

"I thought all kinds of crap would hit the fan at full speed after the book scandal made the news," Coop said.

Two days after he'd confronted Ella, he had to call Angelique with his tail between his legs and confess the truth. After she ripped him up one side and down another, she made some comment about being impressed that his sexual prowess was good enough to end up in a bestselling series of erotic novels. Then she told him to stop being an idiot and to start thinking with his brain instead of his prick. Every warped female in the world would want a chance to get in his bed now. And when crazy groupies thought there was money to be made, they'd line up to take a shot at him.

He shuddered at the thought, and not just because he didn't want to be accused of anything else he hadn't done. When he thought about getting in bed with a woman, Ella's face was the only one he could picture in his mind.

"Why didn't Kim and her attorney try to use it against me?" Coop scrubbed a hand over his jaw.

"Oh, he wanted to, pal. But your new girlfriend's offer to testify as a character witness in your defense stymied that strategy."

Coop's conscience prickled. "You mean Ella?"

"Yep." Papers shuffled in the background.

"She's my ex-girlfriend, and what are you talking about?"

"Uh, I thought you knew." Angelique hesitated. "She called me. Offered to testify that the, uh, things in the book didn't actually take place in your office, but in a cabin you own jointly. It was the deathblow to Kim's case. Her attorney knew they couldn't win, so he talked some sense into her."

Coop inhaled and rubbed his eyes with a thumb and index finger. Ella had stepped up for him.

"I talked to my connection down at the police station, and they said Kim came in with her attorney." Angelique's voice got a little sing-song tone to it. "She was sporting about a two-carat diamond on her left hand, and was all fake-weeping and clinging to her new dentist-fiancé. Said they didn't want the pain of going through the ugly details in court. They just wanted to get on with their new lives together."

"Poor schmuck," mumbled Coop.

"Yeah, looks like she found herself another sugar daddy that she doesn't have to sue for attention. My friend at the precinct said her fiancé followed her around like a lovesick puppy."

"Sounds like a match made in heaven," Coop said.

"So, my friend, case closed. All we have to do now is get your license back. I'm drafting a letter to the state board as soon as we hang up. Oh, and Kim sent you a message through her attorney. She said to tell you 'no hard feelings.' Funny, huh?"

Yeah, hysterical. "That's the best news I've heard in a long time, Angelique. Thanks." He looked down at the deed in his hand.

"Sure thing, bud. Just keep your nose clean, would you? You got seriously lucky this time. Not heeding my advice about sleeping with your roommate could've come back to bite you in that nice little ass of yours that she wrote about." More papers shuffling from her end. "It's not my place to tell you this, but I'm a nervy Italian so I'm going to say it anyway."

He smiled to himself. Nervy females who didn't think twice about putting him in his place were growing on him lately.

"You kind of made yourself a target, ya know? If you'll exercise better judgment when it comes to your love life, you won't need me again. Find yourself a nice girl and settle down. Sorry it didn't work out with Ella, by the way. She seemed to really care about you, and you two obviously had a lot of, uh, chemistry together."

"What about you, Ang, are you interested?" he joked.

"Not even a little," she bantered back. "Seriously, it's not like you don't have the goods to make it happen."

"You're one to talk," Coop said playfully. And she was. Angelique Barbetta was a thirty-year-old beauty of Italian descent. Dark, exotic looks, long legs, knockout figure. Yet she was still single. A highly intelligent attorney with a killer instinct, most men were probably scared to death of her.

"I'm seeing someone, actually. Another attorney here at my firm. I think he might be the one. We'll see. He's an Italian that moved here from New Jersey, so my mom's already planning a huge Catholic wedding."

"That's great, Angelique. I hope it works out. Just invite me to the wedding."

He heard her nails clicking against a keyboard. "Okay, enough about me. I gotta go, so I can actually do my job. I'll let you know when I hear from the board. Oh, and I might see you up in Red River sometime. I'm about to close on a vacation property up there."

"Will do. We can hit the slopes together this winter. Does your boyfriend ski?"

"Yep." The clicking got faster.

"All right, Ang. See you soon."

"Not if I see you first, Wells."

He laughed and hung up the phone. Now he had everything he'd thought he wanted just two months ago. Full ownership of the cabin, no criminal record, no lawsuit pending against him, his career and his life back, and, most of all, no woman in his life. Everything he thought he wanted before Ella Dennings showed up on the doorstep soaking wet and nearly blinded him with pepper spray.

So, why did he feel like dirt?

Refolding the deed, he returned it to the envelope along with the necklace. Coop picked up the phone and dialed a number he hadn't even thought of dialing most of his life. It rang a few times, and then an older female voice answered.

"Mom? It's Coop." He heard her stifle a gasp, and he hesitated. "How are you?"

"I . . . I'm good, honey." Her voice shook. "How are *you*?"

"I'm good, Mom. I just wanted to talk to you. You know, hear your voice. It's been a long time."

And for the first time since he was ten, his heart opened to the prospect of forgiveness and love.

Chapter Twenty-Eight

Ella sat in the waiting room at Ross's garage while he finished the maintenance on the Xterra. She opened her e-reader, but shut it off again after staring at the same page for fifteen minutes without reading a word.

She'd hoped Coop would stop by the cabin when he'd cooled off. Or at least call. Ella didn't want to leave things so . . . so fouled up. And that's exactly what it was. "F'ed" up in the worst possible way. Even if he couldn't forgive her, she'd wanted to at least talk one more time before going their separate ways. And Ella had a few things she needed to say to Coop, some of which he probably wouldn't want to hear because it involved words like "double standards." But, no. Nothing.

It was over.

And, really, what had she expected? Coop wasn't the type to fall in love or get entangled in a long-term commitment, but he'd been willing to *try* with her. He hadn't said he loved her, but he'd shown her in so many ways, and she'd let him down. Now she'd have to pick up the pieces of her own broken heart all over again, because she'd fallen so hard for him.

He just looked so damned good in those midnight-blue boxer briefs the first night she got to the cabin. And it had been so long since she'd . . .

Her face grew hot.

Yep. She was definitely a blockhead. Having two degrees and graduating summa cum laude might be proof she was intelligent. Didn't make her smart, though.

But it was so true. Sex with Bradley had always been good. Great, in fact. But different. Falling for the bad boy this time around had sent her pulse racing at speeds that broke the sound barrier. And the way Coop touched her, the way he made love to her, went far beyond affectionate, tender lovemaking. It was hot and seductive and seared her to the core until she never wanted to let anyone else touch her but him. Never wanted to let anyone else love her, because she'd never be able to completely get over Cooper Wells.

She sighed.

Never was a long time.

Okay, she was far more stupid than a mere blockhead. She was a complete imbecile. She just wished Coop would give her *some* credit. She'd believed him, his innocence had never been a question in her mind. Shouldn't her loyalty count for something?

She blew out another heavy sigh.

He'd been awful and cruel and lashed out at her in front of the entire town. And why? Because she deserved it. *Selfish ass.* Okay, not really, but it made her feel better to think it.

If he was a selfish ass, then she was pathetic.

And she was pathetically in love with that selfish ass.

Another hearty sigh had the customer sitting next to Ella shooting worried looks in her direction, like she thought Ella was some psycho who needed medication. Well, she probably did, if there was medication for stupidity. The other customer scooted a little farther away.

Ross walked in, wearing coveralls. He wiped his greasy hands on an even greasier towel.

"Mrs. O'Connor, your car is ready. If you'll wait out front, we'll drive it around to you."

Mrs. O'Connor darted for the door without so much as saying "Thank you." Not one hair in her beehive hairdo moved when a cold rush of air blasted through the open door.

"Ella, I'm almost done servicing your Xterra. It's in good shape, being new and all."

"Thanks, Ross. It was too far to drive it back to the dealership in Santa Fe, and I just wanted to have it checked over before I get out on the road. East Texas is a long drive."

"Always smart to check the tires and fluids before a trip." He hesitated, studying her. "You sure you have to go so soon? I can let you stay in one of my rental cabins as long as you like."

She smiled at him. "That's sweet, Ross, really, but there's no reason to prolong the inevitable. I might as well get on with my life." And she should, because she didn't have a future in Red River. Memories of Coop would overshadow any chance of a future with someone else, the same way memories of Bradley would have if she'd stayed in Albuquerque.

Starting over in a new city, making new friends, meeting new people, maybe even finding a group of romance writers that she could connect with now that she'd been outed as Violet Vixen, would all take time. She might as well get started right after a trip to see her family. Preferably in a town that contained a healthy population of straight guys who didn't mind that she was an erotic romance novelist, because she certainly wasn't going to try to hide it anymore. And she definitely wasn't going to feel guilty or ashamed, either. Her writing was what got her through some pretty dark times during Bradley's illness. It had saved her, really.

So she had allowed herself to get sidetracked briefly when she thought she might actually have a future with Coop. Back to her original plan. It was a good plan. Why not stick to it? She'd lived dangerously for a few months, gotten it out of her system. Obviously, she sucked at living life on the edge.

Boring and predictable. That was her.

"I just hate to see you leave town this way," Ross said, still wiping his hands. "Can I at least take you to dinner tonight? Your going-away party isn't until tomorrow, so you can at least let me feed you."

Ella pasted on the best fake smile she could manage. "You've been a good friend, Ross. I'd like that."

Back at the cabin, Ella loaded a few suitcases into the trunk and slammed it shut.

She looked around at the landscape. The sky grew vaguely dark to the north, and the scent of late summer rain hung in the air, hinting at a coming storm. Great. If it rained tonight, she'd have a hard time leaving the day after tomorrow, but she had a four-wheel drive now. That would help. She wandered up onto the porch and gathered her windbreaker around her.

It was mid-August, and summer was still raging around most of the country. But out here in the Rockies, a few leaves were already tinged with yellow and orange, and the distinct scent of autumn rose in the evening air, tickling the walls of her chest with a sense of yearning. A good time to go, she guessed, before the temperatures dropped, chasing away the last remnants of summer.

Ella walked back inside. She stopped at the bar, and frowned.

Something was different than when she left here earlier for Ross's shop. She looked around, and a light dawned.

The deed was gone.

She searched the floors, the countertops. Nothing.

Huh. Had Coop been to the cabin?

The sound of a truck thundering down the drive had her peeking out the window, just as Coop pulled in next to her SUV. Her heart thudded. This was what she'd wanted, a chance to talk to him one more time. A brave woman would stand her ground and look him in the eye. Say her piece, apologize again, even if it fell on deaf ears.

Ella turned and ran for the basement.

You're a wuss, Dennings.

Yes. Yes, she was, because she was afraid of the hostility that might show in his eyes again. Bravery was in short supply these days. She'd used up too much of it already seeing Bradley's illness through to the end, then losing her heart all over again to Coop. He was probably just here to pick up more of his clothes, anyway. She'd let him and stay out of his way.

Wuss.

Calling Winston to follow, Ella closed the basement door and prayed Coop would think she was out for a walk.

She sat for a moment, listening. She tensed when Coop's footsteps sounded above. Slow and shuffling, not someone who was there for a specific purpose. She looked at one of the boxes she'd brought with her. A box of photo albums that she hadn't wanted to put in storage. Pulling one album out, she flipped through it, waiting for Coop's footsteps to recede as he left.

Mostly pictures of her and Bradley. A few of her family.

When she looked at Bradley's picture now, she felt love, but she also felt closure. Well, mission accomplished. She came here to let Bradley go, and she'd done that. Too bad she'd fallen for his best friend and messed up her life even more.

Ella wondered if Bradley would be disappointed that she'd had an affair with Coop. Probably not, if it had worked out. He'd loved them both. At first she'd felt guilty about lusting after his best friend. But then lust turned to love, and she knew Bradley would've approved.

Winston whined and bounded for the door. Urgent scratching came from the other side. Frick. The basement door opened and footsteps sounded on the stairs. Atlas and Winston wrestled and chased each other back down the stairs, so happy to be together again.

She held her breath.

And then there he was. All brooding and hot in his faded jeans and plain red T-shirt. His caramel hair and five o'clock shadow, just long enough to look carelessly seductive. He crammed his hands into his pockets.

"Hi." That's all he said, and then he just stared at her and blinked. Several times.

"Um, hi." She stared back.

"What are you doing down here?" he asked, looking at the photo album in her hand.

"I, um, put these down here when I first arrived. They're photos of Bradley, and I didn't want to leave them in storage." She shrugged. "I wasn't sure how long it would take me to get settled, you know, how long my stuff will stay in storage. So, I brought these with me. They're irreplaceable." To stop rambling, Ella bit her lip.

He just stared and brooded some more.

"Well, uh, I'll be out of your way day after tomorrow. You can move back in and all."

"Why didn't you and Bradley have a kid?" he blurted.

"I . . . um . . . what?"

"You love kids, right? You want a few, I guess. Why didn't you and Bradley have one?"

A few raindrops pinged the outside of the cabin, and Coop's words pinged around in her brain. She had no clue what he was trying to say. "We tried for a few months. Then he was diagnosed."

"Is that why you weren't on birth control?"

She bristled, a hand going to her hip. "Yes. That, and I didn't need to be, since I wasn't sleeping around. Until I met up with you, that is." Her confusion started to turn to anger. "Wait. Why?"

"Bradley would've been a great father. I would probably suck at it."

Now she was furious. On top of everything else he'd said, all the vile things he'd accused her of without giving her a chance to explain, without listening to her apology, he was throwing *this* in her face? "Is that what you thought I was doing? Trying to get pregnant?" A tremble started at her core and spread through her, the emotions she'd kept pent up for the last week ready to spew like hot lava. "Because I told you before we slept together that I wasn't on birth control. I was completely honest about it, and you didn't seem to mind at the time."

"No!" He ran fingers through his already-tousled hair. "No, it's just that there were a few times that we weren't very careful, and I was just thinking . . ."

"Thinking what, Coop? That I might try to trap you, the way your last girlfriend did? Because I assure you, if I were pregnant, I wouldn't ask you for a thing. Don't worry, I know what you're thinking. You're thinking that you don't want a kid, especially with me."

"Actually," he almost whispered, "I was thinking that if I ever did have a kid, I would only want to have it with you."

Chapter Twenty-Nine

The photo album swooshed from her hands and smacked the floor. Ella stared at him open-mouthed. Then the luscious strips of pink flesh that formed a perfect O thinned into a frown, and her eyes burned like hot coals.

A few pictures had shaken loose when the album hit the cement slab flooring. Ella bent over to gather them up. When she stood upright again, her green eyes had turned darker and looked ready to unleash a thousand fiery darts right at his chest.

"You've got to be kidding me." She clutched the album to her chest like it was a precious treasure. And he supposed it was.

That was the problem. He knew he loved her when they'd visited Aguas Rojas. Even though he hadn't told her, he still knew, and it scared him. Bradley was a great guy. The best. A good husband, would've been a great dad if he'd had the chance. An icon that Coop couldn't compete with. Wouldn't even try. And after he spoke to his mother, he had to admit to himself that that was his biggest fear of all. Not that Ella would let him down, because she wasn't that kind of woman. She stayed with Bradley through it all; she was loyal and good to him. And Coop knew that once she gave her heart to *him*, she'd do the same. She had done as much when she believed him, saw through his bullshit to his core and knew he wasn't a criminal. She'd given him her trust when all of his friends and colleagues back in Albuquerque had turned their backs on him. The ones he'd thought Bradley was an idiot to trade in for Ella. Turns out, Coop was the idiot, and Bradley knew exactly what he was doing.

Case in point—Bradley was a terrific guy, and Coop didn't hold a candle to him.

He was scared that he wouldn't ever measure up to Bradley. And as soon as Ella figured that out, she would grow tired of him. It wouldn't take long for Ella's superior intelligence to kick in. Coop could see that day coming in the not-so-distant future, and finally understood just how far out of his league Ella really was.

"You're here to talk about kids that we're never going to have together?"

"I—"

Ella cut him off.

"Well, let me tell you something, Cooper Wells." She clamped one hand to a curvy hip. The other clutched Bradley's photos so tight her knuckles turned white. Her face glowed crimson with anger. Still, in the fitted black leggings, black UGG boots, and long-sleeved Under Armour shirt that fit her like a second skin, he wanted her. She was gorgeous. And she belonged with him, even if he was just figuring that out. Coop had to confess, he'd been pretty slow on the uptake when it came to women, but Ella loved him. She'd said so when she thought he was asleep. He took a step closer to her, because if he could just pull her hair loose from that ponytail and run his fingers through it, taste her tongue with his, she'd stop being angry with him.

Right?

She held up a hand and glared at him. "Don't you take another step closer. I wanted kids. More than anything. With Bradley. Because, you're right." Her words clipped out, quickly gaining momentum. "He would've been a great dad. Loyal, trustworthy, there when the kids needed him and always there for me, even if I were wrong or made a mistake. But you wouldn't know anything about any of those things, would you, Coop?"

He eased another step closer.

"Do you have any idea what it was like watching him die a little more each day? Watching the real Bradley disappear until he was just an empty shell who didn't even resemble the man I married? No, you don't, because you weren't around. And you know what? I got over you not being there, because Bradley never held it against you. That's just the kind of guy he was. So I figured if he could understand and forgive you, then I could, too. And you know what else?"

Another step.

"Maybe I was even a little jealous that you didn't have to be there, watching it all happen the way I did. Because it was so hard, so hard that I wanted to run away some days and pretend that I'd never met Bradley Dennings." Her body started to tremble, her voice shook, and angry tears pooled in her eyes. "And then I'd get out these photos and sink into overwhelming guilt over having those thoughts about him."

Another step. She was just out of arm's reach, and the flowery soap she'd used in the shower this morning teased his senses, spiked his desire. She smelled fresh, like a summer breeze, and he wanted to fold her in his arms right there in the basement where they'd kissed for the first time so many years ago.

"That's why I escaped into those novels. They were a release for me. And not in a sexual way. They were an escape into a fantasy world of things I'd never had the courage to do. Writing those stories and creating those characters became my salvation. They saved me from the depression that was suffocating me and robbing me of my desire to live."

He took one more step, and he could touch her if he just reached out.

"So don't expect me to apologize for what I had to do to survive. I'm sorry that I hurt you, and even sorrier that I may have made your troubles worse. But I didn't want to have the same regrets with you that I had with Bradley. So I tried to actually *live* a few of those fantasies with you, because I didn't know where the future would lead us—"

And then he was kissing her, because, really, it seemed the only way to shut the woman up. His mouth moved over hers, tasting and exploring. And for a brief moment she was kissing him back, threading her fingers through his hair, something she loved to do every time they were together. That small sexy sound she made whenever they kissed escaped and he pulled her tight against him. Then the moment was gone, and she tensed, pulling out of his embrace.

It wasn't the first time a member of the female persuasion tried to slap his face. Her hand rose high in the air, but as it came down, he grabbed her wrist in midair. Their eyes locked, angry tears spilling over and streaking down her face.

"I love you, too," Coop said.

Ella's forehead wrinkled as she tried to process his words. "Huh?"

"I love you, too," he repeated, still holding her wrist.

"'Too'? I never said I loved you."

"Yes, you did."

"Uh, *no.* I didn't."

He nodded. "On your birthday, after we got back to the cabin. We made love, and when you thought I was asleep, you said it." His eyes raked over her face, her flame-throwing eyes, her hardened jaw. Her full lips that begged for a deep, hard kiss. "I love you, too, but I can never be the kind of man Bradley was. I lived and he didn't." It was bold and harsh, but it was true. "You said it yourself at Aguas

Rojas. We both loved him, and he would want us to move on. But I don't think either one of us has completely let him go. Can you do that, Ella? Can you really let him go? Or will I always feel like a cheap imitation of the real thing?"

A flicker of something dark raced through Ella's eyes, and he waited for a response. Slowly, she pulled her wrist from his grasp and took a step back.

With a fury that rocked him to the core, she breathed out a whisper. "Get. Out."

***

"You sure you want to stay here?" Ross asked later that night as they slid into a booth at Joe's. "We can go somewhere else, if you're uncomfortable."

Ella shook her head, her eyes bouncing quickly to the bar where Coop was working the evening shift, then back to Ross. "Nope. I'm good."

Coop's look had turned to stone when Ella walked in with Ross, and it had pricked her heart.

Miranda sauntered over to their table, handing out their usual drinks without waiting for them to order. Her thick black hair slid around her shoulders like a bolt of silky fabric. "Hey, you two. Out on a date?"

"Just friends," they said simultaneously and laughed.

"You two make a cute couple. I think you should call it a date." She raised a silky black brow.

"I know you want Coop to suffer a little, but I wouldn't use Ross that way. He's been too good a friend."

"I wouldn't mind being used." Ross shrugged playfully. "Probably be kind of fun."

Ella laughed. "Let's just keep it friendly, okay? I need friends more than I need a boyfriend right now."

"Sorry, buddy," Miranda said to Ross. "I tried."

Ross and Ella ordered, and Miranda walked toward the kitchen with a slinky saunter.

Donna stormed in and stalked toward them. She slid into the booth next to Ross, pushing him against the wall.

"Sure, have a seat," Ross said.

Donna ignored him. "Can you believe it? Hank has threatened to leave me if I don't stop reading your books. Says he's tired of being used like a sex toy. I mean, really? What straight man in his right mind wouldn't want his wife reading your books? After every chapter, I give him the best sex a guy could ask for. Only that's the problem. He doesn't ask for it, and he acts like it's an imposition for him."

Ross slammed down half his mug of beer in one large gulp.

"Um, Donna, maybe we should talk about this later." Ella gave Ross an apologetic look.

Donna plowed on without missing a beat. "I mean, come on! Our sex life was always good, in an ordinary, okay sort of way, but now it's soooo good I can't wait for him to get home every night after work."

Ross downed another huge gulp.

Lorenda walked up with her kids, but redirected them across the restaurant when she picked up the gist of the conversation. "Sorry, guys. Got to keep it G-rated tonight." She pointed to her two boys, who strolled to a table on the other side of Joe's.

Ella nodded at Lorenda and returned her attention to Donna. "Maybe that's the problem, Donna. I mean, those books are fiction. They're not real-life stories about real-life people." Well, okay. Some of it was based on real life, which was precisely the reason her own love life was in shambles. "Maybe you should dial it down a little. You know, give Hank time to catch up with you."

"Yeah, I think you might be scaring the poor guy. Just go a little slower, and eventually I'm sure he'll see the uh . . . fun in it all." Ross turned a little pink across the cheeks.

Andy and Brianna walked in holding hands. "You two want to join us?" Donna asked as they strolled past.

"No, we're on a date tonight," said Brianna.

"Yeah, we're on chapter eight." Andy winked at Ella. "Thanks, Violet."

She laughed. "Sure thing, buddy. What are friends for?"

Brianna and Andy found a spot for two in a secluded corner and held hands across the table.

"See?" huffed Donna. "They look like new lovebirds that just started dating. Why can't Hank get with the program?"

Ella shrugged. "Men can be numbskulls." She glanced at Ross. "No offense, bud."

"None taken," he said and took another swig of beer.

And speak of the devil—Hank walked in, a bouquet of flowers in his hand. He was dressed to kill in a new pair of finely starched and pressed jeans, a western shirt, and a black Stetson. He walked toward them sporting a determined look.

"Uh, Donna." Ella nodded in Hank's direction.

When Donna glanced over her shoulder, she stood and faced him, her mouth hanging open. Her hands went to her hips.

"Uh-oh," Ross said.

But instead of berating Hank, Donna threw her arms around his neck and all but screamed, "They're beautiful, Hank!"

"They're not for you," Hank said, with his trademark bland expression and monotone voice. "They're for her." His eyes still locked on to his wife, he thrust the bouquet at Ella.

"Uh, thanks?" Ella slowly reached out to take the bouquet, afraid she might draw back a nub by the glower on Donna's face.

"No," Hank said. "Thank *you*, Ella." He glanced at her with a strange look. "Or Violet . . . or whatever your name is." Then his eyes grew husky with lust as they latched on to his wife again. "Thank you for what you've done for our marriage."

A lilt of feminine "awws" circled the room.

"I've been an ass, Donna. Can you forgive me?"

"Of course, you handsome man, you," Donna said. "But what changed your mind?"

One side of Hank's mouth curved into a smile. "I read chapter three."

"Oh," Donna said with a knowing smile. "I definitely forgive you, then."

"Then this, little lady, is for you." Hank captured Donna in his arms and sank her back into a dip that would've made Fred Astaire and Ginger Rogers weep with pride. He laid a dreamy kiss on his wife. And stayed there. For a long, long time.

A round of cheers and claps went up around Joe's.

"Miranda," Ella called. "A round of drinks for everyone on me." It was the least she could do, after all. When her eyes grew wet, she picked at the flowers and cleared her throat.

"Okay, okay, you two, get a room," Dylan said as he walked by to deliver a tray of drinks for Miranda.

Without breaking the kiss, Hank flipped him the bird and then grabbed his wife's ass.

When they finally came up for air, Donna whispered, "Let's get outta here."

"Oh, thanks be to Jesus in heaven." Miranda rolled her eyes as she delivered another tray of drinks to the booth next to them and made the sign of the cross, but her mouth twitched up into a smile.

"Well, there you go." Ross raised his glass to Ella. "Who needs marriage counseling when they've got Violet Vixen?"

Ella smirked and glanced at Coop behind the bar. Serving up an endless supply of drinks, he still wore the same stony expression.

Some marriage counselor she'd make. Violet Vixen might be winning friends and influencing marriages around the globe, but she'd also cost Ella her heart. Her life was a bigger mess than anyone else's, and she had no one to blame but herself.

———

The next day Ella sat on the old fallen log in back of the cabin and stared at the shifting stream. She pulled Coop's gray hoodie tight around her, breathing in his scent. She'd leave it in the cabin when she moved out tomorrow, but tonight, just one more time, she wanted his presence wrapped around her.

On the highway, a vehicle slowed and turned onto the driveway. She held her breath until Butch's truck appeared and pulled to a stop. A sigh of relief escaped her, and she waved him over.

"Hi, Butch," she said, giving him a warm smile as he joined her on the log. "If you came to pick up more of Coop's things, I'll be gone soon, and he'll have the place to himself again."

"Nope." Butch shook his head, and stared at the stream, too. "I came by to see how you're doing." Crossing his legs at the ankles, he scratched his whiskered cheek. "It's peaceful here, isn't it?"

Ella nodded. "I'm glad I got to spend one last summer at this cabin." She let out a heavy sigh. "I'm sorry I made such a mess of things, Butch."

"It takes two, Ella." Both arms crossed over his chest as he gazed at the rustling leaves overhead. "You know, Bradley would be a tough act for anybody to follow. That kind of pressure might make any man have second thoughts."

She frowned. "I never compared Coop to Bradley." But Coop had accused her of it anyway.

"You don't have to. Coop knew Bradley better than anyone except you. The male ego is an interesting thing. More fragile than we men care to admit." He chuckled. "Take it from someone that's been married as many times as I have, we don't like being runner-up."

Ella bristled. "I didn't intentionally give Coop that impression, and the accusation is insulting, quite frankly. He won't listen to my apology for the things I *did* do wrong, I'm not about to apologize for his imagined offenses, too."

He patted her hand. "I'm not accusing you of anything, Ella. But I suspect Coop is doing a fine job comparing himself to Bradley all on his own."

"Well, it doesn't matter now. Coop doesn't want my apology because I've caused him so much trouble."

Butch exhaled. "Yeah." He nodded. "Yeah, you have. But he did a pretty good job of getting himself into trouble before you got to Red River. Seems to me if you found it in that big heart of yours to stay by Bradley's side until the end, you might be able to dig a little deeper and try to get that hard-headed son of mine to listen just one more time." He brushed a bug off his pants. "Just a thought. Your call." He stood. "So I'll see you tonight at the going-away party?"

Ella stood and gave him a hug. "Sure thing."

Waving as Butch backed up and drove away, she sat down on the log and covered her face with both hands. She just didn't have any more fight left in her. Even if Coop was ready to hear her apology, maybe even try again, how could she live torn between the love she'd had for Bradley and Coop's absurd fear of being second-best?

Tears spilled over and trekked down her cheeks. Damn it to hell, she was tired of crying over men. She'd arrived in Red River crying over the memory of one man she'd loved. Now she was leaving Red River crying over another man that she loved just as much.

She shook her head and dropped her forehead into her hands. No. Actually she loved Coop much more. Guilt washed through her. Coop was right. Neither one of them had let Bradley go. Not completely.

Chapter Thirty

Joe's was decked out with balloons and confetti. A banner hung over the bar that said, "We'll miss you, Ella," and the drinks and merriment flowed.

Becca, Carissa, and Marilyn drove up to Red River for the party and were spending Ella's last night at the cabin so they could see her off in the morning.

Lorenda and Becca discussed the real estate market and a possible venture between the two of them.

"Okay, you two real estate gurus. Stop talking shop," chastised Marilyn. "Tonight is about fun."

Becca rolled her eyes, turning her attention back to the crowd around their table. "So, are there any cute guys in East Texas?" she asked. "*Straight*, cute guys?" she clarified, since her first husband had inadvertently forgotten to tell her that he was batting for the other team.

"Who cares? I'm still pissed that our best friend in the whole world forgot to mention that she is a famous erotic romance writer." Carissa almost hummed. Even though she wore a scolding expression, the pride was evident in her tone. "How could you hold out on us like that?"

Ella shrugged innocently.

"Ella, you're my husband's favorite author, and he's never read your books," said Marilyn. "So, I forgive you."

"Me, too," said Donna. "You're my hero." Donna raised her mug and her voice so everyone at Joe's could hear her. "Here's to Ella and Violet. May you find happiness in your next home, and keep writing juicy stories."

"Hear, hear," rounded the place and glasses clinked in harmony.

"You guys are so sweet." Ella bumped mugs with her friends and took a long drink. "I'm really going to miss you. But, I'll be back eventually to get my things out of storage in Albuquerque, so I'll stop in Red River then. I'll just need a place to stay."

"I told you, you can stay in one of my rental cabins whenever you want," offered Ross.

"Of course she'll take you up on it, as long as her Albuquerque friends can tag along," said Becca. "You got room for the rest of us gals, Ross?"

He smiled wickedly. "I'll make room, vacationers can stay somewhere else."

"Well, Ella, your cabin might be vacant, because Coop's legal problems are over," said Miranda. "I'm sure he'll move back to Albuquerque soon."

An uncomfortable silence settled over the group.

"What?" Miranda asked, looking around at the annoyed expressions.

Lorenda glared at Miranda. "We weren't going to bother Ella with all that."

"Sorry," Miranda offered an apologetic smile.

"Wait. Coop's case is closed?" Ella's eyes went wide.

Everyone looked at each other, and Ross tried to excuse himself.

"Sit," commanded Ella. Ross slowly sank back into his chair, mumbling. She glared around her circle of friends. "And you all were saying?"

"His ex-girlfriend found a dentist. Said there were no hard feelings because it was all just a big misunderstanding," Lorenda explained.

"No hard feelings, my ass," Marilyn huffed.

"So when is Coop moving back to Albuquerque?" Ella's mind raced.

"He hasn't said, but I'm sure he will. He can open up his practice again," Lorenda said. "So if you have the cabin all to yourself, you could stay longer if you wanted, or come back for extended vacations."

The energy drained from Ella's limbs, and she slumped back in her chair. "It's not my cabin anymore."

The circle of friends went quiet again.

"I gave it to Coop." She spun her mug around in a slow circle.

"Beg your pardon? You didn't just say you *gave* it to Coop, did you?" Becca asked. She looked around the circle of people. "Someone tell me she didn't just say that."

Ella shrugged sheepishly. "The cabin wasn't ever really mine. I wouldn't have felt right keeping it. I think Bradley would be happy with my decision."

"Bradley would've also kicked his buddy's tail if he heard the way Coop talked to you," said Marilyn. "No matter the circumstances."

"You're probably right." Coop's voice startled all of them. "Bradley had four inches and at least twenty pounds on me, so I would've been dead meat. Plus, he was a lot smarter than me. Smart enough to know a good thing when he saw it."

Coop stood at the edge of the circle like an unwanted guest. He gave Ella a gentle look. Her pulse zinged to life, sending tingles through her body all the way to her fingertips and toes.

"What are you doing here, Coop?" Lorenda asked.

"Since you all did such a good job not inviting me to the party, I just wanted to stop in and say good-bye to Ella anyway." He stared at the guest of honor, his eyes searching hers.

"Good-bye," Ella whispered, and then clamped her mouth shut.

Miranda cleared her throat. "Seriously, Coop, it's a *party*. Nothing personal, buddy, we're your friends, too. But you being here does kinda put a damper on the festive atmosphere."

"Exactly why Coop's not staying, are you?" Donna said to him, but Coop didn't answer. He just kept looking at Ella.

Finally Ross started to ease out of his chair. "Why don't I walk you to the door, Coop."

"I think I can find my own way, thanks," Coop said, his cloudy eyes still locked on to Ella, soft yet penetrating to her soul.

Ella's heart thrummed, and her girlie parts broke into a waltz. She swallowed and tried to steady her uneven breaths.

"But first, I just wanted to ask Ella myself if she really wants to leave Red River." He let a beat go by. "Do you, Ella?" Uncertainty flashed in his hazel eyes, but he plowed on anyway. "Do you want to leave? Because look around, there's a lot of people here that love you and want you to stay." He ran a hand over his jaw before continuing. "Most of all, me."

All eyes turned to Ella, and she choked back tears. He was so beautiful standing there asking her if she wanted to stay, and all she really wanted was to kiss the daylights out of him.

"I . . . I—" Ella fumbled for words. Any words would be fine right now.

Ella looked around the circle of people. Somehow, they'd become her family. She'd never imagined being happy in a small town, but she was happy here in Red River. With these people that got in her business and tried to run her life, and defended her when someone hurt her.

Ella sniffed and shook some more, but warmth spread through her, because she belonged here.

"Excuse me," Coop said, trying to sidestep past Miranda.

Miranda didn't budge.

Lorenda and Ross closed the gap even further.

"I need to see Ella," Coop protested.

"Sorry, buddy," said Miranda. "Not until we get the word from Ella." A few more people joined the blockade.

"I just need to ask her a question, if you don't mind." His voice rose a notch, still trying to push through the human wall of friends that'd formed a defense line around Ella.

Her heart beat a little faster. "It's fine, guys. Let him through."

Miranda put two fingers between her lips and a loud whistle ripped through the room. "Let the man through. He's got a question for Ella." The crowd parted like the Red Sea, and he pushed his way to her.

"Jesus, they're like the Mafia." Coop shot a thorny stare around the crowd.

The coldness in Ella's chest drained away when she looked at him. He was so cute when he was angry and under pressure from the mob.

"They used to be my friends, too. Do you have them on your payroll or something?" His eyes cloudy, his brow wrinkled like he was unsure of himself, he turned his attention to her. Only her, and Ella's heart skipped again. "Can we have this conversation in private, please?"

She stood up, and Coop took her elbow, pulling her along into the ladies' room. Thank God it was vacant. When the door closed, he moved her in front of it, and placed a hand next to her head, anchoring the door shut.

"Coop, before you say anything else, there's something I need you to hear." She took a deep breath. "You're nothing like Bradley."

Coop bristled.

"I didn't get what you were trying to say at the cabin the other day. I thought you were insulting *me,* accusing me of treating you like a stand-in. But I get it now. I think." God, she hoped she got it. "You don't have to try to measure up to him. You're a completely different man. That's what I like about you."

His lips parted but no sound came out.

"Actually, I love that about you." Ella's voice was almost a whisper. "I love *you.* Just the way you are."

The wrinkles between his brows deepened.

"So, um, that's all I had to say. Um, you had a question?"

He pinched the bridge of his nose, processing what she'd said. Finally he looked into her eyes. "Will you stay?"

She tried to swallow, but her throat started to close. "Do you want me to?" she all but choked out.

He was quiet for a second too long. Hope ebbed from her grasp. Slipped through her fingers like water through a sieve.

Coop ran one hand through his hair. "The truth is, you probably shouldn't stay."

Her heart deflated, the air wringing from her lungs. She looked down at her trembling hands.

"I acted like an ass," Coop said.

Ella's head shot up. "Me too."

"I've always acted like an ass with you," Coop went on.

Ella swallowed hard. "Me too."

"But that was before I got to know you. You're probably better off without me."

This time Ella didn't agree. Instead she shook her head. "No, that's where you're wrong. I'm so much better off *with* you."

Closing his eyes, he leaned his forehead against hers. "I can't believe I'm about to do this in the john, but here goes." He took her hand in his, her left hand, and stroked the empty space on her ring finger, staring at it.

"I'm asking you to stay. I don't want to go home to the cabin if you're not there. I don't want to get in my bed if you're not in it." He looked deep into her eyes. "I don't want you to have another man's last name anymore. That's probably selfish, but I want you to be Ella Wells. Maybe I even want to change dirty diapers eventually. With you."

A tear slipped down Ella's cheek, and Coop reached up to dry it. His hand was so warm against her cheek, and he cradled her jaw in his palm.

"So what do you say?" he asked her, the pad of his thumb caressing her bottom lip.

"Yes to all of it," she said. She couldn't stop a smile so broad it made her cheeks hurt.

Coop placed a warm kiss on her mouth, and then he retrieved the tiny heart necklace from his pocket and placed it around her neck. He encircled her with his arms and she leaned into him. He pressed a kiss to her forehead.

"I don't want to move back to Albuquerque. I want to live in Red River," she whispered against his chest.

He laughed. "So do I. I can open a practice on Main Street. Now can we please get out of this bathroom? This isn't how I pictured asking you to marry me."

Ella pulled back and gave him a sultry look, her mouth quirking at the corners. "Then let's go to your truck."

A spark of lust ignited in his dusky eyes, turning them a dark shade of green. "Research for the next book?"

Her hands smoothed over his hard chest, and she looked up at him through starred lashes. "If you'd like. From now on all my books are subject to your approval before I send them to my editor."

He kissed her hard. "Then let's go."

Coop grabbed Ella's left hand and fingered the wedding band he had slid onto her finger when they exchanged vows. "The ceremony was inadequate," Coop mumbled, and pulled at her hand, trying to tug her down onto their bed.

"It was perfect," Ella said, and swatted his hand away to put more winter clothes into her suitcase. She'd just unpacked a week ago, when she'd decided to stay in Red River. Then she called her entire family, explained the reasons for her new career choice, and asked them to get their butts to Red River to attend her wedding. To her surprise, every last one of them showed up two days before she and Coop got married at a small informal ceremony in back of the cabin, overlooking the stream. Reverend Morgan from the Red River Lutheran Church performed the ceremony with Ella's family, her friends from Albuquerque, and most of Red River's residents looking on. Winston and Atlas cuddled by the stream while their masters exchanged vows, content to be together.

"You are a strange woman, Ella Wells." Coop smiled when he said her new name. "What do you have against big weddings? Aren't most girls planning them by the time they hit puberty?"

"I'm not like most girls." She tossed another sweater and some hiking boots in her suitcase.

"You can say that again." He tugged at the hem of her shirt.

"I'm not like most girls," she parroted. "And you, buddy boy, need to start packing for our honeymoon." She eyed him suspiciously. "Or are you already backing out on your promise?"

"A chance to see the American Flag-Raising Site in Sitka, Alaska. I wouldn't miss it." He raised a brow playfully.

"There's also salmon fishing, and hiking in Denali National Park. And don't forget whale watching. That should be interesting."

"Especially if it's mating season." He tugged a little harder, and she fell on the bed, landing on top of him.

His hand found the waistband of her shorts and he dipped underneath.

Her skin prickled under his touch.

"We need to pack before we go see my family off."

"Uh-huh." His words were muffled as he found her mouth. She kissed him deeply and lovingly, then she broke the kiss. Looking down at him, her heart filled with joy. And something else, too.

"I love you, Cooper Wells."

That was it. It was love filling her heart, a mirrored reflection of the very thing that danced in his hazel eyes. Love. Bright and colorful and alive.

Acknowledgments

A huge thank-you to two tough and incredibly talented critique partners, Shelly Chalmers and Katherine Fleet, who aren't afraid to tell me when I can do better. Thank you to my friend and mentor in this business, Tamra Baumann. Everyone needs a Tamra in their corner. Thank you to Stephanie Thompson, the Steady Editor, in San Diego, CA, for fighting my duel with the dreaded comma. And last but certainly not least, my deepest gratitude to my agent, Jill Marsal of the Marsal Lyon Literary Agency, and my editor, Kelli Martin of Montlake Romance/Amazon Publishing.

Every one of you rock!

IT'S IN HIS TOUCH

Chapter One

"Drop the panties, or the octopus gets it." Angelique Barbetta held out the plush doggy toy, a bottle of bitter antichew spray pointed at its overstuffed head. She used the predatory tone usually reserved for courtroom opponents as she glared at her four-legged adversary.

A soft breeze whispered through the trees, wrestling autumn-hued foliage to the ground. The draft of cool air caught the silky neckline of her robe and sent a chill racing through her. Late afternoon sunlight filtered through the shedding branches, and a silhouette of the snowcapped Sangre de Cristo Mountains glittered in the background. Her long black hair up in hot rollers, a sudden gust pulled a thick tendril loose, and she blew it out of her eyes, refusing to lose a staring match to a dog.

The ten-pound weenie dog's posture tensed, his tail wagged a fraction, and his jaw clamped tighter around the black thong panties he'd snatched from her suitcase while she was unpacking. Hence, the reason she'd scurried outside half-dressed and sporting curlers so big they could pick up a radio frequency from three states away.

Why'd she bring skimpy panties on an extended vacay to Red River—population 475? *Pfst.* Insulated long johns would've been a more practical choice.

She shivered against another nippy gust of autumn breeze.

It wasn't like she'd ever wear the string bikinis currently lodged between her dog's teeth. They'd been part of the risqué honeymoon trousseau given to her by her best friend, Kimberly, and the horde of female Barbettas. Of course, that was before she caught her fiancé, Gabriel, screwing their legal assistant on top of his desk. *While* Angelique was recovering from invasive breast cancer.

Asshole.

Come to think of it, she should let the dog have them. Let Sergeant Schnitzel chew up the underwear and every last memory of what she thought she had with Gabriel.

Just like she'd *accidentally* let the dog chew up Gabriel's Armani jacket. And his Tumi briefcase. And the crack in his brand-new fifty-five-inch widescreen—a testament to his insecurity and belief that size really did matter—may or may not have been an accident. Golf clubs sometimes slipped out of one's hands midswing. It happened.

Sergeant Schnitzel whined, his tail wagging at lightning speed.

"Come on, Sarge. Drop 'em. *Please*."

Jeez, she was pathetic. Had she really been reduced to begging a dog?

Okay, admittedly, destroying Gabriel's personal property had been a vindictive reaction, but her momentary lapse in emotional restraint was understandable. While she was in the process of moving out of their rented condo, Gabriel announced his shotgun wedding to their legal assistant because he'd knocked her up. Then he actually expected Angelique to attend along with the rest of their law firm because *cohesion* looked good for the junior partnership he'd just landed. So much cruelty at once probably would've pushed Mother Teresa over the edge. That was Angelique's story, anyway, and she was sticking to it, because Gabriel deserved it times ten.

About the Author

Photo © 2014 Frank Frost Photography

A 2014 Golden Heart® finalist, Shelly Alexander grew up traveling the world, earned a BBA in marketing, and worked in the business world for twenty-five years. With four older brothers, she watched every Star Trek episode ever made, joined the softball team instead of ballet class, and played with G.I. Joes while Corvette Barbie stayed tucked in the closet. When Shelly had three sons of her own and no daughters, she decided to escape her male-dominated world for some "girl time" by reading romance novels and has been hooked ever since.

Now she spends her days writing steamy contemporary romances while tending to an obstinate English bulldog named Lola. Her debut Red River Valley series is set in the quaint mountainous area of northern New Mexico, where fun, quirky characters and beautiful landscape embody the essence of small-town life. Find out more about Shelly and her work at http://shellyalexander.net/